Nath Doughtie

ALL RISE

Trafford
PUBLISHING

Order this book online at www.trafford.com/06-2116
or email orders@trafford.com

Most Trafford titles are also available at major online book retailers.

Note for Librarians: A cataloguing record for this book is available from Library
and Archives Canada at www.collectionscanada.ca/amicus/index-e.html

ISBN: 978-1-4251-0359-0

*We at Trafford believe that it is the responsibility of us all, as both individuals
and corporations, to make choices that are environmentally and socially sound.
You, in turn, are supporting this responsible conduct each time you purchase a
Trafford book, or make use of our publishing services. To find out how you are
helping, please visit www.trafford.com/responsiblepublishing.html*

*Our mission is to efficiently provide the world's finest, most comprehensive
book publishing service, enabling every author to experience success.
To find out how to publish your book, your way, and have it available
worldwide, visit us online at www.trafford.com/10510*

 **Trafford** PUBLISHING www.trafford.com

North America & international
toll-free: 1 888 232 4444 (USA & Canada)
phone: 250 383 6864 ♦ fax: 250 383 6804 ♦ email: info@trafford.com

The United Kingdom & Europe
phone: +44 (0)1865 722 113 ♦ local rate: 0845 230 9601
facsimile: +44 (0)1865 722 868 ♦ email: info.uk@trafford.com

10 9 8 7 6

AUTHOR'S NOTE TO THE READER

This book is intended to provide light entertainment for the reader. It is totally a work of fiction and all the characters are imaginary and not based on any real person living or dead, but any real person wishing to claim identity with any character should feel free to do so. The places named are real and will be familiar to local readers.

Despite the cavalier attitude displayed by some of the judicial characters on occasion, the author's experience with real-life judges finds them to be very conscientious in general and aware of the awesome responsibilities entrusted to them by the public.

As Judge Learned Hand once said, "A judge's life, like any other, has in it much of drudgery, senseless dickering, stupid obstinacies, capricious pettifogging, all disguising and obstructing the only sane purpose which can justify the whole endeavor." He goes on to say that once the turmoil stops and the judge can sort things out and make his mark, that "That is a pleasure which nobody who has felt it will be likely to underrate."

Anything Judge Hand says sounds as wise as a tree full of owls, and I have to admit I can take pleasure in a few of my rulings from the bench. I can also take pleasure in leaving the "senseless dickering" in the hands of others.

Nath Doughtie, Gainesville, 2006

Acknowledgments

Many thanks to Edward, Polly, Jean and Rick for their help in editing and proofreading this book.

Thanks to the people of the Eighth Judicial Circuit of Florida for trusting me to serve as a judge for many years.

The author would like to thank the following writers who are referenced in this book in one way or another.

Edgar Allen Poe	Hunter Thompson
Joel Chandler Harris	Jonathan Swift
William Shakespeare	Harper Lee
Robert Browning	Garrison Keillor
Ernest Hemingway	Hoyt Axton
James Joyce	Winston Churchill
William Bartram	Benjamin Franklin
Patrick O'Brien	Patrick Conroy
Walker Percy	Tom Wolfe
Archie Carr	George Orwell
P.C. Wren	Marjorie K. Rawlings

All profits from the sale of this book are to be donated to the Guardian Ad Litem Program of the Eighth Judicial Circuit.

Cover photo by the author

I

Judge Alva Cason sat in his chambers holding his face in his large bony hands and pressed his eyes. It was early on a Monday morning. The opening of court was almost a half hour away, and he felt some obligation to review the files stacked before him. These were for the cases he would hear later in the day, after detention hearings. The thought depressed him. Shirley Bloch, his judicial assistant, had made coffee and was working the daily crossword puzzle. Judge AC, as he was called outside of court, knew he did not really need to review the files as they were all about the same. He had been on the bench for many years and knew none would present a unique legal issue or produce a case of lasting jurisprudential precedent. Judge AC was a circuit judge assigned to the family division of the Eighth Judicial Circuit of Florida. He had taken to referring to his assignment as the division from hell. *Hell*, he thought opening his hazel eyes, maybe I should at least thumb through them.

"Hey, Shirley. What do I have after detention hearings?"

"Judge, your calendar on top of your stack of files on your desk shows a hearing at ten-thirty."

Good, that would give him time for a cup of coffee with Judge Ira Moss, the chief judge of the circuit. He needed to talk to him about judicial assignments. Particularly his own. He was accustomed to snippy remarks from Shirley, and ignored this latest.

As Judge Cason walked down the corridor on his way to juvenile court he wondered why juveniles could not just be "arrested" like everybody else, but had to be "detained" ; why they were not found "guilty", but "adjudicated delinquent." Hell, it's the same damn thing. *Modern day juvspeak* thought AC, as he took the bench clad in the same threadbare black robe he had worn at his swearing in, almost twenty years ago. All detained juveniles had to be brought to court within twenty-four hours for a judge to determine whether to release them to a parent or keep them in secure detention. This morning's catch was the normal run of bike thieves and sibling slappers. "He won't mind me. He don't do nothing I say, and I don't want him home," was not an atypical parental plea.

After the bailiff opened court, Judge AC went into his usual routine with the first case.

"Good morning. I am Judge Cason and this is a hearing to advise you why you are in custody and what your rights are. You are charged with auto theft and have the right to remain silent and the right to a lawyer and if you cannot afford one, please sign the form in front of you and one will be appointed."

Judge AC thought a retired actor could do a better job at a much cheaper price. No wise or learned judicial decisions were needed. The release criteria for the juvenile detainee were determined by how many points were scored on a form prepared by the Department of Juvenile Justice. Points were scored for the seriousness of the offense, prior crimes and whether the child was on probation, or community control as it was called in juvspeak, at the time of the new offense. No points were scored for not minding parents.

After only six cases, Judge AC's mind began to wander. He thought he could do this job in his sleep, but remembered he sometimes did just that, which was generally frowned upon. A quick glance at his docket sheet told him that he had no more cases, and as soon as the public defender finished signing up the last defendant, he could go finish the crossword for Shirley and slip off for coffee with Ira. The atmosphere in the courtroom was relaxed. The soon-to-be retired bailiff was chatting with an attractive social worker from Juvenile Justice, and the clerk had loaded all the morning's files in a push cart for return to the central office. Suddenly the doors to the hall swung open in a manner not in keeping with judicial decorum. Everyone perked up. Although criminal courts were perceived by the public as dangerous, all in this courtroom knew that the emotions in family court ran much higher and most incidents of violence occurred here.

"Your honor, your honor, I need to talk to you about a case," the intruder said as he approached the bench, holding up his hand like a schoolchild.

The speaker was wearing green work pants and a tee shirt with a Miller's beer logo.

There was a three-inch gap between the two, showing a belly in keeping with the shirt's promise of happy times. He looked to be about fifty, but AC thought he had been "rode hard and put up wet" and was probably much younger. The bailiff immediately came to life and positioned himself between this potential menace and the judge.

"Who are you, and what case is it?" Judge AC asked.

"Me? I'm Ricky Jordan, but it's about my daughter. The H and RS people got her baby girl and won't tell us what's going on. Either you order something or we're gonna sue."

AC glanced down at his docket sheet, then looked at the clerk, who shrugged. There were no dependency cases listed, although they would normally be heard at this time. Just like juvenile delinquents, all children who have been sheltered against possible abuse must be brought to court within twenty-four hours for a determination as to the necessity of future shelter, or whether a return to the parents or other relatives would be appropriate. This work was done by the Department for Children and Families, which had formerly been the Department of Health and Rehabilitative Services or HRS. The old name prevailed in the community and was commonly pronounced "H and RS," (like H&R Block, Judge AC thought). Well, that is as good as calling the new entity "decaf", like coffee, the way the insiders did.

"Mr. Jordan, who told you to come here this morning?"

"Judge, what happened was this. Mary Beth and some of 'em were hanging around the landing, and then the next thing they knew the law was there. I got a call from Suzie, who said the H and RS had came and took Mary Beth's baby. I went down there, but we can't find out nothing."

Judge AC, of course, could not tell who Suzie or Mary Beth were at this point but pressed ahead. "Mr. Jordan, who told you to come here this morning?"

"I don't know. Some lady gave me a card or something, said there would be a court hearing, but I left it down in the truck. Do you want me to go get it? What I can't understand is how they can just run off with the kid without a hearing or nothing."

Judge AC reflected a bit. Here was Ricky Jordan with sweat beads all over his enlarged brow, dressed for the Gatornational drag races, and evoking the essence of constitutional law. This was awkward. He knew that if what Ricky said was true, there should have been a scheduled hearing, but there was not. Were the representatives from DCF simply late? "Mr. Jordan, your daughter is Suzie, right?"

"Yeah, uh, yes your honor. I mean no, your honor. Suzie's a friend. My girl is Mary Beth."

"Well, where is Mary Beth and her husband?"

"She's in the hospital, and she ain't married."

"Well, what about the father of the baby?"

"You mean Duke? He ain't got nothing to do with this. He's in the service, stationed up in Lejeune."

The time allocated for detention and shelter hearings was now over. AC thought, *why should I involve myself in this?* Judges are supposed to remain detached. Their job is to adjudicate, not to investigate.

"Mr. Jordan, if what you say is accurate, the DCF people should be here by now. By the way, did all this take place here in Alachua County? And why is your daughter in the hospital anyway?" This statement, followed by a compound question, fazed Ricky Jordan not a whit.

"That's what I been saying. It ain't right. Them Palm Landing boys went after her, and they think her collarbone is broke. They got the baby right here in Alachua County for sure."

Lawyers would want to get all the "theys" straight, but Judge AC had no problem. He could surmise the rest of the story. There was a drunken tussle and the baby was in close enough proximity to get DCF involved. It would make no difference as to who threw the first beer can, so nothing further was needed from Ricky Jordan.

"Mr. Jordan, I will make a couple of calls to see if I can find out what is going on. You should call the person named on the card you have. You need to understand I am not in charge of DCF. I rule on cases that are properly brought before me. I do not conduct investigations."

"Judge, your honor, all I know is that they got our baby and you can make them give her back."

When Judge AC got back to his chambers, he immediately called Ira Moss.

"Hey, Ira. How about a quick cup at Emiliano's?"

"Sure," replied Ira, who had grown up in Tampa on Cuban cuisine. Ira Moss was currently the chief judge of the circuit and responsible for all judicial assignments. He was very bright, and some thought bound for higher places. He had assigned himself to the felony division, but carried only a small portion of the caseload due to his demanding responsibilities as chief judge.

"What's with the division from hell?" asked Ira as they met in the corridor.

"Ceased to exist. Evaporated. We felt it was not fair to hoard such a treasure, so now we call it by its true name, the duck soup division. What's with the criminals?"

"Who knows? All I do is thump the heads of the attorneys. It's like the public defenders and prosecutors are only interested in playing macho games with each other. Neither side even bothers to make a realistic assessment of a case until docket day. Still, it beats cutting up babies. I don't see how you put up with that day in and day out."

They passed the security station where a metal detector helped deprive entering litigants of guns, knives, scissors, and suspicious pointed objects of unknown use. The morning was extra humid and, upon leaving the courthouse, Ira removed his small reading glasses which, being cooled by the air-conditioning, had fogged up. He wore these glasses on the end of his nose, and when he peered over them it caused him to raise his eyebrows so that he expressed the traditional look of incredulity. There is no doubt that this was a natural response to much of the testimony he heard, but it once caused an attorney to request that the record reflect that the judge was leering at the witness.

Emiliano's was deservedly popular with the courthouse crowd. A former dry goods store, the decor was now exposed brick and wire-backed chairs. The staff all had hairdos designed to annoy adults but were young and cheerful. The coffee was rich but not bitter, and the pastry was minutes from the oven.

Ira said, "Grab a seat by the window and I'll get coffee. You want a roll or something?" AC did not, having eaten two micro-waved sausage biscuits while driving to work.

"OK," said Ira as he slouched into a wire-back, "Tell me the secret of remaining sane after two years in the family division."

Ira Moss was a tall imposing figure. He was a few years younger than AC, but his balding head made them look about the same age.

"It's very simple, Ira. You begin by learning a set of maxims I will share with you as a future family judge. These are not taught in law school, so perhaps you should take notes."

"Perhaps your tie would look good with coffee stains," said Ira with a mock tilt of his cup.

"Family division ties come issued with dried blood, so coffee should blend in fine. The first rule is detachment, and I do not refer to judicial demeanor, but to true mental detachment. Perhaps an example would help."

"Perhaps a Tequila Sunrise would help, but go on," said Ira.

"Take child custody," said AC. "You non-family judges agonize over this issue as though every case required the wisdom of Solomon. Think for a second. If both parties are fine folks and would do a good job of raising the kid, then how can you go wrong? If both are nasty, then the kid will suffer no matter what you do. If one is good and the other bad then there's no dilemma."

Ira thought for a minute in sincere reflection. "What you say is logical, but I still get caught up in the emotion of the thing. Back when I suffered through my only year doing family, I had one case where everything pointed to the dad as having sexually abused his teenage daughter, but she still preferred him over the alcoholic mom. Rather than go to the mom and step-dad, she ran off to Orlando and lived on the streets. Naturally, all the social workers refused to consider the dad's home as suitable."

"Case in point. It's a lose-lose situation. Assuming the kid is old enough to protect herself from an alcoholic mom or a perverted dad, you need not fret over the greater of the two evils. She knows and can decide. All you have to do is to ensure that there is no coercion."

"That being said," said AC looking at Ira with his most serious expression, "even though it's simple work, it may be time to share some of my joys with others. I really think by the end of the year I may need a break."

"Well, AC, as you know, our administrators are working on a reassignment plan. How about civil?"

"I'm willing to serve where needed, but civil sounds great for a change."

After a bit more idle chit-chat they mutually pushed back the wire-backed chairs and Ira sprang for the tab. This was OK with AC as he had just had coffee and Ira had ordered fancy Spanish pastry to boot. AC thought what a fine fellow Ira was. Never, like Will Rogers, met a man he did not like. This was not really true, but he never complained about, or gossiped about lawyers the way most of his fellow judges did. Lawyers did raise the ire of Ira to their great regret, but his frustrations were more situational than personal.

Later, in his chambers, Judge AC looked at his morning's schedule. He had noticed several groups of litigants clustered about his door, but did not know if they were his cases or if they belonged to Judge Lee across the hall. He did want to follow up on the Ricky Jordan matter, but knew he needed to clear up a few uncontested matters first. These could be handled expeditiously, but he did need to spend enough time with each litigant to ensure that the public felt his empathy. After all, his was an elected office.

Adoptions were made for baby kissing. Uncontested divorces often produced tears from big burly men who were being left by their wives and vice versa. These couples were entitled to a sympathetic handling of this big event in their lives. The retired actor image again came to Judge AC's mind. Eventually the traffic subsided, and Judge AC went into the office behind his hearing room and began to try to sort out the Ricky Jordan matter.

He was annoyed at himself for not knowing the child's name. It was a boy, wasn't it? No, Jordan had said "girl." Anyway, he could assume the last name was Jordan, but no, the baby may have the last name of the marine stationed up at Camp Lejune. He was not even sure the case was in his county. Palm Landing had been mentioned by Ricky Jordan, but it was in an area where the corners of three counties met and the incident could have happened in any of the three. Alachua County was the only one of the three which was even in his circuit. He could not very well call a receptionist at DCF with such a vague inquiry. The District Legal Counsel was a possibility, but he was new on the job, and AC's initial impression was that he was an unctuous prick. He could hear him defending DCF and stating that "all sheltered children were always brought to court as the law required." The DCF had been under a lot of public pressure recently due to lax supervision of dependent kids. Then Judge AC thought of Vicky Carter who was a supervisor now, but who had formally been a case worker in his court. She was the best bet, thought AC as he reached for the phone.

Just as he touched the phone it rang and he briefly recoiled.

"Judge, they're ready on your conference call," said Shirley when he had picked up the phone. They normally just shouted back and forth rather than using the intercom, and Judge AC was somewhat annoyed at this new procedure.

"What call? What case? Do I have the file?"

Judge, it's the 11 o'clock hearing in the Nazell case, and the file is in your hearing room with the rest of today's files," said Shirley in a slightly condescending tone.

Judge AC was slightly miffed, but he could shift gears in a hurry. After entering his hearing room, a quick glance at the file told him all he needed to know.

"Hello, this is Judge Cason."

"We're ready on your conference call sir, and thank you for using AT&T."

"You're quite welcome. Who do we have on the line?" asked Judge AC in his professional tone. Cordial, but not designed to put people at ease exactly. Telephone protocol when calling a judge's office required that the lawyers should be on the line before the judge.

"Judge, this is Ron Baker on the Nazell case, and I really appreciate being able to do this by telephone."

"Judge, this is Lawrence Buckman of Clearwater representing Mr. Nazell, and we would like to strenuously object to this matter being heard by telephone and on inadequate notice. We have a number of substantial matters to present, and our client insists on a full and adequate opportunity to be heard."

This kind of posturing went on all the time. Judge AC often wondered if the lawyers really considered it effective or did it just to impress the clients.

"Mr. Buckman, you can assure your client that this court will allow an ample opportunity for all parties to be heard on all issues. I would like to proceed with the wife's motion to strike your motion for change of venue, and, if necessary, reserve time on the court's calendar for any unresolved matters."

"Thank you, judge," chimed both lawyers in unison.

Judge AC's quick review of the file showed that the husband's attorney had filed a motion to transfer the case from Alachua County to Dade County where the parties had been divorced. The attorney for the wife had moved to strike the husband's motion as legally insufficient. Judge AC would normally have allowed the attorney for the wife to present his argument on why the husband's motion to transfer should be denied or stricken, but in this case the husband's motion was so obviously spurious he jumped right in.

"Mr. Buckman, your motion to transfer or dismiss is not signed or sworn to by your client, nor is there an affidavit attesting to the factual matters alleged."

"Your honor, that's due to the inadequate notice given to me of this hearing by opposing counsel. There was not time to get an affidavit, and my client is not available to testify in person."

This, thought Judge AC, *was just so much nonsense.* Lawyer Buckman had filed the motion to transfer and should be prepared to defend it. On the other hand, there may be no contested facts, and it may be possible to rule on the motion as a matter of law from the record.

"Mr. Baker," said the judge, "are there any contested facts from your standpoint?"

"No, your honor. For purposes of this motion we are willing to accept the record as it now stands. As you can see from the pleadings, the parties were divorced in Dade County, and my client now lives in Alachua County. She is only seeking to enforce child support from her ex, who lives in Citrus County. The statutes and rules clearly provide that she can bring an enforcement action in the county of her residence. Furthermore, Mr. Nazell, acting as his own attorney, filed a *pro se* answer to the petition and also a counter- petition seeking a change in child custody. He has thus waived any right to object to venue in

Alachua County. The fact that he has now hired a lawyer to try to move the case makes no difference."

Judge AC mentally noted that this was a valid legal argument. He did not bother to point out the obvious fact that Mr. Nazell, now living in neighboring Citrus County, had no real interest in moving the case three hundred miles south to Dade other than to delay matters and frustrate his former wife. Judge AC knew he should give the husband's lawyer another opportunity to argue his spurious motion, but instead announced: "Gentlemen, the motion to strike is granted and the motion to transfer venue is denied. Mr Baker, please prepare a proposed order for the Court to sign. Goodbye gentlemen."

"Yes, your honor," they again chimed. Mr. Buckman asked Mr. Baker to stay on the line to discuss matters. He probably wanted to try to buy a little time for his client to catch up on the delinquent support thought AC.

Shirley Blotch appeared in the doorway and announced, "That's all we have before lunch. You have the final hearing scheduled in the Andrews case starting at one and lasting the rest of the afternoon."

Judge AC could easily have read his own calendar which was on desk in front of him, but he knew he had let himself in for this kind of treatment by his earlier remarks to Shirley. He picked up the Andrews file and noted the names of the attorneys for the parties. He drew a deep breath and prepared himself for a long afternoon. By six-thirty he had forgotten completely about Ricky Jordan.

II

Carlo Proenza took a sip from his second Bloody Mary of the morning as he squinted at the shimmering early morning Atlantic Ocean framed by the sliding doors to his tenth-floor condominium in Vero Beach Florida. He had risen early and enjoyed a Bloody Mary while seated on the balcony, but now the bright sun had driven him inside. Life was good. Vicky Carter was in the shower, and in a minute or two, would emerge drying her curly blond hair. He briefly contemplated the thought of trying to get her back into bed, but knew he should not push his luck. Mixing business with pleasure was always risky. Still, he thought, maybe an early-morning drink would work as well as the ones last night. There was plenty of time before the big meeting. One look at Vicky told him to forget it.

Her expression was one of vexation mixed with a slight hangover. She did, however, try to be pleasant.

"Hi, sweetie. What's for breakfast other than booze?"

Not all *that* pleasant, Carlo thought. "We have OJ and fresh mango for your early morning dining pleasure, *y tambien café Cubano especial.* This can be served in bed at madam's request."

No harm in trying, thought Carlo.

"How about some Danish or something?"

"There is a place across the street that's OK, if you can put up with the clientele. Usually a bunch of retired stockbrokers talking about the relative merits of BMWs versus Porsches."

"Let's do that. I need a walk."

Vero Beach had undergone considerable change since Carlo first visited it. Located about half-way between Daytona and the South Florida Gold Coast, it had been transformed over the years from a tranquil village into a high-rise hideaway for the wealthy. Not as bad as Naples, perhaps, but no longer a slice of Old Florida. Carlo still loved the place, and found it convenient for his somewhat covert enterprises. There would be no *Miami Herald* reporters hanging around his door, he thought, and the condo itself met all his needs. From his oceanfront balcony, he could look up and down the beachfront for miles. Looking to the west, from the window over his kitchen sink, he had a view of the broad Indian River which separated his island from the mainland. On the beach side, the rooftops of the Driftwood Inn were visible. Built in 1934 by Waldo Sexton from Buzzards Glory, Indiana, it had helped put Vero Beach on the map, so to speak. "The Inn," and Waldo's nearby "Ocean Grill," had, so far, refused to succumb to the ravages of Atlantic hurricanes and beach erosion. Carlo often wondered how much longer that would last.

Carlo and Vicky took the elevator down to ground level and walked out of the shade into the glare of an early morning Florida summer. Vicky winced and put on her sun glasses. Carlo felt it would not hurt to try to soften her up a bit.

"Look, honey, about last night, it was…"

"Carlo, I don't mean to sound curt, but we have work to do. Last night was last night. I don't think either of us should dwell on it. I really don't know why I got involved in this business with you, but I'm in it now, and it's too late to back out. Once we finish I plan to go my way and expect you to go yours."

Carlo sighed and thought, *oh well, she's just nervous*. A1A was almost traffic-less this time of year. They crossed over it to "The Combers" and sat at a small round table for a while, then realized they had to serve themselves from the counter. Vicky chose a croissant with orange marmalade, and Carlo had a bagel and cream cheese.

"Let's have tea. Coffee makes me sweat," Vicky said.

"Fine with me," Carlo replied. He really preferred stronger Cuban-style coffee, but agreed to the tea to humor Vicky, as she was indispensable to his current venture as well as a delightful companion. He wanted to keep her in good spirits as he could feel her apprehension. They found the small round table again, and, as Carlo predicted, the idle retirees at the adjoining table were talking about sports cars with the enthusiasm of high school boys talking about jalopies.

"Carlo, I just don't see how we can ask these people for really big bucks without seeming to be on the take. Not that we aren't, but I mean, crap, anyone can see that a baby adoption does not cost two hundred thousand bucks. This gimmick of yours about the money going to charity is so transparent. Really!" Despite her apparent agitation, Vicky was speaking in hushed tones. Street-side sparrows watched for every fallen crumb of bagel.

"Sweets, we don't need to convince them. In fact, I already have the money in trust. What we do, is to present a plausible picture, and they will convince themselves that everything is fine. What they want is a result. They won't fret over the details. You know your role. You do this sort of thing for a living."

Vicky jumped in at this point. *"I do not do this sort of thing for a living!"*

At this exclamation, several of the retirees turned and looked over, and Vicky reddened. Carlo lowered his voice.

ALL RISE

"I know, I know. What I mean, is that the Cunninghams are just like any other adoptive parents. They merely want to move to the front of the line, cut all the red tape, and there's nothing immoral about that. Look, we've been over all this before. There's nothing illogical about it. We know the woman in charge of the adoption process. She's a fanatical anti-abortionist. She's willing to let our friends move to the front of the line for a contribution to her favorite charity, the Sara Beville Foundation, which carries out many fine anti-abortion activities. The fact that there is no such woman or foundation does nothing to defeat the logic of the deal. We're not selling babies. All the approvals will still be required, but look, these folks have more money than Croesus. Wait until you see their layout. A semi-retired investment banker and his lovely trophy wife. Any kid would be only too lucky to end up in such a home. And, Vicky, it's not just the house and money. Reed and Rita Cunningham are really delightful people. Charming, if I may say so. I know you'll approve of them."

Carlo Proenza had emigrated with his family to the United States from Cuba when he was six years old. It was 1962, the year of the great missile crisis. Before that, his father had been a lawyer in Havana and had known Fidel Castro in high school. He and his much younger wife rejected all that Castro stood for, and by 1961, knew that things in Cuba were not going to improve for a very long time. They were lucky to escape to Mexico and then on to Miami, where they had friends. Sadly, the lawyer never learned to speak English which was necessary back in the 1960s in Miami. He ended up working as a dishwasher in a Cuban restaurant in Little Havana. Carlo's mother had been a sheltered member of the Cuban upper class and could have been expected to live out her life as an exile in poverty, but a strange thing happened. She experienced an epiphany of the spirit and began to see Florida as a land of opportunity. She got a job in real estate and was very successful. She became a broker and formed her own office, and brought Carlo on as a runner while he was still in high school. Later, after taking several courses and passing an exam, he became an associate. His quiet, easy-going manner, and his ability as a natural mediator, helped him in working with both sides of the ethnic split of Miami. To the Anglos, with his perfect English and light brown hair, he did not appear Cuban. To the Cubans he was still one of their own. After Carlo spent several years with the real estate office, his mother encouraged him to attend the University of Florida. He graduated ahead of schedule with passable grades in political science and, being unemployed, signed on as an unpaid worker in the campaign of Hector Suarez, who was running for Congress from Dade County. Carlo, as a young fellow-Hispanic immigrant, quickly became his chief aide and a close confidant. Suarez won the election and took Carlo, who was now on the payroll, to Washington. It did not take Suarez long in the nation's capital to realize that the people who were polite to his face were not necessarily his friends when his back was turned. He wanted to help out his constituents back in Miami, but he felt no loyalty to his fellow congressmen who snubbed him, and really not much loyalty to his newly adopted country. He was re-elected twice, and Carlo's influence grew along with that of his boss. Finally the old pre-Castro ethics, with which Suarez had been imbued in Cuba and had transported to the States, caught up with him. Although charges were never filed the handwriting was on the wall and, after the usual "pack of lies" statement of denial, he quietly resigned from office and went home to spend more time with his family. This left Carlo with a large number of influential contacts, but with no influence to peddle and no paycheck.

As Carlo was packing for home, he was struck by a bolt of good fortune. A wealthy developer from Dade County called and invited him to lunch. He knew Carlo from past dealings with Suarez and had always liked the thoughtful young man. He also knew that Carlo knew something about the persuasive power of well-placed money. He felt some need to check out Carlo's sensitivities and understanding of the delicacies involved in handling such transactions, so arranged a face-to-face meeting. During lunch at the developer's private club, Carlo learned that the Seascape condominium in Vero Beach needed to expand its parking garage and tennis courts onto an undeveloped area of sand dunes and scrub oaks along the oceanfront. The preliminary application for this project had been denied, as a citizens group wanted the property for beach access. The developer felt out of touch with the in-and-outs of Indian River County politics and wanted help.

Seascape had been purchased for a surprisingly low price, and then it was soon discovered that the parking was inadequate and that more recreational facilities were needed to compete with the newer condominiums.

"And so, my friend, you can see we absolutely *have* to be able to expand our facility. To be frank with you, I have no business involving myself in Vero Beach affairs, but that's where you come in. You can live in the condo a few months and get a feel for what's going on. Hell, with Suarez in office, development in Dade was a cinch, but with *these* people, who knows?"

Carlo had visited Vero Beach during his college days, and, compared to Miami, found it to be very pleasant. He knew nothing of the politics of Indian River County, but was sure he could learn. His fee, if he was successful in obtaining approvals for the expansion, was to be a condo unit at Seascape. If he was unsuccessful, he would have had an all expense-paid vacation for several months. Carlo discreetly asked about expenses of a non-personal nature and was assured that they would be no problem, but to wait until the time was ripe to discuss the details. A handshake, and the deal was done.

As things turned out, Carlo got his vacation and Seascape condo as well. Not exactly a vacation perhaps. After all, he did have to wine and dine a few Vero Beach "persons of influence", but Carlo enjoyed every minute of it. He did incur a few expenses of a non- personal nature, but these were paid without question as promised. After the successful completion of his assignment, he sat on the balcony of the top floor condo unit now titled in his name, and knew he had found a new home.

***

"How did you find this Cunningham guy anyway?" Vicky asked. "How did you find me, for that matter?"

"Hey, Vicky, I know a lot of things you don't need to know about. It's how I make my living. You make your living protecting children. I make mine protecting myself. You have ways of finding out when children are at risk. I have ways of finding out when people need problems solved in an unorthodox manner. You could call me a fixer I guess, but I always work by charm not intimidation. My mother once called Florida the land of opportunity. I call it the land of opportunists, and they often need my help. Let's go get dressed for the big meeting."

The traffic along A1A had picked up as they crossed over and entered the condo.

"Now Vicky," said Carlo, in a nervous, stilted voice, as they changed from shorts into casual business dress, "I know you do child protection and not adoptions, but you know what goes on there. You do have all the forms don't you?"

"Yes, Carlo, yes Carlo. I have all the forms and I can handle my end of things, but I don't want to have anything to do with the money talk. You know why I got into this and it has nothing to do with money. I thought about not taking my share, but realized that then I would do all the work, and you would get all the money."

She is *really* getting testy, thought Carlo. *Probably still nervous.* Not at all like last night when she unexpectedly slipped between his sheets. They had never made love before, and Carlo was utterly amazed at her passion; maybe it had been the wine, maybe it had just been a long time for her. Carlo then realized that it was he who was setting a hostile tone by suggesting she was unprepared. He immediately apologized. She smiled.

"It's nice to know that Mr. Cool can get antsy at times. You look fine. Not at all like I would expect a con man to look." (She had been afraid that he would be wearing one of those embroidered Cuban shirts that are not tucked in at the waist.) What about me?"

Vicky was dressed in navy slacks and a beige printed blouse showing the smiling faces of children of all ethnic backgrounds.

"Perfection personified. What a team," said Carlo, who paid much attention to his dress. He felt he projected a dignified but relaxed look in his navy colored trousers and light blue polo shirt with what appeared to be a yacht club emblem on the pocket.

***

After Carlo's successful negotiation of the Seascape parking lot application, he was glad he had decided to continue to live in Vero. He knew something about real estate from the days he worked for his mother and from a few classes at UF, but his years in Washington were now proving more valuable than college in what he saw as his true mission in life. Mediating, bringing people together, creating. He had the zeal of a Baptist missionary. He became a man about town. No one was quite sure what he did for a living, but that was not uncommon in Vero Beach, where everyone seemed to have a lot of money earned or obtained from other places. The locals who ran for office were split between the pro-development group and the greenies. Carlo did not seem to fit into either category. Word got out as to Carlo's ability as a fixer. He could fix anything but a leaky faucet, so they said, but there was never a hint of impropriety. He was invited to charity golf tournaments and ribbon cutting ceremonies. He prospered, but eventually Vero became a bit small for his chosen occupation. It was a great base of operations, but eventually he ran out of local charities to support and local commissioners to exploit. Through a bit of research and through carefully cultivated contacts, Carlo expanded his "operations" throughout Florida.

Carlo was somewhat introspective and certainly not self- delusional as were many entrepreneurs who had achieved success by total luck. He knew he had to pursue his clients diligently, but he knew one thing about himself: he never wanted to work a regular job for a living. He privately referred to himself as the "Prince of Bribes."

Carlo's particular venture with the Cunninghams had come about following a large ad in the local newspaper. The text condemned abortion, and described a couple wishing to adopt unwanted children. There was something suspicious about the ad that caught Carlo's trained eye. He did not have much experience in the adoption business, but had been approached twice by people wanting to see if he knew any way around the rules. A quick assessment of these potential clients told Carlo they did not have enough money to bribe a meter maid, but he had looked into the way adoptions worked. He knew there were many wealthy people, movie stars and the like, who wanted to adopt children and would not mind paying big bucks for the privilege. He opened the yellow pages and found quite a few ads for adoption agencies. The names of the agencies were sprinkled with loving words such as "miracle", "angel", and "godmother," and were usually directed at mothers seeking to give up their children without feeling guilty about it. He read more and learned about foreign adoptions. Carlo thought, why not cash in? He found out as much as he could about this Reed Cunningham who had placed the adoption ad. The more he found out, the more the newspaper ad reminded him of similar ads he had seen in *Soldier of Fortune* magazine asking for someone willing to undertake a "special assignment." Through computer research, Googling, he learned that Reed Cunningham had made millions in the savings and loan business in Texas. He had been prosecuted for certain improprieties and spent several months in prison in the Florida Panhandle. The federal prison there was known as "Club Fed." There were, of course, large fines that had to be paid, and a number of civil judgments, but Florida and the Cayman Islands had welcomed Mr. Cunningham and his leftover millions.

Carlo sensed that Reed Cunningham would be a good person to get to know regardless of the adoption issue. The Reed Cunninghams of the world certainly needed accountants and asset protection lawyers, but they did, on occasion, need persons with special expertise in, well, bribery, thought Carlo, so he answered the ad and called for an appointment which was granted the next day.

Carlo was met at the door by a slightly built balding man wearing the typical retiree's uniform of yellow trousers and white shoes. Reed Cunningham introduced himself and his handshake was firm as rock. Carlo noted the man's features. His thin nose and hard hawk-like eyes. This guy was a chairman-of-the-board type.

The meeting went well. They spoke the same language, and had a number of mutual acquaintances from Carlo's days in Washington. Mrs. Cunningham was there as well and was, indeed, a trophy. She was not only pretty, but gorgeous. Carlo noticed a number of real trophies on a bookshelf. He learned that Rita had been a champion swimmer at the University of Georgia and had earned a law degree from Emory. She described meeting Reed in Atlanta during the S&L boom days, and how she had flown down to Vero in his private jet for a real estate closing. "He proposed to me on the balcony of a penthouse atop some place called Seascape." (Just above Carlo's condo, as it turned out.)

One key to Carlo's success was his easygoing manner. His role was not that of the aggressive hard-charging dealmaker. He was a facilitator, not a negotiator. He flattered; he stroked egos. After only a short while the parties saw eye-to-eye and things could be laid on the table. Reed was a convicted felon, and despite his wealth, the public agencies would not approve an adoption. Carlo tactfully did not inquire of the Cunningham, about other reproductive means of acquiring a child. He agreed to check out alternatives to the standard process of adoption. The conspirators discussed all this and, upon parting, Carlo and Reed exchanged a hearty handshake and Rita gave Carlo, they were on a first name basis now, a big hug. Not a Palm Beach kiss, but a sincere hug. After this initial meeting with the Cunninghams, Carlo had met Vicky and developed a possible plan of action. The meeting between the Cunninghams and Vicky was supposed to be a preliminary contact. Everyone would then have to wait for a suitable dependent child to become available for adoption before things could be finalized.

***

Carlo drove Vicky's five-year-old Honda since he knew the way to the Cunningham estate, and since he was currently in-between cars. He could not make up his mind between a convertible or a sedan, or possibly a Lincoln Navigator with golf clubs always on display in the rear compartment.

He told Vicky as they crossed the high bridge over the Indian River he had "Cased the joint." She failed to see the humor and told him so. "This might be a lark for you, Carlo, but my career is involved." She could feel her anxiety level increase with every mile they drove.

The sea breeze had not yet come up and the mirror-calm river reflected the trees along the bank, as well as the sprinkling of white yachts dotting the surface. Indian River was really a lagoon, just like Mosquito Lagoon farther up the coast, or perhaps a bay, like Apalachicola or a sound, like Santa Rosa or Cumberland, but not really a river.

Regardless of how it was designated, it was a boater's paradise. The Cunninghams could have lived wherever they chose, and, indeed, had other residences in addition to *Kissimmee Kiss*, but it was their favorite. It was on the west bank of the river and they were able to dock their yacht, *Osprey II*, in the back yard. The boathouse could double as a guest cottage and was connected to the main residence by a covered walkway.

Kissimmee Kiss was not part of one of the gated communities typical of the area, but was a single residence surrounded by a limestone fence with an elaborate wrought-iron gate. Much like an English manor, there was a gatekeeper's cottage which could serve as servants' quarters. Vicky felt a pronounced sense of intimidation as they approached the imposing entrance.

Suddenly she shouted, "Quick, stop the car!"

Carlo did as he was told, thinking there must be some female emergency. As soon as the car came to a halt, Vicky sprang out and yelled at Carlo, "I'm not going to do it. I'm just not. I can't. Find somebody else." She slammed the door and began walking back in the direction toward town.

"Vicky." Carlo pleaded, "Get back in the car. It is *your* car."

Vicky kept walking along the side of the road on the freshly mowed grass in front of the Cunningham mansion. She somehow knew if she had entered the estate grounds she would have crossed the point of no return. She had made a few mistakes in her life and might make a few more, but this was not going to be one of them.

Carlo had to do a U-turn and when he pulled along side Vicky said "Vicky, please. I won't push it. We have an easy out. I don't need the money, I was just trying to help out a friend. I was just trying to help you." He knew this last line was a lie and a transparent one at that.

"You were just trying to help me commit a felony? Trying to help me lose my job? Trying to help me go to jail? Shit, Carlo. You keep the car. I'm walking."

Carlo remained calm and drove slowly beside Vicky waiting for her to cool off. "Vicky, come on, get in the car. I'll take you anywhere you want to go. Please."

Vicky continued walking for a minute or two, then got into the Honda and scrunched over to the far side away from Carlo. They were both silent as Carlo retraced their way back across Indian River. Finally Carlo said, "Vicky, I really am sorry. Really sorry. I hate to sound mushy, but you mean more to me than this adoption thing."

Carlo thought *what am I saying?* Do I *mean* this or is it just habit? He still rushed ahead. "It's just that I've seen so much corruption that I've become very cynical. I admit that when all this started I looked at you as just another chick that wouldn't mind pulling a few strings for a few bucks. That's the way I make my living you know. But hey, I'm just a middle man, a facilitator, a bagman. I don't really commit the bad act or pay the money. I just deliver it. I do realize that what I was suggesting you do could be considered wrong. You know, like morally wrong. Well, I was wrong about you and I'm glad I was. You make me feel better about people."

"Carlo, I'm sorry I'm so upset. I appreciate what you are saying and I do like you, but I need to get back to my own element. I need to pick up my things at the condo and get home. I trust you, but if any of this ever gets out I'll die." (And kill you) she thought.

They were both very quiet for the rest of the time they were together. Vicky got her things from the condo and Carlo walked with her back to the Honda.

"Can I get a hug?" asked Carlo.

Vicky said "Yes", and threw in a kiss on the cheek that lasted a bit longer than the pecks he was used to in social circumstances.

"Carlo," said Vicky, looking directly into his eyes, "Thanks for understanding. I'm not cut out for this business."

As Vicky drove back to Gainesville, she thought of how far she was from her native West Virginia and how she had ended up in a place like Vero Beach, Florida. She had been a social worker for all of her professional career. As a girl growing up in Welch, West Virginia, that career had gotten off to a slow start. Girls there had jobs, not careers, and jobs were expected only because a family needed two incomes to survive. Women were still expected to take care of their men, raise kids, and go to church, in addition to working at the minute mart. Vicky had big brown eyes that saw a lot. She saw the lives her friends led and dreamed of something more. As things worked out, she could have served as the role model for the old mountain ballad about "Nancy Brown" which she occasionally hummed to herself.

"...along came a city slicker waving hundred dollar bills// took little Nance in his Packard car and drove up to the hills// She came home next morning early more a woman than a girly, and her daddy kicked that hussy out of town// Now she's living in the city, well she's living in the city doing swell, and them West Virginia hills can go to hell."

Vicky had indeed moved to the big city and married the cad in the Packard car who remained a cad, and a few years later was left standing in a cold Charleston rain as Vicky drove off never to look back. She hoped he had filed for a divorce, but did not really care. Armed with her degree in social work and a suitcase full of clothes, she drove south until she reached Gainesville, Florida, where she had a friend from school and where she decided to stay for awhile. "It's hot as the dickens, but at least there are no damn hills," she wrote home.

As she thought of Carlo she was reminded of her West Virginia snake oil salesman/husband. Still, she couldn't help feeling some affection for the guy. He had good looks for sure. Smooth Latin skin and a head full of soft brown hair with just the right touch of gray. Maybe a bit soft around the middle, but not fat at all. Certainly he had a self-assured charm. Maybe the gold necklace was not exactly West Virginia, but she remembered her city-slicker husband had worn such a chain.

Carlo had watched from the condo's parking lot, as Vicky crossed A1A and turned toward Highway 60 and home. Why had she been so special? He felt an unusual depression fall over him. He walked all ten flights up to his condo and sat for a long time on the balcony swirling and sipping his Manhattan-on-the-rocks and watching the charter boats as they returned to port.

***

Carlo had met Vicky at a Gainesville fitness center where he had a non-resident membership. They had a nodding acquaintance for a few days, and then he had looked at the sign-in sheet to find out her name. He was in town on business for only a few days, but it never hurt to know a pretty girl in case he came back to town. The day after he saw her name he saw her picture in the local newspaper with the caption, "DCF Under Fire."

Carlo normally liked to read about people being under fire. After all, his job was to quench the flames of passion and bring people together. Being under fire for taking kickbacks was another matter as that could involve himself.

The article was apparently one in a series involving a child who had died under suspicious circumstances. The child had been taken to Shands Medical Center at the University of Florida where the child protection team had been called in, and upon autopsy, confirmed the initial suspicion that the child had been shaken to death. Carlo skimmed through the details of how it was possible to tell if a child had been shaken to death, and concentrated on the part about Vicky Carter, a DCF supervisor. The child had come to the attention of DCF several months previously due to unexplained injuries, and had been removed from the home and placed in shelter care. The mother had been required to take parenting classes and ordered by the court to have no contact with her live-in boyfriend, or "paramour," under DCF terminology. Substance abuse classes were also ordered. Home inspections were made and, after a period of time, the mother and child were reunited, subject to continued DCF monitoring. The DCF caseworker had failed in her responsibilities and the mother and paramour were now in jail facing most serious charges. The negligent caseworker had been fired and her supervisor, one Vicky Carter, was left holding the bag. Even though the case worker had filed false reports of home visits, everything had happened on Vicky Carter's watch and she was left to answer questions and to receive the brunt of the criticism. A distraught Vicky Carter was quoted as saying there were some cases in which parents should not be given a second chance.

"One strike and you are out should be the rule in cases of severe abuse," she said.

"Children should not be subjected to a cycle of neglect and foster homes, but should be placed out for adoption without the delays currently prevalent in the system. Children are entitled to permanence," she said. She had no comment when asked whether DCF would be sued. Carlo wondered where the natural father was. He could possibly make a good plaintiff if he could be located.

A few days later Carlo had asked Vicky to go get a snack after a workout, and she accepted. After a few preliminaries, Carlo broached the subject of DCF adoptions and Vicky opened up with a passion. It was obvious after a few minutes that Vicky would not finish giving her opinions on DCF funding, overworked case workers, court delays, federal mandates and so forth, for several hours. Carlo suggested that they continue the discussion, but it had to include some time when he could take her mind off her work. She agreed and they set time for a real date.

Both Carlo and Vicky thought their first real date went well. Carlo found Vicky much more lively than he had expected. It turned out he was only a few years her senior. He had thought her much younger. She was enthusiastic about things in general, once her mind was diverted from her job. They exchanged the usual information about backgrounds and schools, but did not delve into prior relationships. They were both over forty and could assume each had not lived in isolation. Neither mentioned children. Carlo made Vicky relax, feel comfortable, even to the point that she wanted to confide in him, but she noticed he was finding out much more about her than she was him. He was born in Cuba, grew up in Miami, attended UF, lived for a while in DC, and now lived in Vero Beach. He had picked her up in a Volvo, wore nice casual clothes, and took her to the elegant Mr. Han's Supper Club, where he seemed to know the owner.

But something was missing. Occupation perhaps? He had said something about problems with some road construction project in town, but he did not look like a paving contractor. Well, he can just be my mystery man, Vicky thought. She continued to relax, she laughed, even giggled the way she had back in Welch.

Carlo knew not to spoil the ambiance of the evening by talking work, but he did want to find out more about the adoption process. It was clear that Vicky felt strongly about not returning children to abusive environments. He did need to check out two areas about her personally. What authority did she have in the DCF process, and whether she could be influenced by money? He knew this inquiry had to come later, so he too relaxed and enjoyed the company of the delightful, vivacious Vicky.

Shortly after their date, Carlo had to return to Vero Beach, but he promised to call Vicky on his next trip to Alachua County. He thought about inviting her to Vero but decided against it. He needed to find out if she was going to be a useful business associate or just a fun date. Vicky intrigued Carlo in a way that was new and different for him. He had generally preferred to date party girls. He had a common understanding with them.

They wanted to go out and have a "good time" as they often told him. This involved spending money which was *"no problemo"* for Carlo. He sometimes found these girls interesting and desirable but never really intriguing. Vicky was new territory. There was no doubt in Carlo's mind that Vicky was a free spirit, a prankster and a risk taker, but there was a quality he was unsure of. She was passionate about her work, and had a high sense of responsibility toward the families she worked with, and, to some extent, to her job with DCF, but he could sense an underlying frustration with how she fit into the whole process. It was this last feeling that led Carlo to ask Vicky one evening how she would like to do someone a small favor and earn half of two hundred thousand dollars? Vicky thought he was joking at first, but then, when he told her something of the plan, she became as serious as he was. He explained the situation with the Cunninghams, but left out a few details. He asked Vicky to come to Vero and see for herself what a fine couple they were. Once she was satisfied with them, all she would have to do was to pull a few strings to, in effect, move them to the front of the line waiting to adopt. Carlo said he knew how Vicky felt about returning children to abusive environments and the seemingly endless cycle of foster homes. Would she at least come with him to Vero?

Carlo had felt a little guilty about partially deceiving Vicky. He did not tell her she might have to cover up Reed Cunningham's felony record, but he did know she would have to do whatever was necessary to complete the deal once a certain line was crossed. *The Prince of Bribes*, he thought. I should write a training manual.

III

Judge AC was at work early the next morning. As he had predicted, the Andrews case had, indeed, been an ordeal. He had known that the attorneys would not finish by five o'clock as was scheduled and as had been promised. Judge AC kicked himself. He knew both lawyers very well and knew that their assurances were as reliable as a used car salesman's guarantee. He could have simply closed court at five o'clock and told them to come back, but that was the problem; they would have come back, and he wanted to finish the case as badly as the parties. Win or lose, parties to divorces are almost always ready to get on with their lives, and do not want to drag the litigation out. During a break in the Andrews case he had placed a call to Vicky Carter at DFC about the Jordan matter, but was told by a machine that she was on vacation.

Judge AC was at work early as he had nothing better to do. He lived alone these days, having sent his son off to college the year before. He had not really started dating since his divorce, two years ago. He had gone to lunch a few times with women who had called him up when they learned he was single, but nothing had clicked. He supposed he would be considered a good catch. He looked OK, didn't he? He liked to think of himself as wiry, rather than skinny. His hair was dark and full. So what if his whiskers were gray? They got shaved off every day. People who did not know him often expressed surprise when he admitted he was fifty-six. At least that was what they told him.

He had called Vicky Carter, the day before, about the Jordan matter as she was a former case worker in his dependency court. They had always had a good rapport, and he felt she could be trusted. This was not the case with all case workers. It was often frustratingly impossible to get a straight answer from many of these dedicated, but apprehensive, public servants. It did little good to rant and rave as that just made them clam up in fright. Vicky was now a supervisor, so was seldom in court, but he inevitably cheered up when he saw her smiling face and blond curls. Most of the faces in dependency court were unsmiling.

ALL RISE

Judge AC glanced down at a note pad lying on his desk. It was full of all the scribbling he had made during the Andrews case the day before. At the top of the pad, in bold print, he read "Call VC." He thought for a minute, remembered Ricky Jordan, and decided to call again. His subconscious mind could have told him that he really just wanted an excuse to talk to Vicky, but, like so many others, AC did not often delve into his subconsciousness. Perhaps, as a judge, he should have. He punched in the DCF number on his telephone, and, having been told to "wait one" by the operator, fantasized about what it would be like to go out with a woman like Vicky or, more specifically, Vicky herself. As he listened to Elton John playing in telephone's background, he considered Vicky's qualities. She didn't have outstanding good looks, but there was a vitality, a warmth and a sensuous quality about her which intrigued him. Voluptuous? Nah. Svelte? Not really. Sensuous? Yeah. Beautifully clear skin, big light-brown eyes, curly fluffy blond hair, an expectant smile formed by perfect cupid's bow lips... This last image reminded him how far his fantasizing had gone. Well, why shouldn't he fantasize? He knew the sexual harassment rules, and he was aware of the invisible barrier between judges and court personnel. Fantasizing was all that was left. More to the point, he knew Vicky Carter would have no interest in a man of his age regardless of the color of his hair. Surely, she lived in a different world. She probably listened to musicians he had never heard of. Kept up with the latest serials on TV. AC's daydreams of the vivacious Vicky were broken by the ringing of his other telephone line.

His usually punctual assistant had not arrived, and then he remembered that she had a dental appointment and would be a bit late, so he hung up on DCF and punched his other line on.

"Judge Cason."

"Oh, Judge, is that you? I expected your secretary."

"Can I help you?"

"Judge, your honor, this here is Mary Beth Jordan. My dad was in your court yesterday and he said you said you would help with my baby. I didn't know what to do but call you. They got her over in Putnam County and won't give her back or nothing. I just got out the hospital yesterday afternoon."

"Ms Jordan," said AC as he thought, *why oh why did I answer this telephone?*

"Where are you calling from?"

"I'm over at dad's house. I was living over at Ted's, but I can't go back there because of the fight."

"Who is Ted?"

"That's my boyfriend, or was my boyfriend. I ain't going to see him no more. He might be in jail for all I know."

"Ms Jordan, I do not think I am going to be able to help you at all. Putnam County is not in my jurisdiction. My court does not go over there if you see what I mean."

"But they told Daddy to come over here," said Mary Beth, sobbing.

ALL RISE

Judge AC paused and thought for a moment. Something did just not seem right. He was due in court in a few minutes. He knew court could start only when he got there, but he believed in punctuality and did not want to keep the crowd waiting.

"Ms Jordan, you are going to need a lawyer."

"But I can't afford one," she wailed.

Judge AC knew Mary Beth Jordan had missed the shelter hearing over in Putnam County the morning before. The judge there had presumably determined that the baby needed to be protected on a temporary basis. Although he felt some sympathy for the mother for all he knew she had placed the baby in a life-threatening situation while getting involved in a drunken brawl at the Landing. Even if that were the case, she needed some help in dealing with the system. *What the hell*, he thought, the baby will be fine for a couple of weeks and this hysterical mom probably brought it all on herself.

"Look Ms Jordan, you need to get over to Putnam County and go to the courthouse and ask for a free lawyer. I have to go now. Good luck," he said as he hung up the telephone. He could not help feeling a twinge of guilt as he thought of Mary Beth Jordan trying to wade through the bureaucracy at the Putnam County Courthouse.

"All rise," announced the large bailiff, a former interior lineman at Southern Mississippi. "The Circuit Court of Alachua County will come to order, the Honorable Judge Alva Cason presiding. There will be no talking or gum chewing in the courtroom. You may be seated."

Judge AC made a mental note to tell the bailiff that it was the Eighth Judicial Circuit Court in and for Alachua County which was in session; and where had Ben gotten that gum chewing line from anyway? Perhaps a holdover from the spittoon days. Where was the discarded gum to go? Stuck under the benches like in grammar school? No cell phones would make more sense. He decided just to ignore the whole episode. He was not big on ceremony anyway, and he certainly did not want an "Oyez, Oyez, Oyez." That would really confuse things. He would take "Big Ben" Stoker just the way he was. Big Ben was large enough never to have to raise his voice. If there was some tension in court, Bailiff Stoker would quietly sidle up to the tense person in an avuncular way and whisper a word or two in his ear. Judge AC never heard what was said, but it always seemed to work. People who are excited in court do not like to lose face. Yelling at them does not quiet them, but incites them. "Please, Mr. Defendant, I want to hear what you have to say," usually works wonders. *Most of them can't talk more than a minute*, thought Judge AC as he looked at the morning's detention docket.

There were no emergency shelter hearings scheduled for dependencies, and Mary Beth Jordan had solved the mystery of the Palm Landing episode. Judge AC looked around the courtroom. It was usually easy to spot individuals who were in the wrong courtroom. The dependency crowd presented one appearance;

the delinquency crowd another, but it was sometimes close. The civil litigants did not always look civil, but were still distinguishable from the criminal crowd. It was a lot like shopping at Sam's Club, AC thought. You could spot the folks buying enough food for a boy scout camp; then the old couple who drove over from Dixie County for their monthly purchases; then the couple buying food for a Gator game tail-gate party; then a socialite with a book or two in her cart feeling proud that she saved three dollars out of her monthly budget of three thousand.

AC prided himself on this ability to recognize the audience. He knew most of the lawyers, but those that he did not know were identifiable in their suits and ties. Sometimes out of boredom they would wander in and watch the proceedings while they awaited their turn in some other courtroom. The traffic court crowd was also easy to spot. They would often have large charts depicting the intersection where they were accused of running a red light. Others would be the UF students dressed for an outing to a local pub or fitness center. When someone looked out of place, Judge AC would ask the bailiff to check discreetly and see if they were in the right courtroom. There was such an out of character person sitting in the back of today's courtroom crowd, but Judge AC thought he would wait and see what happened. At times the misplaced person would realize something was amiss and leave, but AC knew, that for many people, courts were as confusing as hospitals, and people could wait for hours only to find they were in the wrong courtroom. This was a short docket, so no one would have to wait long.

"Your Honor," said Assistant State Attorney Susan Workman, "We have one matter we would like to take out of order for the convenience of Officer Walsh who has to get back to duty."

"Of course," said Judge AC. "What case it that?"

"It's the Shilling case on page two of the docket, your honor. Mr. Shilling (Judge AC wondered why twelve-year-olds were referred to as mister) and his co-defendant are charged with auto theft. The state feels that they should remain in detention even though they do not score enough points on the scale for secure detention."

"OK, tell me more," said Judge AC as he quickly scanned the file of Sedrick Shilling.

It seemed that Sedrick and his co-defendant, who was his half-brother, had stolen a thirteen-year-old Ford Crown Victoria and had driven it into a ditch after a joy ride of two hundred yards. Judge AC looked for the defendants. Just as he was about to ask where they were, he saw two small faces barely peeking over the defendant's podium. The file showed no prior juvenile problems for either and, under the current scoring system by the Florida Department of Juvenile Justice, the children should not have even been taken into custody, but should have been released to their parents with instructions to report to court the next day. Obviously, thought Judge AC, there is more to come.

ALL RISE

"Judge," said Assistant State Attorney Workman, "These defendants need secure detention. They not only stole their uncle's car, they wrecked it and ran from the scene. When Officer Walsh arrived the parents were non-cooperative and refused to say where the kids were. There would be an obvious security risk if the defendants were returned to such a home. Officer Walsh located the defendants and, in the process of taking them into custody, was called a white MFer and was spat upon. I have officer Walsh here to testify if necessary. The state has nothing further."

Patience in a judge is not a virtue, thought Judge AC, it is a necessity; an essential quality, just as agility is in an athlete.

"Ms Workman, I've read the file and appreciate your concerns. Let me hear from the counsel for the children."

The Public Defender had, by this time, been appointed to represent the juvenile defendants. The parents, had they shown up, would have been required to sign a statement that they were without funds to retain a private lawyer. That usually presented no problem as almost all parents of juvenile defendants were in debt up to their necks and credit cards were not an option in retaining lawyers. The state had hired an overseer for this appointment process to ensure that rich people were not getting free legal counsel at taxpayer expense. This enforcer of the law had no staff and was responsible for six counties and thousands of cases. About all he could do was to check the financial affidavits of the defendants and look for errors. AC remembered one case where counsel was denied on the basis that the defendant earned, according to his sworn affidavit, five thousand dollars a month working as a busboy. Misplaced decimal; misplaced logic, thought AC.

There were two assistant public defenders assigned to juvenile delinquency court in Alachua County. Judge AC felt he was the most fortunate judge in the whole state when it came to handling juvenile delinquency. His defenders and prosecutors were highly professional; they were courteous to one another and the court; they did not raise sham issues; they did not delay proceedings; and were all, in Judge AC's semi-lecherous mind, beautiful young women. He knew that the only reason Susan Workman had asked for secure detention in this case was to salve the ego of the arresting officer. Judge AC felt that this was important too. The assistant public defender knew it was important, too, but all knew that secure detention was prohibited by legislative law. This was strictly a financial decision by the legislature, but it took all discretion away from the judges who were on the front line. Judge AC could anticipate the headline: "Judge releases juvenile car thieves who spat on officer."

The representative from The Florida Department of Juvenile Justice was in court and spoke up. "Your honor, we would like to be heard. In all due respect to your honor, the law permits the court no discretion in this matter. These defendants must not remain in secure detention, (*at many dollars per day, thought*

AC), but may be held in home detention in the custody of their parents."

"What says the defendant?"

"Your honor, these children meant no harm. It was their uncle's car and we intend to raise consent as a defense. What they may have said to officer Walsh was inexcusable, but they are not really felons. They do need some discipline, but they do not need to be locked away awaiting trial in this case. We request that they be released to the custody of their parents. Home detention is not necessary. They're not going anywhere."

Judge AC knew it was up to him. The parents had not even bothered to show up in court so he could not lecture them or even feel them out for possible future problems. He had six other cases on his detention docket and less than one-half an hour to deal with them. Should I fret over this, he thought? This is why I get paid the big bucks, to take the heat.

"These children are entitled by law to be released on home detention. I direct the department to conduct a home study to determine if they even have a home and report back to me no later than tomorrow morning. If the parents will have them, they may be released. If the parents are not to be found, or will not take them, then DCF should be alerted. And, as a point of personal curiosity, how did these kids even manage to steal a car? They don't appear able even to see over the dashboard."

"Your honor, they are alleged to have cooperated by one of them steering and the other holding down the accelerator," said Susan Workman the vicious prosecutor.

The rest of the docket was uneventful.

"There being no further business before the court, court is adjourned!" Judge Alva Cason announced in his best senatorial tone. This was repeated by Bailiff Stoker. The unidentified and unclassified person on the back row rose and left. Judge AC felt a moment's curiosity pass over him, but then, he too, rose and left through the side door that took him through Judge Lee's chambers and into the hallway.

***

A few weeks, routine weeks from Judge AC's perspective, passed. The events of these weeks were not, however, routine, uneventful or without trauma and tribulation for the litigants passing before the family division of the Eighth Judicial Court in and for Alachua County. AC could, perhaps, remain detached, but the mothers and fathers and children in his court could not. It was not quite certain that AC met his own ideals of detachment, but he tried. One day, to get away from the courthouse and its turmoil, he walked the three blocks down to the lunch counter at Wise's Drug Store. Founded in nineteen thirty-eight, Norman Rockwell could almost be pictured in the corner with his sketch pad. One could, in the words of Walter O'Connor, a local attorney, still get a real American sandwich there. Tuna salad on wheat toast, hold the mayo. BLT. Turkey. Cream and olive on white. Bar-B-Q with pickles on the side. And, best of all, a milk shake made from scratch. Two scoops of vanilla ice cream, malt, a few squirts of chocolate and a pint of milk, all stirred up in a Waring blender.

AC loved Wise's. Its location and ambiance attracted all sorts of local citizens. It was Gainesville's own version of the Chatterbox Cafe as immortalized on *Prairie Home Companion.* Your counter-mate could be your stockbroker, your accountant, your cardiologist or your yardman. Retired professors met there. Society dames dined. Vicky Carter sat next to the only empty stool at the counter, and AC did not hesitate to grab it.

"Ms Carter, is this seat reserved?"

"Why, yes, judge, just for you. How have you been?" she asked, with her customary smile.

"No complaints really. I'm about ready for a transfer to civil, but family has treated me well. I'm sorry you got elevated to the upper echelons, but that was to be expected. Can you share any gossip about the new district legal counsel? My lawyers are naturally protective, but I gather he is, shall we say, a real martinet."

"Judge, I'm not sure what that means, but it doesn't sound flattering. I'm more interested in what you think of our workers. We've caught a lot of heat lately. I can understand the public's reaction, but do you feel you can rely on us?"

"Let's talk about new movies instead," said AC. There were some things he did not wish to share with Vicky, and he wished he had not asked her about her boss. Not really her supervisor, he thought. She reports to Department of Children and Families staff, and the DCF attorneys report to the district legal counsel.

"I would love to," said Vicky. "but I really don't get out that often."

"Well, how 'bout them Gators?" asked AC hopefully. The UF football team had been ranked in the top ten in preseason polls.

Vicky was even more at a loss with this and did not even know a witty reply, so mumbled something and sat in silence as they finished their sandwiches. Polite departure remarks were made and they paid their bills and left for work.

As AC walked back to the courthouse he thought well, *I had my chance and blew it.*

Damn, what a dummkopf. The Gators! Of all things. She likes kids, not jocks. I don't even like the Gators that much. Well, let's not be delusional. Polite is one thing; interest is another.

Vicky walked back to her office along the same street, but on the side north of AC's path. *You are really cool*, she thought. You know absolutely nothing about new movies. Not even enough to carry on an intelligent conversation. The Gators? Well, on football weekends the traffic is impossible. I do know that. Well, so what, she thought. The judge was just trying to be polite. That's the way he is in court. Polite. Polite to everybody. Polite is one thing, interest another. As she waited for the light to change at Main Street she fantasized about what it would be like to go out with a man like AC, or more specifically, AC himself. She considered his qualities. He did not have outstanding good looks, but there was a vitality and warmth about him that intrigued her. That tag of unkempt brown hair that flopped down on his brow could have been sprayed up in place, but she liked the casual image. His hazel eyes were usually gentle, and often, during a hearing he looked like he had to suppress a smile on his rather thin lips. She had seen him, on occasion, take a very firm stance in court but had never seen him explode or degrade anyone. Her daydreams of the austere AC were broken when the Main Street light changed, and she crossed over with the usual crowd of lunchgoers.

IV

Judge AC's responsibilities within the Family Division of the Eighth Judicial Circuit Court included work in three of the six counties of the circuit. His home port was Gainesville, the county seat of Alachua County. There he handled all of the juvenile delinquency cases, one half of the dependency cases, and an occasional divorce case, referred due to some conflict of interest with the assigned judge. On two mornings each week in Alachua Judge AC presided over what was known as "detention court" which was the initial proceeding for people taken into custody for reasons other than being an adult charged with a crime. These detainees included juvenile delinquents, minors placed in shelter for reasons of dependency, and civil contempt cases involving both people delinquent in child support and the occasional unfortunate witness who failed to respond to a subpoena. Ricky Jordan had intruded into AC's detention court, but had been long forgotten. Judge AC also traveled west to Levy and Gilchrist counties at least two days a week where he handled all family matters including civil injunctions against domestic violence, an unpleasant chore he was spared in Alachua.

Scheduling cases has always been a major problem for the courts. No one knows how many juveniles will be taken into custody on a particular day, or how many cases of domestic violence will occur. All family cases need to be handled expeditiously due to the dislocation of the families as well as a potential for future violence. A special source of frustration in dependency court is the request for "TPR" trials. Termination of parental responsibility. A deadly term from the standpoint of the family of a dependent child. Dependency can result from abuse or deliberate neglect but it can also be due to an inability to care for a child due to chronic poverty or mental illness. This is serious business. To permanently remove a child from a parent or parents and place the child up for adoption ranks at the top part of the scale of serious judicial proceedings. In practice, however, few cases ever proceed to a contested trial. If the case is weak, the DCF backs down. If the case is strong, the parents recognize their inability to care for the child, and do not contest the proceeding. The problem facing the courts in all this, is bringing the case to a head.

Neither side is ever willing to concede until a firm trial date is set by the court. Once a firm trial date is set, and the parties know that no continuances will be granted, everyone involved will be forced to make a realistic assessment of the evidence, and a mutually acceptable resolution can usually occur.

Judge AC understood all of these human dynamics and would set firm trial dates even though he knew he could not possibly cover all of the trials which had been set. Judicial politics then came into play. The chief judge of the Eighth Judicial Circuit had the responsibility of assigning judges to their jobs. Judge AC was able to convince the chief judge to guarantee a backup judge for all TPR trials that Judge AC set and could not cover personally. This created a certain resentment among some of AC's fellow judges who guarded their own calendars with jealous zeal. Their cases were important too, as well as their time away from court. They were, after all, entitled to a bit of relaxation. Judge AC, of course, knew that judicial availability was only part of the equation. Courtroom space was limited as well as the number of attorneys who would be available to handle a trial. All this resulted in a game of "who blinks first," and was played in all the divisions of court; in civil, and criminal, as well as family.

As a result of his strict application of time standards, Judge AC had to spend much less time in trials, and his cases did not back up in a logjam. He remembered the famous baseball movie line, "build it and they will come." He thought, "set them and they will go away" would be a good motto for the courts.

One day as Judge AC sat in Alachua dependency court he thought about the minutes ticking away into hours, and the hours turning into days, and the days to months, and the months to years. The wheels of justice, he thought, slow, but really much faster than glaciers. As he looked out over the crowd he saw a familiar face. This was not uncommon as he saw hundreds of faces every month. They all remembered his face as he was the only judge they knew. The reverse was not true, but this particular face rang a distinct bell in AC's memory. The cases were called, and Judge AC tried to exhibit the concerned expression of a person with hemorrhoids as one of his seniors had suggested. Finally, the last case on the docket was called; In re: Justine Jordan. It was then that AC remembered his previous contact with this family.

"Your Honor," said Margie Maguire, one of the DCF attorneys, "this case is a transfer from Putnam County and is before the court for judicial review."

Judge AC looked at the group clustered in front of his bench. Margie McGuire was standing at the podium dressed in a rather formal dark brown pants suit. Behind her was what Judge AC presumed to be the case worker. This was a new face, but her facial expression read "apprehensive new case worker" all over it. To the Judge's right stood Ricky Jordan looking much the same as he had several weeks earlier. Next to him stood a young woman who made AC think Mayella Ewell had stepped out of the pages of "*To Kill a Mockingbird*" and come to court. She had an expectant expression on her face as if she had been waiting to tell her side of the story for a long time. Beside "Mayella," who turned out to be Mary Beth Jordan, stood Jane Jennings. Jane was one of the more reliable of the guardian ad litem volunteers who assisted in dependency court. Judge AC thought, thank goodness there was not the usual cortege of aunts, uncles, and other family members that usually came to court on these occasions. Also noticeably absent was anyone from Justine Jordan's father's side of the family. Judge AC knew he was derelict in his duty in not having read the DCF report as well as the guardian's report prior to court, but he was a speed reader and had gone over these materials as the parties approached the bench.

"Judge," said Margie Maguire, "as you can see from the file this case arose somewhere near Melrose near the county line. The incident leading up to the alleged neglect started in Alachua County, but the case ended up over in Putnam County where the mother had been staying with a boyfriend. She really has no permanent residence, and the putative father of the child is in the armed forces, stationed out of state. Paternity has never been formally established. At the shelter hearing over in Putnam County, Judge Hood determined that the child was at risk, due to this incident and to the mother's prior history with the Department. The child was placed in foster care because of lack of a suitable relative placement. We are asking the court to continue the case for one month to give the Department time to investigate more and to determine whether to seek a termination.

"Why," asked Judge AC, "is the case now in Alachua County?" He suspected simple case dumping from Putnam.

"Judge, I'm really not sure. I just saw the file this morning, and I don't know the exact history of what led to the transfer to Alachua. That's one reason we need a continuance. We need to review all the facts and circumstances, but we do see the potential for a termination proceeding."

"What says the guardian?" AC asked.

"Judge, we just received the file, and have not assigned a guardian. I'm only here as a stand-in until we can get someone to take over the case. I would point out that an attorney for the mother has never been appointed. If the Department has been considering a TPR, that should have happened over in Putnam County. We cannot contest a continuance, but we think there should be a review of relative placement without delay. This baby has been away from the mom for some time now. There has been supervised visitation, but that's not much help for a child deprived of its mother. I would point out that this case doesn't involve direct abuse of the child at all, but merely alleged neglect by the mom. If an appropriate relative placement can be found there's no reason for the mother and child to be separated."

"Ms Jordan, I am Judge Cason. I believe we spoke over the phone one time. Do you have any comments to make at this time?"

"Judge, your Honor, I got a lot to say. I think this whole thing is trumped up. I ain't never done nothing to harm my baby. I think H and RS has got something going on. "There ain't no reason she can't stay over at my dad's. I agree I need some help, but that ain't no reason to keep me from my baby the way they done."

Judge AC assessed the situation. He believed in the sincerity of the DCF employees before him, but he knew that due to the recent transfer of the case, they did not know much more about this case than he did. He had no desire to embarrass them by a lot of pointed questions. All they were asking for was for some time to evaluate the case. Still, he was curious about the relative placement decision. What was wrong with Ricky? he thought.

"Mr. Jordan. You were in court a few weeks ago I believe. What is your situation? Where do you live? Could you care for this baby until all this is resolved?"

"Judge, I don't mean to sound disrespectful, but something fishy is going on. Them folks over in Putnam have not treated us fair. I can see what they are saying here about needing time to straighten things out, and I ain't got no problem with that, but there ain't no reason the baby can't stay over to my place. Mary Beth's staying there now, and we got lots of room. We got a big double-wide with a single wide attached. I work and my old lady stays home. We raised four kids, and none of them ever got in trouble except Mary Beth, and she ain't really done nothing bad but hang out with the wrong crowd."

"Ms McGuire, has this been investigated?"

"Judge, the file reflects that Mr. Jordan lives with his paramour and has a criminal history dating back to nineteen seventy."

"Judge," snorted Ricky, "that is just so much BS, excuse the language. Back during Viet Nam I got arrested at a veterans for peace protest march, but that was it. I might have had a couple of run-ins, but nothing serious like. I got no idea what they mean about living with some paramour. Me and my old lady have been together for over twenty-five years."

"Mr. Jordan," inquired AC, "have you, or, that is, are you married?"

Ricky actually scratched his head. "Judge, it wasn't really fashionable back then, but no. The answer is no. We ain't never been formally married."

Judge AC shifted into his formal tone and granted the continuance. He directed DFC to conduct an updated placement investigation of Ricky Jordan's home and to report back in one week. He also requested more information about the putative father supposedly stationed at Camp Lejeune. He had always felt some special kinship with fellow Marines.

***

After the mutual disaster at Wise's Drug Store, the next contact AC had with the intriguing Vicky Carter came at the local Publix supermarket. There she was in the vegetable section hefting a bunch of collard greens packaged in plastic.

"Them greens taste good cooked with a bit of bacon," he said in a cornpone accent from her back.

"Oh, Judge, you scared me. Do you really like collards?"

"Not only the greens, but cornbread dipped in pot liker."

This was a bit better, AC thought. The conversation with Vicky at Wise's had been running through his mind for some time. He was determined to do better if the chance ever arose. Vicky was dressed in shorts and a tank top, instead of her usual professional courtroom outfit. AC was not accustomed to this and hoped he did not ogle. She was wearing her habitual sunny smile to which he was accustomed, and, as he struggled for something to say, he remembered that his old lawyer friend, Doug Smith, had once been spotted shopping for vegetables in Publix with a young woman not his wife. Well, perhaps one could sit next to a girl in Wise's and not arouse suspicions, but to be seen shopping for vegetables together could mean something else. AC was not about to be deterred.

"Actually, I'm a big veggie eater. I think I could live off sweet corn all year long."

"Well, Judge, that's a good thing to know. I have a couple of rows in my garden. I'll bring some to court the next time I'm there, if you take bribes."

AC stammered out an unintelligible reply, and. as Vicky walked off, she looked back over her shoulder and repeated her smile, AC watched her as long as he dared. Again he thought what a dunce he was. Everyone was polite to judges. Everyone laughed at judges' jokes no matter how bad or old. Still, there seemed to be something special in her smile, but then he thought of Browning. What was it? The Duchess' smile for "what e're she looked on," was the same as her smile for the Duke, so he had her eliminated. Some people just smiled a lot. Vicky's smile for AC was the same as her smile for the bag boy he thought as he checked out.

As she went through the checkout line Vicky thought, I think he might like me. He could just be shy.

Not long after AC's Publix encounter with Vicky, the most amazing coincidence occurred. Gainesville and the surrounding area has a population of over two hundred thousand people. AC was at the Home Depot. "Agent Orange," as it was sometimes called, was not a home town place like Wise's so chance meetings with acquaintances were rare. AC was bending over looking into a bin of bolts that had been shuffled around so that many of the three inchers were in the two-inch basket. He felt two probes in his back and heard a voice say:

"Señor, thees ees a steekup. One false move and you are a dead mon."

AC turned, and to his shock, amazement and delight there was Vicky Carter, grinning like a porpoise.

"Why, Mees Carter, I never knew you were a bandito. I never even knew you were Mexican."

"Señor," said Vicky will a twitch of her eyebrow, "there ees much you don know about me."

"Look," said AC laughing, "we've simply got to stop meeting like this in public. People will start to talk."

"I agree," said Vicky, "Why don't you come out to my farm, it's nice and private, and you can help me fix my mower. I'll fix you a BLT as good as Wise's."

AC was prepared for light banter this time, but Vicky sounded serious. Was she? All he could do was gulp, "When? I mean, what's wrong with your mower?"

"Well it's that plastic thing on the side where the grass blows out. The bolt or whatever was holding it fell off. I need to get some kind of rod to stick through the holes and some kind of way to hold it and keep it from falling off." Judge AC was more in his element now. He mentioned a grass deflector, a six inch long one-quarter inch bolt with a lock nut to hold things in place. When this purchase had been made the cheerful couple walked out of Home Depot and AC followed Vicky to her car like a puppy. They agreed on a time for the repair job, and this time it was Vicky who watched AC out of sight before driving off.

ALL RISE

Vicky had given AC the directions to her farm. It was south of Gainesville near the town of Micanopy, which claimed to have been founded in eighteen twenty-one. This whole area was rich in Florida history. The Seminole Indians, who had been called Creeks before they had been driven out of Alabama, settled the area during the time the Spanish were still in control of Florida. When the Spanish left, the Seminoles took charge of the abandoned wild cattle and kept them on a vast prairie later named Payne, after one of their leaders. William Bartram had walked through the area on his travels as a naturalist in the seventeen hundreds. War inevitably broke out between the Seminoles and the United States leaving many Florida cities named after forts and military heroes on both sides of the conflict. Micanopy was one and Gaines was another. Marjorie Kinnan Rawlings Baskin had lived over in Cross Creek a few miles to the east, and her house and orange grove were still there. This area was truly special in AC's mind, but he had no idea what to expect when he arrived at Vicky's farm. He knew he should not really be seeing one of the court personnel, but his elated spirits squelched all thought of any adverse consequences of his actions.

Later, driving home from Vicky's farm, AC felt his visit had gone quite well. Extremely well, he thought. Vicky had met him at the front door of her ranch style house with a big glass of iced tea in her hand. "I hope you like it sweet. I'm so glad you could come.

I really love my place, but, except for my animals, I really have nobody to talk to. Come on, I'll show you around."

She actually took his hand like a teenager, and AC began to feel like one. They saw the stables where Vicky kept three Tennessee Walkers and a fenced off area for chickens, complete with a roost and hen house.

"I grow my own eggs," Vicky bragged.

"Well, the hens participate I suppose," AC threw in as a bit of wit, and Vicky giggled politely.

The farm looked to be about fifteen acres consisting of three five-acre parcels lined up in a row, away from the county road. There were scattered pines and a grove of oaks along the rear of the property. Vicky showed AC the dove cote she had built herself and where she planned to keep homing pigeons some day. There was a high fence surrounding the goat pen which held a miniature alpine mountain made from limestone. The goldfish pond needed attention as did much of the rest of the farm, but the rundown aspect of the place gave it a homey ambiance not found in the pampered and manicured horse farms to the south, around Ocala.

After the promised BLT, the offending mower was tackled. AC had brought his own tool kit just in case. This was fortunate, as Vicky's tools were a haphazard jumble piled in a cardboard box. From a practical standpoint, AC could have done the job with only a pair of pliers, but his vise-grips came in handy for holding a spring in place while he gingerly eased the new bolt into its slot and tightened the nut with his ratchet wrench. This spring allowed the glass deflector to kick up when a foreign object was hit and then push the deflector back down into position. AC was at ease fixing the mower, and refrained from his usual string of curses when the deck spring popped out during the process.

After washing up he felt his former uneasiness return, but Vicky's West Virginia charm came to the rescue, and before he knew it he was laughing and swapping old tales about country life he had heard from his mother. There was no need to talk of the Gators, movies or court proceedings. Vicky had thanked him, maybe a bit too profusely, for fixing her mower and held both of his hands as he got into his pickup. AC had felt a strong urge to hug Vicky but did not trust himself to do so. He was still worried that her smiles were not a signal to him but merely a manifestation of her warm nature. AC's drive home took him back across the vast expanse of Payne's Prairie. It periodically flooded and became a lake when its draining sinkhole became plugged, but it was now a wetland full of wildlife. His already elated spirits now soared as high as the hawk he spotted cruising the prairie looking for a late lunch.

V

Carlo Proenza called Reed Cunningham soon after Vicky left to apologize for the missed appointment. At first he considered some phony excuse that would keep the door open, but he realized that Vicky was gone forever. He decided to level with Reed and tell him the whole story. He knew Reed was a man of the world and would not like phony excuses. Their conversation turned out unexpectedly pleasant, and Carlo was invited over for an outing on *Osprey II* the following weekend.

Carlo arrived at *Kissimmee Kiss* driving his brand-new silver-gray Volvo convertible.

The weather had cooled off somewhat but not enough for Carlo to lower his convertible top. He was greeted warmly by Rita, who said Reed was down at the dock checking out the boat. The *Osprey II* was a thirty-eight-foot cruiser and still smelled like a new car. There were a couple of rod holders near the stern, but she was not really equipped for fishing. Simply motoring up and down the Indian River and occasionally into the Atlantic on a calm day was her style, although a run to the Bahamas would not have been out of the question. Rita had graduated from the Coast Guard boating school and held a captain's license which would allow her to take out six people on a charter basis. A "six-packer" as it was called. The *Osprey II* had two sleeping cabins and a luxurious dining area. Carlo had been on bigger yachts in the Chesapeake, but they had required a crew and lacked the intimacy of the *Osprey II*. An intimacy soon formed between Reed and Carlo, but it had more to do with mutual interests than the ambiance of the yacht.

"What's our first port of call, Captain Rita?" called Carlo once they were under way.

"This is more like a shakedown cruise. We need to check out all the equipment every week or so. I thought we would just look for a quiet cove and have lunch. Somewhere away from the jet-skiers. Reed even brought lettuce for the manatees if we see them."

After finding Rita's quiet cove, they dined on sushi along with a very fine Chablis.

After lunch Rita left the men to talk while she busied herself about the boat in her role as captain, bo'sun and navigator.

"Carlo," Reed said, having been relaxed by the wine, "Tell me about yourself."

Carlo rather eased into the subject although he instinctively felt that he could trust Reed as a fellow traveler. They talked of the Washington days and people they both knew. How some of the mighty had fallen and how some of the simpletons had risen to power. Reed tactfully told Carlo how he knew from the start that Carlo was a con, and Carlo replied that it was essential that people understand what he was up to, but that no one actually come out and say so. This, he explained serves several purposes.

"When law enforcement engages in activities that induce a normally law abiding citizen to commit a crime they break the rule against entrapment. Remember John DeLorean? Automotive genius who named a car after himself? He got charged with dope dealing supposedly in an effort to save his failing automobile company. He was acquitted since someone must have felt he was improperly lured into misbehavior."

Reed said he agreed and wondered why his lawyer did not argue that theory during his late unpleasantness with the law.

"Same thing could happen in prostitution stings. I would never want to come out directly and suggest an illegal transaction. I guess it's like a game. The cops don't want to suggest a crime and the guy on the make doesn't either, in case he is talking to a cop, or they're listening in. I like to somehow convey the impression of guaranteed results without explicitly saying so."

At this point Carlo got up and walked over to the port rail and looked at a white heron poised in the shallows waiting for lunch to swim by.

"Never rush things. Be as patient as that heron over there."

Yeah," said Reed with a burp. "If I was one of those birds I'd starve to death."

Carlo gave a polite chuckle.

"Another reason never to mention the specifics of the transaction is to provide an internal face-saving device for the participant. Self-delusion is a strong human instinct. Some people taking bribes do so with full cognizance of what they are doing, but most want some moral justification for doing what they do. If a spade were called a spade this justification would be lost. This was just the case with my friend, Vicky. She had a moral justification for her actions, but was overcome by what she considered to be an immoral act."

The *Osprey* gave several gentle rolls in response to a passing cruiser that was ignoring the no wake zone that applied in the manatee protection area of the river.

"Take for example," Carlo continued, "the cop who turns his head to a dope deal. We have a willing buyer and a willing seller. All the cop has to do is to be somewhere else when it takes place. You don't want to come up to him and say, 'How much of a bribe do you want to keep quiet on this?' You use words which convey that message without saying so directly."

"Carlo, my friend," Reed said, as he opened another bottle of Chablis, "I really appreciate your efforts on the adoption business. Now that Rita's not working she really wants to be a mom. After all, she's just 37. She wants to do the soccer thing and all the rest. As you might gather, what Rita wants, Rita gets. I'm 57 myself, and would really like a taste of domesticity. When I was working, it was all work. All day, every day. I still manage to stay busy, but with Rita and a nanny I think I would enjoy that part of life I missed earlier. Now tell me," he said as he handed a brimming glass of the first-rate wine to Carlo, "what other tricks of the trade are you willing to share? Well, let me come directly to the point. As you know, I claim to be retired, but I do have friends in businesses who occasionally need a helping hand. How do you go about finding out whether or not people are susceptible to your form of persuasion?"

Carlo thought for a minute and sipped his Chablis.

"Often it's a simple question of greed, but sometimes it's vulnerability. Politicians are almost always greedy, so are naturally vulnerable. They're not paid much, so they always need money, and they have to raise a lot money to run for election. I know this is elementary, but a little research helps a lot. Much of the information I use comes from public records.

ALL RISE

I took a course at UF called fact finding. Most of the kids did just enough work to pass, but I kept all my materials and have expanded on 'em ever since. It's easy to find who's behind paying taxes, who's being sued for an increase in alimony and so forth. I find it entertaining even if there's no foreseeable use for my research."

"You could always get a job as a gossip columnist." Reed threw in with a chuckle.

"Take judges, for example. They're relatively well paid and rarely have to run for election in Florida, but they sometimes have the heel of Achilles. Alcee Hastings, who was a federal judge for life, was impeached after being acquitted on a bribery charge. I guess I should call him Congressman Hastings now. I never figured out his motive in the case. Maybe it was a race thing."

The heron's patience, poise and perseverance paid off as the onlookers saw what appeared to be a small mullet wiggling in its sharp beak.

"Now comes the time for the most patience," said Carlo. "He's got the prize right in his mouth, but has to flip it up just right so it will slide down his throat head first. One slip and it's back to the waiting game."

Reed sat back and let his new friend rattle on.

"You probably don't remember the big scandal on the Florida Supreme Court a few years back. The loser there was a guy named McCain or something, who ended up in the dope trade after leaving the bench. I can't remember the specifics of his case. I don't think it was monetary bribery, more like ruling in favor of someone to gain political influence."

"So you're saying money is not the only root of evil?" put in Reed.

"Well, take Benedict Arnold for example. He apparently felt he was not appreciated by the rebels. His moral justification for selling out was that he had fought with the British against the French and didn't want to fight with the French and Americans against the Brits."

Reed quietly assessed his new friend and liked what he saw and heard. Carlo was suave, philosophical and at the same time unpretentious. They talked in generalities for some time more when Carlo, looking up at a waving Captain Rita, said, "It looks like Captain may need us to do our thing with the ropes and stuff. Reed, this has been a pleasure, a fine cruise. I hope you invite me again. I do enjoy my work. Give me a call. I'm like those trial lawyers who say, 'no recovery, no fee.' I'm still working on that adoption situation. I thought Vicky was perfect, but who knows?"

***

After waiting a few days after the lunch at Vicky's farm, (AC did not want to seem overly eager,) he called Vicky at work.

"How about eats and a flick tonight?"

"I thought you'd never ask," said Vicky. "What time?"

"Why not meet at Ballyhoo's at six? You know where that is? The place in front of Royal Park theaters on University? There're a couple of movies there that don't look too bad. l'm not really big on car chase scenes, but one looked like a comedy."

"You've got it," said Vicky "See you at six."

As AC pulled into the parking lot at Ballyhoo's, he almost wished he had chosen a different restaurant. One with a quiet candlelit corner table where patrons were addressed as "Sir" and "Madam." Then he saw that Vicky was already there, looking so young, warm and friendly, that he immediately relaxed. Relaxed to some extent that is. She grabbed him by the arm and said,

"This is one of my favorite places. How did you know?"

They were seated in a noisy table in the middle of the room directly under a dripping air conditioning vent. The waiter, wearing shorts and suspenders, gave them the ubiquitous, "Hi, guys, what'll it be for drinks? It's two-for-one happy hour until seven."

Vicky ordered sweet iced tea, and AC, who really felt he deserved two Margaritas, joined her. The menu listed many of the fish dishes at market price. AC was not about to ask how much the grouper steak actually cost. He was not going to be a cheapskate on his first date. Instead, he suggested to Vicky, "The grouper steak was really good the last time I was here."

Vicky, too, thought about asking about the price, but decided AC was a big boy, really a worldly-wise gentleman, and said, "AC, that's perfect. I love fish, but never have them at home."

"The secret is in the freshness. I really prefer to catch my own, then I know just how long it's been since they were swimming in the ocean."

"Will you take me? I mean, take me fishing with you," blushed Vicky, flustered at her wit.

"Absolutely. Are you a fisher girl? I'll tell you, let's let the water temperature cool off a bit then the mackerel will migrate south along the coast. When they're off the reef, they practically jump in the boat with you."

Vicky smiled and silently assessed her date, as he rambled on about fishing. His boyish enthusiasm, coupled with his self-possessed urbaneness, pleased her. The word 'urbane' did not actually cross her mind, but the image depicted by the word did. She felt she had made a good choice in men for once. God, I hope he's not gay, she thought.

The movie portion of the date went as well as the meal. The new couple saw AC's comedy, and he felt Vicky's head on his shoulder during two particularly hilarious sequences.

"That was my kind of movie," said AC as they left the marquee and walked out into the crowded parking lot. "Where are you parked?"

"Practically next to you out by Ballyhoo's."

Vicky unlocked her door with a click of her remote, and AC gallantly opened it for her and beckoned for her to enter, but Vicky just stood by the door saying nothing.

AC tried again.

"You know, you really take a chance on movies these days."

Vicky was silent as the tar baby.

"I'll tell you what," said AC "let's meet at Wise's this Thursday for lunch. It's their 'chicken and rice special' day."

"I would love to, AC," said Vicky without moving toward the car seat.

"Then it's a date?"

"Yes."

There was a long pause when Vicky finally said, "AC, I'm going to stand here all night until you kiss me."

"Oh. Well, yes."

The kiss was not one of voracious desperation of the Hollywood variety. It was peaceful but lingering. Long lingering enough that AC was the first to come up for air. Before he recovered his composure, Vicky had slipped into her seat closed the door and rolled down the window. As she started the engine AC heard, "Night, night. Sleep tight. "Don't let the boogies bite."

And then she was gone.

The couple's lunch at Wise's was not at all like their first meeting. The food was the same. The crowd was the same. The conversation, however, flowed like the Suwannee. Finally, the presence of the crowd waiting for stools at the counter forced them to leave. As they walked back toward the courthouse, Vicky took AC's hand. After a minute he found some pretense for dropping hers, but she did not let him get away with it.

"Judges worry about their image, don't they?" she asked, looking directly at his face, but not retrieving his hand.

"Well, I guess we do. So many people recognize us. I mean, not like movie stars or anything, but gossips are out there."

"You're not ashamed of me are you? I'm not a society girl."

"Hey, I'm the guy that drives a pickup, and asked you to the movies, and stood smooching in the parking lot like a college kid," said AC as they entered the courthouse.

Judge AC knew he would be noticed when he walked with Vicky past the bailiffs at the security station. Big Ben Stoker was on duty and gave his usual genuine smile. AC was not holding Vicky's hand in public or anything, but bailiffs had keen eyes. They knew. Whether they gossiped he did not know, but so what if they did? This was not like Eisenhower and his driver, or Kennedy, or Clinton or somebody. He was not married or anything. Well, there could be a conflict if he presided over a case involving Vicky, but all they had done was have lunch at Wise's.

The next day while dictating an order into his recorder, AC heard a buzz.

"Judge," said Shirley Bloch over the intercom, "There's someone on line one for you. Says her name is Vicky. Won't say what it's about. 'Just tell him it's Vicky' she says,"

"Thanks, I'll get it'," said AC glancing up to make sure his door was fully closed.

"Hey, Vicky, what's up? Problems with the mower? All my work is fully guaranteed."

"Forget the mower. This is a real problem. I have a flank steak at my place that's desperate for company. Like, maybe a bottle of Bordeaux. There'll be valet parking from six to seven this evening. Oh, I almost forgot to mention, this is a slumber party. Bring a toothbrush."

There were no highway patrolmen on Payne's Prairie which was fortunate for AC as he drove south. His mind was not on his driving, *This was not polite chit-chat or polite smiles* he thought. Could he have misunderstood? Lumber party? Number party? You don't need a toothbrush for those. He checked his face in the rear-view mirror. What was it? Mature good looks? Twinkling hazel eyes? Engaging smile? Well, he was not fat or bald and that was the truth. Power? He had heard some women liked men with power. Ben Franklin and Henry Kissinger, for God's sake, were supposedly lady killers. It was certainly not money. How was this going to work? Would they actually go to bed? And scariest of all, how would he perform if it came to that? Would he remember what to do? After all, AC and his former wife had given up on sex some time before giving up on marriage.

As things transpired it was like riding a bicycle; something you never forget. They ate, drank AC's wine and watched a TV movie. Vicky sat very close and rested her head on AC's shoulder. She put her hand on his thigh. After the movie they went into the bedroom like an old married couple. Vicky had a new toothbrush for AC, and while he brushed his teeth she slipped into a nightgown and into bed. AC joined her and held her face in his hands and looked into her light brown eyes.

"I can't believe this is happening," was all he could say.

"Less talk. More action," was Vicky's simple reply. Then she added with a giggle as she squirmed around.

"What do they say in court? All rise?"

***

Monday morning found Judge AC driving to Bronson, the county seat of Levy County. The books-on-tape presentation of *"H.M.S Surprise"* sat neglected on the seat beside him. The insipid rendering of the news by NPR was unheard. AC sang snatches of songs from the wonderful musicals of the Fifties. The first two lines of "Some Enchanted Evening" was about as far as he got with the original words, and this proved to be the same with "Oh, What a Beautiful Morning" and the rest. Vicky. Vicky, the voluptuous vixen. Vicky of the golden locks. How did the line go about "nothing like a dame?" Curves where there ought to be curves or something. Fortunately for AC the road had few curves and he was in Bronson and emerging into reality before he knew it. AC often rationalized about Monday mornings in Bronson where the week began with an hour of domestic violence hearings. Depressing, yes, but the week could only get better. Suppose they were held on Friday afternoons? Today with his high spirits he was undaunted by the prospect of this unpleasant event until he saw the number of cases that had been scheduled for this time slot. Domestic violence injunctions were issued ex-parte, meaning that the respondent had been kicked out of the house without a chance to rebut the allegations in the petition. Naturally it was only fair to require that these cases be brought back to court without delay.

An hour seemed about enough time to allot to hear a week's worth of cases in Levy County, but a full moon was said to affect behavior in strange ways, and AC had noticed the full moon through Vicky's window the night before. Fortunately he had time to read over the petitions in the clerk's office and make a few notes. He also had the advantage of being able to talk to Peggy White, the clerk who had provided the injunction forms to the petitioners and who knew everyone in Levy County. AC often joked about these cases, but he had a dead serious approach to them. These cases were not for a retired actor. Retired shrink, perhaps, but one with a Marine drill instructor's authority. By talking to Peggy White out of court he was, in a way, violating a basic principle of jurisprudence. Parties have an inherent right to confront their accusers or anyone offering testimony against them. AC was aware of this, but he had to administer justice expeditiously as well as impartially. The judge in these cases was more like a European inquisitor or a Sicilian godfather than an American jurist. Usually there were no lawyers involved to ask questions, and the litigants had little skill in cross-examination. Peggy often gave him a little background information to help him frame a pertinent question.

Domestic violence cases had to be analyzed from several perspectives. The initial consideration was whether the parties had any need to have contact in the future. Couples with children had this need although in extreme cases all contact had to be prohibited. Next-door neighbors presented a problem as well as co-workers and others who would inevitably come into contact in the future. The safety of children was of utmost importance, as adults in abusive relationships often made up and drove home from court in the same pickup truck. Many cases involved a simple power play in which the judge was the parent or teacher who was supposed to tell the offending party to behave, or else. Young couples with domineering parents were common. These cases presented the greatest hope for resolution. A little good counseling away from the extended family worked wonders. The true battered spouse syndrome cases were the most frightening. The petitioner, usually the wife, presented like a zombie. Many of these cases did not involve the knock down, drag outs so common in rough communities, but involved a more subtle intimidation. Subtle, but deadly.

Judge AC noted that three of the six cases on the docket involved criminal charges.

These would be simple. The criminal court had already enjoined contact between the parties, and the perp was probably in jail anyway. Often the victim wanted to drop charges, and AC had to caution the victim that to do so could create further problems if children were involved in the violence. One case presented somewhat of a problem in that it involved boy-friend, girl-friend college students. It would have been nice if he could simply have told the kids to stay apart. There had been no physical violence, just a lot of yelling. Idle threats from people who felt themselves threatened were very common in domestic violence cases. I will kill you, burn down the house, take the kids and you will never see them again. All this from someone who has never harmed a fly or been out of Levy County in his life.

The best thing about the parties coming to court in these cases was that it exposed the issue to public review, and possibly beneficial counseling. The bad thing was that it could prove to be a permanent stigma on the respondent's record. The college kids presented this exact problem. The boy had filed the petition, but AC knew the fight had probably been mutual. A domestic violence injunction directed against the girl would be on her record forever. It could bar her from teaching or other employment with the State. Mutual injunctions had been abolished by the legislature as the cops did not know whom to arrest when there was future contact. Judge AC could hear the wimpy boy now, "Judge, she threatened to kill me, and I believed her. This is not the first time either. I need an injunction for my safety." The minute I dismiss it she will shoot him; hopefully they will not show up, AC thought as he was escorted down the hall by a seventy year-old bailiff no one had the heart to fire.

Judge AC's prognostications held true. None of the criminally charged respondents showed up. The college students had made up. One divorce case now involved counsel and they presented a voluntary dismissal, with a promise to work things out in the future. This just left one case that had a familiar ring in the caption: "Amy Jordan; Petitioner, vs. Richard Jordan, Respondent." Judge AC directed the bailiff to show the Jordans in.

"How's that, Judge? There ain't nobody left outside. Not as I can see anyhow."

"Look a bit harder. They may be sitting around the corner away from each other. Peggy saw them in the courthouse earlier."

"Judge," said the loyal Peggy, "I don't really know these folks. I don't think they are from Levy County. I was a little nervous when the wife came in as I saw some man hanging around the lobby as if he was watching her. I asked her if I should call the bailiff and she said no, that it would be alright."

ALL RISE

"Judge, I ain't found them anywhere in the courthouse," said the ancient bailiff.

"Well, dismiss it as a no show," said AC as he perused the stack of files which would occupy him for the rest of the day.

By four o'clock Judge AC had completed his docket, which had been routine, and uneventful. Routine from the perspective of a judge. A couple of happy adoptions; a couple of unhappy dissolutions, and various motions to compel discovery. Discovery was the process by which each side to a legal proceeding could learn what cards the other side held prior to trial. Bluffers never want to show cards early. Maybe a card or two, but not the whole hand. *Buffing, huffing and puffing*, thought AC, as he waded through the morass of demands and objections. "Your Honor, it would be extremely burdensome and oppressive to produce all the documents counsel has requested. Some of the data contains trade secrets and is otherwise privileged. They are on a fishing expedition and are simply trying to run up costs as a leverage toward settlement." And so forth and so on. Judge AC wished he had the latitude of the television judges and could say what he really felt. Sometimes he did, but it was usually safer to simply say "Motion granted," and keep a poker face. He had no need to bluff in this game as he did when setting trials. "Remain detached" he had told Judge Moss. Sooner or later this baby will come to trial and you can render a fair and just decision and in the process do what you damn well please to stick it to the obstreperous party. He knew that in many cases it was the lawyer and not the client who threw up roadblocks, but he noticed that bulldog clients liked barracudas for lawyers.

"Oh, Peggy, do you still have that file for the no-show folks from this morning?"

"Judge, I took it back to records over lunch, but you sit still, I'll fetch it in a minute."

Judge AC would do anything for the clerks in Levy County. Never ever a surly expression. Never a "Why?" They even gave him a Christmas gift. Not one, but two ties, and he could really do nothing for them in return. No raises or promotions, but he did bring candy at times. He was curious about this no-show from the morning. Peggy had made some comments about residence and it also sounded like someone was in the courthouse and left before the case was called. The name Richard Jordan rang a distinct bell but he heard thousands of names a year. Intimidation could play a major role in domestic violence cases, and if kids were involved he wanted to report the situation to a protective agency.

The case file came as requested. Amy Jordan, Petitioner, Richard Jordan, Respondent. The first page of the form petition contained all the usual information concerning place of residence and whether there were prior cases and marital status. Then came the narrative: "My husband Ricky Jordan have abused our daughter and I think he may be the father of her baby but I don't know for sure. He verbal abuse me all the time. I have come over here to Levy to stay with my sister, but he won't leave me alone. Mary Beth got into trouble and come to stay with us but she left. I am skeert of Ricky as he is violent and has guns. I want him kept away from me and my sister."

"Thank you, Peggy, I'm out of here," said AC as he thought, *crap*. He felt sure this was the same Jordan family he had heard of in Alachua County. What should he do with this mess? The grandchild certainly should not be living in this household, but probably was not. Amy had not even alleged a specific violent act by Ricky so, technically, the injunction should not have been granted in the first place. Good old Judge Berry, the county judge who issued the injunction, did what he knew was right, regardless of the law. This jumble of facts rolled around in his brain on the drive to Gainesville, but soon, thoughts of the delectable Vicky Carter erased them from his mind.

***

Judge AC was concerned about the Jordan case, but certainly not distraught. He dealt with similar situations year in and year out. Things would work out. This was not something he should discuss with Vicky. In fact, Vicky posed an ethical problem. She did not regularly appear in his court but did supervise the case workers he worked with. He expected a transfer to the civil division at the end of the year, or at least by the end of June the next year. Still, it might not look too good if some high publicity case presented itself and he was found in bed with a DCF supervisor. Of course he had known that from the minute he crossed Payne's Prairie heading toward their first rendezvous. Maybe she could transfer to the other division. He would inquire. He was not about to give up Vicky. He did not think in terms of love, but she was a bright spot, a beacon, a refuge, a haven in the sea of misery that surrounded him. He would look up from the bench and there she would be on the back row of the courtroom, with her eager, toothy smile and a quick wave of hand. No, he was not about to give this up. They met for lunch when they could. One of their favorite places to tryst was at Bivens Arm Park which was only a mile or so south of the courthouse. They would always part with a quick kiss and a promise for more to come.

As the weather cooled Vicky would wait for AC in the plaza in front of the courthouse. One day as she sat in the shade of one of the large oaks, she heard a familiar voice.

"*Hola*, Vicky, q*ue pasa*? Long time no see."

"Oh, Carlo, how are you? You look fine. Did you join the clean hands club?"

"Hey, Vicky, you know me. When people need a hand Carlo is there. Helping hands don't have to be clean. What's up with the dependents? I stopped by court a while ago hoping to see you. I think I was in the wrong courtroom. It was all about delinquents. I didn't envy the judge."

About this time AC walked up with a big smile on his face and an expectant look toward Carlo.

"Well, it's about time," said Vicky. "I'm about starved." There was a momentary awkward pause then she said, "AC, this is my friend Carlo Proenza from Vero Beach. Carlo, this is Judge Cason, one of our family court judges."

The men shook hands in a pleasant but wary fashion, and did not engage in the usual pleasantries. AC started to ask Carlo where he might have known him from, but thought better of it. After all, he saw thousands of new faces each year under circumstances that were often far from pleasant. Vicky grabbed AC by the arm and explained how they had to run or she would be late for a meeting. "Cordial Carlo" voiced a reluctant *adios* as they parted and murmured a *c'est la vie* to himself.

Vicky had brought a huge sub from Subway which they enjoyed at Bivens Arm Park on a wooden bench at the far end of the raised walkway that ran beside the marshy pond. Vicky always sat very close to AC, and even when it was time to part she would cling to him and force him to be the first to draw away. Today she did not seem to sit as close, AC thought. Eventually he asked, "Who is this Carlos what's-his-name?"

Vicky thought for a few seconds wondering how much to tell about her past. Finally she gave a smile she hoped did not look fake and replied, "I met him at the fitness center. We went out on a date, but he wasn't my type. Say, do we have time to make out in the car or do you have to go back and kick ass?"

They did have time to make out a bit in AC's pickup, but not in a way that would have embarrassed any passing park visitors. As they snuggled, AC noticed Vicky's seeming preoccupation, but did not ask "You OK?" in the manner of soap operas. His skill at reading body language had not been taught but was the result of listening to countless hours of courtroom testimony. He watched as she entered her offices after being dropped off. Her smile of departure had definitely changed to frown. He shrugged and drove back to the courthouse. If there was something going on with Carlos whoever, she would tell him when the time was right.

These were idyllic days for AC. Vicky called him daily and even developed a friendly relationship with Shirley Blotch, which was not an easy undertaking. This was fortunate, as it would have been impossible to hide the relationship from a judicial assistant. One day Shirley walked in looking a bit sheepish.

"I'm afraid I opened this by mistake. I'm happy for you."

She handed him a greeting card with clouds and a bluebird on the cover. The note inside read "Anywhere, anytime, anything, but only with you, Love Vicky."

VI

Judge AC did not consider himself to be a particularly hard worker. He seldom worked past five in the afternoon, but he did take pride in ruling on his cases in a timely fashion. This kept him in good graces with the local bar association. Lawyers liked to win, but also really liked for cases to move along. Those South Florida lawyers who made a practice of delaying cases were often surprised to find Judge AC's orders on their desks by the time they reached home. AC was not trying to win any type of judicial promptness award; he simply did not like work to pile up on his desk, and at times it was worth it to come in and work at off-hours. The last Sunday in September was one of those times. AC reached the courthouse about church time, based on the sound of the bells about town. He noticed one car in the judges' reserved parking area and assumed it was the duty judge for first appearances. Must be a large docket, thought AC, as these proceedings were usually over by ten, or at the latest, by eleven. He took the elevator to the third floor where his office was located and immediately noticed a light glowing from the door to his clambers. This gave him a pause, but what the heck, lights were often left on by mistake. When his door opened without a key he took a second pause and said, "Hello?"

Each of the judge's clambers in the Alachua County Courthouse was located adjacent to a courtroom. The judges routinely had to use courtrooms other than the one next to the judge's own chambers so it was not unusual for another judge to pass through the judicial assistant's area on the way to the back entrance to the courtroom. Standing at the doorway Judge AC again repeated his hello, and who should come out of AC's office but AC's colleague, Judge Asner. Jack Asner's face blanched for only a second then broke into a supercilious smile.

"Hey, AC. This is a Sunday. Did you forget? I've got the duty. What excuse do you have for being at the factory?"

AC, as the expression went, laid low.

"Well, I've got to work on a couple of files. Can I help you find something?"

Judge Asner was quick on his feet if nothing else. "Well, yes. I was looking for a file they said was in your office. Jerdon or Jordan or something. The clerk said it was reassigned to me and there's a review hearing scheduled Tuesday. Have you seen the file? Normally they send them up ahead of time for the judge to review, and I always like to review all of my files ahead of the hearings."

AC's mind began to click. Jordan. Palm Landing. Putnam County. Mary Beth. Levy County.

"No, I don't remember that case. I usually review all cases prior to court too. I don't remember a reassignment in this matter, but then I am not sure I remember the case. I'm sure I will when I see the file. I'll have Shirley check on it in the morning. Jordan you say? What's the deal on a reassignment? I don't recall a motion or order or anything about a reassignment."

"I have no idea. I just saw it on my docket." said "Judge Jack-the Ass" as he slithered out of the office.

***

After this unpleasant episode with his colleague, Judge AC tried to concentrate on his work but his mind kept creeping back to Judge Asner. His opinion of his fellow jurist was not at all flattering. As an assistant state attorney, Asner had been devious, although never rude. AC was especially disappointed when Asner was appointed by the governor to the Alachua County Court bench. He felt Asner was, as the old expression went, an "accident waiting to happen." His manner was always friendly, but it was more ingratiating than warm. Asner had run for the Eighth Circuit Court unopposed and had never stopped running. Well, thought AC, judges *are* elected officials, but there is an impropriety in constantly suggesting to constituents that the judge is "ready to help out however I can." About all a judge could ethically do to help a friend was to postpone jury duty. He recalled there had been some courthouse rumor abut Asner trying to get a friend's case assigned to him, personally. AC thought he would check this out with Judge Clem Weaver whose mind was a virtual floppy disk of such gossip. These thoughts were so distracting that Judge AC finally left the courthouse without finishing all his tasks.

Judge Asner was still on AC's mind early the next morning, when his favorite attorney from DCF came into his office looking down in the mouth. He would normally have been in Levy County on Monday, but this was the fifth Monday in the month so nothing was scheduled there.

"What's up, Cindy, why so glum?"

In her mid-to-late-forties, Cindy Sapp was one of the more senior staff attorneys handling dependency matters. She was a newlywed, and, to Judge AC, always seemed genuinely happy in her life and in her work and never downcast. The DCF attorneys were like all attorneys employed by the government. They did not have the luxury of being able to decline to accept a case or fire a client. If lawyer-client disagreements arose, the staff attorney could appeal to a supervising attorney, who could discuss the matter with senior staff. All bureaucratic hierarchies experienced similar conflicts. Engineering versus advertising perhaps, but the lawyer's role as an "officer of the court" placed an extra heavy burden on the attorneys. To run a misleading ad was one thing; to mislead a judge, quite another. Cindy Sapp had always maintained a high degree of credibility with Judge AC, so her mission to Judge AC's office was especially hard on her.

"Judge, I'm afraid I am the bearer of ill tidings. This is not my call, but comes from Mr. Grimmage, our new district legal counsel. I think you may have met him."

"Yes, I have," was all AC said, but Cindy knew from his tone and grim expression that he understood the situation perfectly.

"Well, it's this Jordan case. The grandfather of the dependent child, some guy named Richard or Ricky, has been spouting off to staff about how he is buddy-buddy with the judge. He claims the judge told him from the start that he would call DCF and straighten things out and said his daughter Mary Beth said the same. I know it's all a bunch of malarky, but he even claims you threw out a domestic violence claim against him over in Levy County. When Mr. Grimmage heard of it, he said the judge should be disqualified right away and to file a motion with all these allegations. Well, I can't swear to any of this and know it's absurd. The last thing I want to do is file a motion to disqualify, but I'm really in a bind. Is there any way you can just reassign this case to Judge Asner?"

Judge AC began to burn, but a quick glance at Cindy's anguished, pleading face gave him the judicial calm needed in such situations. He told Cindy, of course he could recuse himself and if she would like to wait, he would have Shirley type the order immediately.

"But, Cindy, you are right. This is all total nonsense. I am curious about one thing though. Does Judge Asner know anything about this motion?"

"Why, no, Judge. I've certainly not discussed it with him. I mean I didn't even know whether you would agree to give up the case or whether I would have filed a motion under the circumstances. I really appreciate your not puling me through all this, and I can assure you we have many more nasty cases to take the place of Jordan. Thanks again."

This new matter gave Judge AC much to think about. The whole question of judicial disqualification was fraught with problems. To begin with, any judge who had any doubt about his ability to be impartial was required to step down without the necessity of a motion. So, simply filing a motion to disqualify a judge automatically questions the judge's integrity. Some judges do, in fact express so much bias that there must be a method to remove such judges from particular cases. The really corrupt judges could be, and are, removed from office when caught misbehaving. Since the filing of the motion to disqualify itself had adversarial overtones, it meant that the judge could not dispute the allegations but only rule on the legal sufficiency of whether the allegations met the legal standards for disqualification. Any argument over the alleged facts would automatically place the judge in conflict with the party making the motion.

Judge AC could not argue against the misleading allegations in the Jordan matter and knew it. He was doubly troubled by the fact that the DCF attorneys could not see through all this. Blowhards like Ricky abounded in legal proceedings. Judges did not really mind relinquishing control of a case like Jordan's, they just did not like the idea that someone like Jordan could manipulate the system. For Grimmage to do so was far more serious. After all the time and hard work he had put into streamlining dependency court, how was it possible that this new jerk of a district legal counsel would accept the allegations of a jerk like Ricky Jordan? These musings were cut short by the day's work which involved an all-day hearing on several motions in a divorce case from Gilchrist County. The hot shot big city lawyers had filed the case in Gilchrist to avoid publicity, but they wanted motions heard in Gainesville, as it had an airport of sorts.

***

The very next day, while Judge AC was still in a stew over recent events, Shirley stuck her head in the office and said, "Some cop wants to see you. Won't say what it's about. Just wants ten minutes or so."

"Does he or she have a name?" said AC.

"Preston was all I heard," said Shirley, the snip, "Can I send him or her in?"

"Why not?" said AC "I get paid by the hour."

"Well, Sergeant Preston," said AC rising to shake hands with his old friend, "heard any good Yukon jokes since your promotion?"

"About ten per day Your Honor. Where do you want me to start? King is outside guarding the sled. I started to bring him in on the pretext of being blind as I know he would like to see you."

Sergeant Jim Preston of the Alachua County Mounted Police was an old friend of Judge AC's. They met through Preston's wife, Valerie, who was an excellent local artist with some recent national acclaim. AC had bought a few of her works at art shows, but now she sold only through galleries. Jim Preston was not really a mounty, but worked undercover and AC sometimes failed to recognize him when he came in dressed in his dope dealer outfit seeking a search warrant. His ability as a horseman led him to work occasionally with the mounted patrol, which was used for crowd control during Gator football games. His black Labrador was named King, just like the fictional husky.

Sergeant Preston carefully closed the door to Judge AC's office and said, "Judge, can we talk off the record?"

"Jim, you know you can talk to me any time about anything, but if it's about a case it can't be off the record."

"Well, Judge, it's not about one of your cases, and if it becomes a case, it's not one you would hear. At least I don't think so."

"Having aroused my curiosity to the breaking point you can go ahead and talk. If it's about a case I can always recuse. If King is having an extramarital affair, that is another matter."

"Judge, do you know a man by the name of Carlo Proenza?"

"Carlo Proenza, Carlo Proenza. Jim, you know I see and hear thousands of names a year. Jurors, witnesses, defendants, cops, attorneys, you name it, but yes, the name does sound familiar. Am I allowed to know more?"

"Judge, he seems to be a friend of Vicky Clark." Preston did not go into how he knew AC knew Vicky. "He lives in Vero Beach but comes to Gainesville on occasion. He's Latino, what I would call clean-cut, well dressed, and in his mid-forties, if that is of any help."

Then it all clicked for AC. The conversation in the plaza with Vicky and the out-of-place man in his courtroom several weeks ago. He knew he had seen Vicky's friend before. He would like to have a chance to talk to Vicky now, but he knew he had to be direct with Jim Preston. Furthermore, he trusted Jim and, obviously, Jim trusted him. He told Jim of the meeting in the plaza and what Vicky had told him of Proenza. He even told Jim of the person in the courtroom, although that did not seem particularly significant.

"Judge, do me a favor. If this guy contacts you about anything just let me know. Definitely do not meet with him without calling me first. I would suggest that you don't discuss this with Ms Clark, but that's up to you. We have no interest in her, but we do in Mr. Proenza. I won't keep you, but please give me a call if something happens," said Sergeant Jim Preston as he handed AC a business card with several phone numbers listed.

"Wait one, Jim, I don't need to, nor do I want to know what's up, but I would like some clue as to why he might want to contact me. I know you would not be here if I were under suspicion or anything."

"To tell the truth, I have no idea. Like you say, he was in your courtroom, but we didn't know that. He is an unsavory character but well-connected. We are sort of helping out other agencies on this one, but no, your name has definitely not come up in any way. I just have a cop's hunch something is up, and you are one judge I know I can trust."

"Likewise," said AC. "Tell King and Valerie hello."

All of these events plagued AC's mind as he tried to get to sleep that night. Vicky was out of town for a training meeting in Daytona. Or *so she said*, thought he, with a twinge of guilt. He really knew very little of Vicky. She was raised in West Virginia in some town he had never heard of. She was effective in court and even more effective in bed, he quipped to himself. She had not told him the full story about Carlo Proenza. He was sure of that. There was no way the police could have linked her name with this guy with only a meeting at the fitness club and a single date. *Well, possibly,* he thought, if Carlo had been under twenty-four hour surveillance. But how could he be linked to Carlo? Why would the police think Carlo would have any reason to contact *him*? Maybe it was just a cop's hunch, as Jim had said. He did have one high profile divorce case involving what appeared to be big bucks. It was the case that had been filed over in Gilchrist County to avoid publicity. There were IRS liens and offshore trusts that neither side wanted to disclose publicly. Possibly, there was some law enforcement interest in that case, but that was it as far as he could figure. He drifted off into an uneasy sleep, without resolving whether to ask Vicky more about Carlo Proenza.

As things turned out he did not need to ask Vicky about Carlo. When she got back from Daytona she called and said he needed to come down to Micanopy that very night. As he drove down he could not help but notice the beauty of the sun setting over Payne's Prairie, but that did not take his mind off his circumstances. Vicky sounded anxious to see him but in a friendly way. He really did not want to tell Vicky about Jim Preston's visit until he found out more about Carlo. When he got to the farm, Vicky was waiting in the yard looking beautiful but distraught. Her eyes told it all. She was never much of an actress, he thought. She did have a professional manner she could don in court, but she was not in court now.

"How was Daytona? Feeling smarter now?" he said, as he gave her a quick brush of the lips. Her response was dramatic. She grabbed him around the neck very hard and did not let go. He could feel her shaking and sobbing as her head pressed against his chest. It took some time for her to stop and pull away. This time he had not been the one to release her. Finally she stood back and looked at him with tears still streaking down her cheeks.

"AC, you are so kind and trusting. You know I love you. You never pry and are always there for me. I've watched you in court all this time and you are so considerate to everybody. I mean it. I really love you. You don't even have to love me back but I have to tell you something."

Well here it comes, thought AC. I knew it all along. Father figure. Young dashing swain ousts over-the-hill nice guy in three sets. "Well, let's get a glass of wine and find a comfortable place to sit and you can pour your heart out."

After following AC's sound suggestion Vicky said, "It's about Carlo."

This was much worse than anything AC expected, and his face showed it. "Oh, yes, that nice fellow you introduced me to on the plaza. I thought maybe you didn't tell me everything about him. He does seem to be a charmer."

Vicky took both of AC's hands in her own and said, "AC, love, it's not what you think but there was more to him than a date. It's a long story."

ALL RISE

Vicky told him the whole long story, leaving out only the part about going to bed with Carlo. She described the Cunninghams simply as "some rich couple." "You can leave me if you want to, but I had to tell you. I worry about it all the time. Suppose something came out? Suppose you heard from somewhere else? I feel so guilty. At this point her sobs began again and AC had to hold her close. Without moving her head which was pressed against his chest, Vicky said, "I don't want to lose you, ever. I meant what I said on your card."

"Well, sweets, now that you've told me your life story, what do you want to do now?"

"I want you to take me to bed, make passionate love to me, and tell me everything will be all right."

AC did exactly as instructed, but as he lay awake listening to Vicky's soft breathing, he was still of a troubled mind.

Vicky served fresh cantaloupe for breakfast. She held his feet in hers under the table. Gone were all the tears and anxiety of the day before. He could not bring himself to tell her about his visit from Jim Preston, or the way her name had been linked with Carlo. He now knew a little more about Carlo, but Vicky had described him as her mystery man. There was one thing they needed to discuss.

"Vicky, love, there is a problem with our relationship." Now it was her turn to quail. "I know we sort of agreed to meet in private, but everyone in the courthouse knows about us. There could be a con-

104

flict if you had some case in which I was the judge and people thought I ruled in favor of DCF due to our romance. I'm scheduled to rotate out of the family division at the end of the year, but there could be a problem in the meantime. How hard would it be for you to get assigned to the other division?" Vicky's stomach unknotted.

"No problem. I can swap places with Rosa. Rosa Banks. She's my best friend in DCF, and I know she would rather be in your division than with what's-his-face Asner."

"Great. Even then there could be a quibble, since you are still in DCF, but at least I wouldn't be hearing your cases."

As they both drove to work Vicky was happy and relieved. AC, on the other hand, was more concerned than ever. He believed everything Vicky told him and felt no need to go into any possible romantic involvement she might have had with Carlo. She had essentially bared her soul without any prodding from him. Still, the cops had linked her with this unsavory character, and now he knew one specific reason why Carlo was unsavory. If some public scandal developed about baby buying, Vicky would be ruined. She had already caught enough flack over the shaken baby case, and any more would be a disaster.

Vicky's meeting with Rosa went very well. Rosa was about Vicky's age, black, hard working and well respected throughout the department. Rosa's only condition for swapping divisions was that Vicky divulge all aspects of her relationship with AC.

"Vicky, I know your tall sexy judge is a fine man, but what I want is the intimate details. How many times a night do ya'll do it? How did you catch him anyway? I might want to catch a judge for myself some day."

Vicky put up with all this in good humor. They debated on the best way to present the matter to their supervisor. It was decided that it was best to leave AC out of it, and to rely on the intuition of Mary Barnes the senior DCF supervisor, who seemed to know everything anyway. They made up a plausible story about schedules, but they knew Mary Barnes had guessed the real reason for the request and thought the swap was a good idea under the circumstances.

After the meeting with Mary Barnes, Vicky and Rosa went their separate ways. As Vicky walked along the sidewalk, she asked herself some of the same questions Rosa had posed. Actually, catching AC had been easy, once she had gotten up the nerve to approach him. Circumstances had worked in her favor on that point. What she was going to do with him was something else. She had always liked his demeanor and, in general, his looks. She thought he was witty, but also soothing, and most important of all, he really seemed to like her. She had instinctively realized she had to tell him about the scheme with Carlo. If anything had come from another source she knew he would have been gone. Vicky caught sight of her reflection in a store window and straightened up a bit. Not bad for forty-three. Who knows?

***

AC felt he could do nothing about the Carlo business, but that he could find out what the hell was going on with Judge Jack-the-Ass. He made a lunch date with Judge Clem Weaver, the supreme historian of judicial gossip and repository of political acumen. They were fishing buddies and had the same approach to judicial responsibilities. Flippant at times, but deadly serious when the situation called for it; they both knew that some cases were decidedly more complex than others and demanded more time and consideration, so did not waste time on routine cases. Clem said he would not only go to lunch, he would do a complete brain search on all Judge Anser's past behavior.

AC knew of course that Clem knew about his relationship with Vicky, although in true judicial fashion had never brought it up. These things traveled through the courthouse faster than the speed of sound. He had no intention of discussing Carlo or the visit from Jim Preston. Despite his own lack of political acumen, AC started thinking about what Vicky had told him about Vero Beach and the rich couple wanting to adopt. He worried about what to do with this information. Nothing had happened. Not even enough for criminal conspiracy, except perhaps in federal court. Certainly enough for a scandal.

ALL RISE

Suppose Vicky was not in the picture. What would he report, and to whom? But Vicky *was* in the picture. And what was going on now in the Jordan case? Could there be some sort of connection between it, Asner, Carlo, Grimmage, and the Vero Beach people? If DCF was going to seek a termination of parental rights there would be an adoptable baby available. This is totally farfetched he told himself. What is this guy going to do? Bribe a judge, a district legal counsel, a caseworker and a guardian ad litem? Why couldn't he go through regular channels anyway? Maybe adopt some Russian kid? This was all too nefarious for Judge AC's trusting mind. He would have liked to have been able to share the full story with Judge Clem, but he was determined to protect Vicky.

Lunch with Clem, short for Clement, Weaver often resulted in dull, repetitious, uninspired rehashing of dull, repetitious, uneventful days in court. Disingenuous argument by counsel, feeble attempts by the legislature to try to micromanage the courts, surly clerks, judges not carrying their load and the like. Still, thought AC as he strolled down the corridor, Clem somehow obtained more gossip than a lady hairdresser, and had the political intuition of Machiavelli. If there was any dirt on Judge Asner, Clem would know of it. Whether he would repeat it was another matter. Even though they were close friends, AC knew Clem was not a common gossipmonger, given to repeating idle rumors just to be vicious. Clem was much more serious. For one thing, he did not want to lose his sources of information, and nothing dried up a source quicker than a pointing finger. For another thing, Clem would be the first to report a truly corrupt judge to the Judicial Qualifications Commission if the circumstances warranted such action. Tidbits might be all AC could expect, but anything would be better than nothing, and his senses were really on high alert, due to the peculiar circumstances surrounding the past few weeks.

Tidbits were about all AC got as the two jurists sat at a booth in the Clock Restaurant. Unlike most Gainesville restaurants staffed by college kids who addressed venerable judges as, "Hi, guys, what'll it be?" the Clock hired middle-aged waitresses who called middle-aged judges "honey." AC and Clem nodded at the few old-time cops they recognized who frequented the Clock, and ordered from the senior citizens' menu.

"You know," said AC, "if Asner weren't Asner, I might not have thought anything of it, but there he was in my office Sunday morning looking for a dependency file he said was being transferred to his division. I kept my mouth shut and sure enough, the next morning I get a visit from a decaf lawyer wanting me to recuse from the case on totally bullshit grounds. No motion had been filed, and she hadn't talked with Asner about the case. Something must be going on between Asner and that new prick of a district legal counsel, Grimmage, who apparently instigated the recusal issue. Well, of course I'm pissed about the recusal shit, after all I've done to straighten out dependency court, but that's not the point."

Here AC paused, wondering how to go into his adoption bribery theory, without appearing as loony as Asner. Clem was a close trusted friend, but he had to leave out parts of the story to protect Vicky and not to appear paranoid himself.

"I really don't know anything about the facts of the dependency case. It started over in Putnam and was transferred here. Before it got here, I talked to the mother and her dad and told them to follow up with DCF in Putnam. Then I get a no-show domestic violence case over in Levy involving the parents of the mother. Typical crap. The dad is nasty and owns a gun. Once the dependency case was transferred here, I granted a motion to continue. The next thing I hear from DCF is that I have improperly helped the mother and her dad, and thrown out a domestic violence case in Levy."

Judge Weaver looked down at his senior menu weight watcher's special rubber chicken and sighed.

"Who are these people? Is there any reason Asner would want to suck up to them?" Clem asked.

"The family name is Jordan. Just salt of the earth crackers as far as I can tell. So far I've only seen the mother and her dad. The kid's putative father is supposedly in the Marines somewhere. The Levy connection is the sister of the grandmother."

"You just lost me," interjected Clem.

"OK, Jordan's wife went to her sister's place in Levy County to get away from him. I think they're all old time Eighth Circuit folks. I have no idea why Asner would have an interest, but I have no idea why he was in my office either. And there's absolutely no telling about the new DLC. I think he's a total flake, hired for political reasons. 'Just say no' to drugs and sex, and Jesus will love you."

The conversation paused while the waitress made a fuss over freshening up the iced tea.

"What was that story about Asner a few years back?" AC asked. "Something about trying to get a friend's traffic case assigned to him. Barbara Jean blew the whistle."

"I think that's about it," said Clem. "It was nipped in the bud so to speak. Asner had some lame excuse, and nothing had really happened. You know, this whole shifting of files is so much garbage. People think I rule in favor of attorneys I like. In reality half the time I can't even remember which side of a case my supposed friends are on."

"Yeah, but appearances count."

"You know I've got the damn Wessex Industries case. As far as I'm concerned, it's the snakes versus the skunks. Still, I am sure one side or the other will try to remove me. At times I wish one side would just go ahead and try to bribe me, rather than to try to get some dirt on me to get me off the case."

AC gave a sympathetic shrug.

"Wait, I do remember something about Asner. He was in some kind of trouble with the State Court Administrator about some travel expenses, but I forget the details. Another time he had a lawyer and the lawyer came to me about some crystals. You know the geodes or whatever the hippies stare into when they smoke their pot. Asner had a collection of these rocks he used to calm his psyche when he had a tough decision to make. He got them over in Porter's Quarters where all the dope dealers hang out and the cops got his license number. Nothing ever came of it. Why don't you call Judge Fox? He was in county court and knows all these details better than I do."

None of this helped Judge AC in his perplexing analysis of Judge Asner's behavior.

"What was this guy's name? Jordan? Not Ricky Jordan by any chance," Judge Weaver asked.

"Yeah, that's the one. Ricky. Looks like a limerock truck driver."

"Well, if it's who I think he is, I've had him in court for the past twenty years. Teenage stuff. Statutory rape when he was eighteen or so. Non-support. You name it. I'm surprised you don't know him. He does have some brass though. I can see him trying to to put one over on some DCF employee."

"Is the Wessex case ever going to get to trial?" asked AC changing the subject back to Clem's big peeve. "During our lifetime, I mean."

"Well, it would if I were the only person in charge. I ordered a bifurcation of the contract issue and all the other junk issues, like defamation and RICO, so we could try a straightforward breach of contract all alone, but our appellate masters ruled otherwise. I know exactly what's going to happen. We'll eventually try it and the multiple issues will get it so screwed up it'll have to be retried several times. I'm sure you'll enjoy dealing with it after I'm retired."

With that the two dispensers of justice finished lunch and went back to work.

***

The gates to the inner sanctum of Judge "Dapper Dan" Fox were guarded by "Brunhilda, Queen of the Valkyries." Normally, judges just brushed past judicial assistants and barged in on their brethren unless a hearing was in progress. This was not done with Hilda Griswald whose icy stare was rarely, if ever, challenged. Judge Weaver would usually call first and ask "can Danny come out and play?" Hilda did not like this but had never been able to come up with a Hildaesque response. Judge AC was even more devious and pretended he came to see Hilda herself.

"We're having trouble getting files from the clerk on a timely basis. Is this just us? I can understand a two-day advance request for scheduled hearings, but we get all sorts of requests for information when we need the file to give an answer. Not emergency stuff, but things that can't wait two days for a response. Oh, by the way, is Judge Fox in?" This puts Hilda in a quandary. She can not very well say, "I'll have to see," or ask Judge AC what it is about, or even say, "I'll see if he is busy." She has to simply announce over the intercom, "Judge Cason is here to see you."

"How about calling Shirley about those files when you get a chance?" asked AC over his shoulder, as he reached for Dapper Dan's hand.

"Dan, Clem says you have the memory of an elephant when it comes to one of our fellow judges."

"Let me guess," said Dapper Dan going thorough the traditional motions of rubbing his forehead. "Jack-the-Ass. Right or wrong?"

"Well, let me tell you this story, and then you can make it a double-or-nothing bet, but you have to promise not to, oh what the hell, of course it's about Asner. But it may not be just gossip,"

"Fart, I hoped you caught him screwing some deputy clerk."

AC paused to regroup at this comment, not knowing how far the gossip of his relationship with Vicky had spread. He relaxed when he thought of Dapper Dan's own catch-and-release policy with women, which he observed as religiously as AC's policy with trout. He would not cast the first stone at AC on this account.

"No clerks, but I do need to check something out about him. My problem is that it involves a case where I recused myself, and if there's nothing to my suspicions, I could look like a fool or worse. I really could give a rat's ass about the case, but I am suspicious about Asner's motives."

"AC, you know how I feel about Asner or you wouldn't be here. I was on the county bench with the s.o.b for four years. He never pulled his weight. We would get requests from the court administrator to cover his docket but it was all one way. He was always too busy to return the favor. But you knew that anyway."

"What about the time he tried to get a traffic case assigned to him?"

"I tried to nail him on that. It's not that I'm out to get him; it's that he's going to bring discredit on us all. Just wait. Well, I guess you aren't waiting or you wouldn't be here. Tell me your story and I'll shut up. The traffic case was all true but got nowhere. If you don't tell me what is going on, I'm going to call Hilda."

Judge AC told Dapper Dan as much of the story as he could risk. He had to leave out any mention of Vicky or Carlo. That would have made him sound as nutty as Asner. This just left the part about Asner being in his office and the curious disqualification issue.

"I mean, how did he know anything about the case at all? No motion had been filed. The clerk could have had no way of knowing of a transfer. All this is awkward. I'm not on the case due to a totally bogus motion to disqualify and now if I interfere it could become a Judicial Qualifications Commission issue."

"Let's back up a bit," reflected Dan Fox. "Let me begin by saying I wouldn't trust Jack Asner with a lollipop. I know he tried to fix a two-bit traffic case for a friend, but I couldn't prove it. Your case is about the same. His story is plausible and you're in no position to attack it. There's not even any motive for him wanting to take on the case, which sounds like a pain in the ass to me from what you say. That name, Ricky Jordan, sounds familiar. Should I know it?"

"Clem says he has been in and out court for years. I missed him somehow. I do remember Ellen Kravitz having some problem with some guy from Waldo, who sounds a lot like Jordan."

"You may be right," said Dan. "I remember a few years back that Judge K. requested a bailiff escort some creep from the time he entered the courthouse until the time he left. Jordan may have been his name. He would call her up at home from the jail. Shit like that. Like she was his personal judge. That was fifteen years ago, but it sure sounds familiar. I'll tell you what. I'll check out the Jordan file and see what I can find out. You need to keep away from it, with the recusal and all."

AC agreed and exited with a kind word to Hilda, who was busy sharpening her talons.

VII

The road from Gainesville to the town of Cedar Key ran southwest beside the old railroad track, which was the first to run all the way across the state from Fernandina to the Gulf of Mexico. The rails and crossties were now all gone, but the grade could be detected by AC and Vicky in places out in the scrub where developers had yet to reach. It seemed a perfect morning. The gray beards of Spanish moss hung motionless from the branches of live oaks. The happy couple had arranged to take a day off to go fishing on a weekday to avoid the crowds of weekend warriors who flocked to the once sleepy hamlet for fishing and relaxing in the quaint charm of a so-called undiscovered treasure.

"Lord help us when it's discovered," said AC. "You can't even find a place to park your trailer on weekends as it is. The taxes are going to kill the locals. How can a mullet fisherman or crabber maintain a shack next to a two-hundred-thousand-dollar lot? The 'save our homes law' will help for awhile, but eventually we can look forward to Naples North. Fortunately, there are no real beaches and you can't play golf in a swamp."

They had driven from Archer to Bronson, passing sand hills covered with turkey oaks and an occasional longleaf pine stand that had reseeded from the few trees that had survived the massive lumbering of the early days. One home-site was called Rosemary Hill.

"When you see rosemary bushes you are looking at the sorriest land there is," AC said. "Still, the old range cattle could somehow survive eating Spanish moss and wiregrass. The old-timers would burn the prairies in the winter to produce new green sprouts in the spring."

AC hesitated to talk too much about the olden days as it provided a clue to his age. He had not told Vicky anything more than that he was the same age as Dustin Hoffman. She cuddled up against him as if he were Hoffman's younger brother.

"What kind of bait will we use? I kind of feel sorry for the worms."

"Vicky love, worms live in West Virginia. We're heading for the Gulf of Mexico where fish eat other fish, and an occasional shrimp of course. We'll use

dazzling lures designed to tempt even the most reticent fish into a rash act. Everything's been rigged.
Well, not like a guaranteed election but the rods all
have jigs and spoons with leader wire and swivels attached. We'll troll along the edge of the reef and the
mackerel will mistake our lures for small fishes and
try to eat 'em. Kind of like streetwalkers trolling for
johns, I guess."

"AC, I never suspected you had such a deliciously
dirty mind. Does your boat have a bedroom?"

The seventeen-foot Wellcraft being towed obedi-
ently behind AC's pickup did not even have a toilet or
marine head as it was called, much less a bedroom.
AC had thought of this and decided Vicky could use a
bucket if necessary. It was still warm enough to swim
over the side, but he was not sure if West Virginia
girls felt comfortable swimming in the company of
toothed marine life.

Bronson, the county seat of Levy County, was
on the edge of the sand hills and the land to the
west turned into a vast timbered lowland. Drainage
ditches bordered the roadway and were now full of
water from the summer rains.

"Oh, look," AC said "a kingfisher. See, on the wire.
That's always my sign of good luck. That and lovebugs
on the windshield. I love the way kingfishers look so
self-assertive. It's interesting about 'em, they nest in
burrows dug into the banks of creeks or ditches."

The object of this mutual attention left his perch,
hovered over the still water, and dove for some un-
seen tidbit, but by the time the splash was over, the

fishing expedition had passed the predator and could not determine his success. Vicky took AC's hand and squeezed it. She had lived in Florida over a decade, but had not paid much attention to nature. Her little farm, with its domestic animals was outdoorsy, but she had not spent much time in the wild. She had driven over to Cedar Key a couple of times with some of the girls from work to sample the renowned seafood, but she had never left the dock or visited the outer islands. They soon passed Otter Creek and crossed US 19/98 which led to Tampa and points south and to Tallahassee to the north. Six miles south down this major highway the Wacassassa River crosses the road at what was once Gulf Hammock, the center of big time logging industry in the early days. It and other sawmill communities prospered until all the cypress and longleaf was cut, then slowly faded away. Rosewood, the next stop on the line toward Cedar Key, was now just a historical marker. It had not faded away like most of the communities, but was burned by citizens of Cedar Key who were irate over a racial incident. Just past Rosewood the land rose to form another sandy scrub before its final descent into the cluster of islands known collectively as Cedar Keys. A few cedar trees remain on the islands and in the surrounding forests, but most were harvested by the Eberhard Faber pencil company years ago. At low tide, the rusting hulk of the pencil factory machinery can still be seen. The town once had a huge plant producing the ice used to cool thousands of tons of fish on their way to markets but it had been replaced by a condo. *Well, why not*, thought AC as he backed his trailer toward the boat ramp. There was no need for tons of ice as the thousands of tons of fish had been reduced to a trickle. AC, the optimistic fisherman, felt there would still be enough left for supper.

AC stopped just short of the ramp and went over his usual check list. Drain plugs in, tie downs released, bow line attached, and so forth. Vicky pitched in and seemed adept at handling the bow line. This was a definite plus for AC, who had seen many relationships stressed to the breaking point at the boat ramp. He knew his motor would start right away, as he had taken the time to crank it in his yard before leaving home. Few things can be more embarrassing to a fisherman than equipment failures at a boat ramp, with a horde of idling spectators looking on. Judge Weaver, AC's fishing buddy, claimed he would sometimes spend his lunch hour eating a hot dog and drinking a coke and watching the loading and unloading process at Newnan's Lake near Gainesville. In some places, slime-covered ramps had been known to launch cars as well as trailered boats into the water without formal christening. Saltwater boaters were definitely more proficient than those at Newnan's Lake. There were no spectators watching AC as he backed down the ramp. The boat, *Go Fish*, slid gently into the water, was tied to the dock by Vicky, and the truck and trailer parked. AC jumped down into the boat, started the motor and briefly went over the controls with Vicky.

"OK, remember '*red right, returning*', got it? said AC, as he eased the boat into the well-marked but confusing Cedar Keys channel.

"I can remember that," said Vicky, "but what does it mean?"

"Look at that channel marker on the piling. The red eighteen. We need to keep it to the right when returning to port. RRR. We're leaving port so we keep it on the left or port. Port side that is. Since we are going out we keep the green markers to the right so we'll stay in the channel. The green ones have odd numbers. Well, not strange odd, but you know what I mean."

"Clear as mud, as we used to say back home."

Now that the channel had been reached, AC increased speed and the ninety-horsepower Johnson quickly had the boat up on a plane.

"Now, see that island to the left," said AC speaking in short loud, jerky sentences above the noise of the wind and motor. "That's Atsena Otie. Seminole name I guess. That was where the original settlement was located before being blown away by a hurricane. That one beyond it is Snake Key. Over there to the right is Seahorse. See the little lighthouse? You can just see Deadman beyond Seahorse. Look past Snake on the horizon and you can see the stacks of the power plant at Crystal River. Nuclear."

The sea presented a light chop from the northeast, which would subside when the Florida landmass warmed up and created a breeze from the Gulf. AC steered a course to the southwest for about five miles from the last channel marker. Soon he saw a few small white dots on the horizon which he recognized as boats on Seahorse Reef. Land was still visible to his stern where he could also see the water tank at Cedar Key. This was always a good reference point unless there was fog or haze. Vicky had moved directly behind him and had her arms around his waist. Her hands occasionally dropped lower and she nibbled his neck.

"What do you want to do, fish or fuck?" said the ever-suave AC.

"Both."

About a mile ahead of the boat, the sea turned a lighter shade of green, indicating the shallower water over the reef. Seahorse Reef was several miles long and about ten feet deep, depending on the tide. It had probably been an island itself in prehistoric times. Predatory mackerel congregated there in the spring and fall following the schools of baitfish which migrated up and down the Gulf coast. Several methods were employed in catching the sleek mackerel. Some fishermen anchored and floated an unweighted shrimp past the reef as the tide brought the water across the shallows and into the area being patrolled by the mackerel. AC chose to troll silver spoons and feathered jigs just behind the boat. The rods could be kept in a holder, but a hand-held rod gave the fisherman something to do, and the thrill of feeling the fish strike added to the excitement. Getting a strike using this method required little skill from the fisherman, but landing a good sized fish required some attention, especially when using light tackle. Vicky, or at least her rod, got the first strike.

"AC, AC I've got one!"

AC quickly put the motor in neutral and reeled in the other line to get it out of the way. Spanish mackerel were usually cooperative, but this one seemed different. The way Vicky's rod was bending, and the whirring sound of the drag as line was stripped away, told AC this was a special fish as well as Vicky's first, and he was determined to get it in the boat.

"Hold up the tip of the rod," he shouted. "Just hold the rod. Let him get tired. If your line goes slack, reel in as fast as you can."

"Son-of-a-bitch," breathed Vicky, realizing she had never used foul language in front of AC, "this mother is going to pull me in the ocean."

AC looked at the reel spool and saw the line was indeed a bit low. Fortunately the Abu Garcia Ambassador reel was one of his larger ones and held well over two hundred yards of twelve-pound test line. Vicky was standing up and AC cleared some of the clutter from the deck so she would have room to maneuver. He also readied the landing net. After several exciting minutes, with both fishermen talking much louder than necessary, the fish swam by the boat close enough to be seen.

"Wow!" exclaimed Vicky. "Look at the size of that fish."

"Hang on. When he sees the boat he'll make another run."

As if on cue, the mackerel shot off again and Vicky was needlessly reminded to keep her rod tip up. At the next pass AC deftly netted the prey and brought it aboard. When he reached for the fish to extract the hook Vicky shouted. "He's mine. I'll do it. Just tell me how."

The mackerel had not yet surrendered and thrashed about becoming more and more entangled in the landing net.

"OK, he's all yours. He's not going anywhere, so take your time. That's the biggest Spanish mackerel I've ever seen. Looks almost like a small kingfish. Actually it's probably a she. They run larger. OK, hold him with this towel so he won't slip, but keep your fingers away from his mouth if you like them. Those teeth are like small little razors. Grab him with your left hand around the gills and use this tool to hold the hook and give it a twist."

Vicky got the hook and jig out, but as she did the mackerel gave a final jerk and was on the deck sliding among the tackle boxes and ice cooler.

"Oh, shit," screamed Vicky. "Get him."

AC grabbed the now exhausted fish just in front of the large forked tail and held it up in front of him.

"Somebody get a camera before he gets away again," grinned AC. "This calls for a beer."

The happy couple caught a few more fish, but none as large as Vicky's first. Actually, Vicky caught four more mackerel while AC, the old salt, caught one. Vicky pointed this out.

"Well, these fish are really pets I keep to please guests. We probably should release them. All but the big one. I've never seen him before. How about a sandwich? I'll anchor and put up the bimini top for shade. Those clouds over land tell me we should head in soon."

"I think we should go into business. The AC/VC Fish Company," beamed Vicky.

Although it was cloudless and calm out in the Gulf of Mexico, the dark clouds continued to build up over the mainland. By the time they got back to the dock and loaded the boat on the trailer, AC and Vicky could hear thunder off in the distance to the east. AC had found that on the road home, after an early morning start and a day in the sun fishing, most passengers dozed off before reaching Otter Creek. He glanced over and found Vicky to be no exception. One thing was different however. She slept with a smile on her face rather than with sagging features and an open mouth. Perhaps she was just a naturally happy person. He remembered the way she squealed with delight at landing *Big Spic* as she named her fish. This put him in mind of Carlo although AC did not normally think of his Cuban friends in derogatory terms. He knew if he told Vicky of his visit from Preston, and the way her name was linked with Carlo, her smile would be gone. She trusted him and confided in him at the risk of his displeasure. Why should he not trust her? *Well, I do trust her,* he thought; I just don't want to make her worried and unhappy. Suppose somehow word gets out, and she finds out I knew about the police and didn't tell her? Tomorrow. Tomorrow I'll tell her all about the cops and Jack the Asner. Tonight I'll broil Big Spic over hot coals and baste him with butter and lemon juice and maybe my secret blend of Greek spices. Then we'll take a shower together, and...and...and he found himself about to join Vicky in dreamland before catching himself and concentrating on the road. He looked in vain for his lucky kingfisher; it was nowhere to be seen.

VIII

The smell of frying bacon. The fact that tomorrow was Friday. Vicky's off-key singing. All these things combined to give AC such a sense of joy that he literally sprang out of bed and into the shower. He did not have his work suit at Vicky's, so he had to rush breakfast and run by his apartment on his way to the Alachua County Courthouse. He did not forget his pledge to tell Vicky about how the police were interested in Carlo. He simply could not say as he drove away "Oh, by the way, the cops are onto Carlo and consider you to be one of his friends." She was more than a friend of Carlo's; from what she told him she had been briefly a co-conspirator. As he drove across the prairie he realized his apprehension could be entirely misplaced. There were always several cops working out at the fitness center during lunch hour. Someone could easily have seen Carlo and Vicky talking and leaving together. That was much more likely than the discovery of a fraudulent adoption scheme that never even got off the ground. Sill, Vicky had to be told, and he knew she would be upset.

Judge AC got to work in plenty of time to prepare for the day, which was a good thing, as he had no idea what was on his calendar. Fridays were his catch-up day. He had no regularly scheduled court events and would sometimes set all-day hearings which were hard to squeeze in during the week, or just use the time to write orders and do other administrative tasks. Shirley Bloch looked up from her crossword.

"I hope you remembered that you agreed to cover for Judge Asner today. He's set some kind of motion in a divorce case for an hour. That's it for the day."

"Why am I covering for him? What's he doing? Long weekend?" asked AC as he peered over her shoulder at the paper.

"Judge, you agreed to cover for him. I don't know what he's doing. Would you like me to call and find out?"

"U-l-a-n as in Ulan Bator. Four down," said AC, ignoring her mild impertinence as he walked into his hearing room. Oh, well, it's just an hour. So what if he did want to take off early? He did vaguely remember a call requesting coverage. Something about an out-of-state soccer game the judge's son was in. The case file for the morning's hearing was on his desk and it was a fat one. Stinson vs. Stinson. This did not ring a bell. Shirley had marked the motion with a blue tab. The first thing he noted was that it was a motion for a rehearing of a motion previously ruled on by Judge Asner. *This is stupid,* he thought. Stupid and totally improper. He glanced at the names of lawyers for the parties. What do they expect me to do? Overrule my fellow circuit judge as if I were a Court of Appeals? Having nothing better to do, Judge AC decided to listen to the lawyer's argument. Perhaps he could find a way to convince them that Judge Asner was right. If Asner was wrong he could always decline to rule.

He read the order that was the subject of the motion for rehearing. It was, in AC's opinion, poorly worded, but it was an accurate statement of the law. The facts were straightforward. A widow with two sons had remarried a professor of sociology at the University of Florida. The widow's sons were entitled to social security benefits earned by their deceased father. Over the years these funds had been deposited into a prepaid college tuition fund offered by the University. Several thousand dollars had accumulated. Based on the pleadings, Judge AC could easily speculate on why the marriage failed, but it was not really pertinent. In the dissolution proceedings the professor husband took the position that the college funds were marital property, and he was entitled to an equitable distribution. After all, he argued, he had supported the stepsons and had not required them to use their social security benefits for their upkeep.

The wife argued that the funds belonged to the boys and was not part of the marital estate like the family home or car. The boys could not voice an opinion as they were not parties to the dissolution proceeding. Somehow or another, Judge Asner had understood the argument of the wife and entered an order allowing the children to bring a separate action to try to establish a constructive trust over the funds which had been paid for by their social security benefits.

This separate lawsuit had been properly filed in the civil division and was, no doubt one of many motions to be paid for from the meager resources of the widow and professor.

Shirley Bloch stuck her head in the door and announced, "The parties are all here, Judge. From the looks of them you might want a bailiff."

"Don't worry. I can handle it but I might not be my usual friendly self."

The parties trooped in with the ambiance of the truce negotiators at Panmunjon. There was really no need for the actual parties to be present as the motion was strictly legal in nature and no testimony would be allowed, but these folks wanted to see their gunslingers in action. They were out for blood. AC sensed this and assumed his formal demeanor. No jokes, no predictions of Gator scores, just an air of concerned wisdom. He knew the lawyers well and certainly could identify the parties, but he made them all state their names for the record. He then announced, "I am Judge Cason, and I have been requested to cover this motion hearing for Judge Asner who is unavailable. The husband, Doctor Stinson, has moved for a rehearing on Judge Asner's recent order ruling that the interests of the children of Mrs. Stinson be determined in a separate suit. Separate from the dissolution suit that is."

This let the attorneys know that he had read the file, and let the husband know the judge knew he held a PhD. Certainly the judge would be impressed with that. Who wouldn't be?

"The husband has moved for a rehearing. Please explain how Judge Asner misapplied the law."

"Judge, with all due respect for Judge Asner, the husband feels the judge was misled by specious arguments of the wife's counsel. I know you've read the file and can see that the funds in question were really part of the household income. My client had no legal obligation to support his stepchildren, yet he provided all the necessities of life for them. These social security payments were designed to cover these expenses. Out of the kindness of his heart he set up this college tuition fund as part of a family savings plan, and it is just like any other asset subject to equitable distribution. Judge Asner seemed to recognize this, but his order is not exactly clear on this point."

"Your Honor," began the attorney for the wife, "the husband's argument vis-a-vis husband and wife, may or may not be correct, but it is the children who claim an interest in these funds, not the wife. The children are not parties to the dissolution action so their rights cannot be determined in it. Judge

Asner recognized this and allowed a separate action by the children to attempt to establish their rights. The husband's argument may have merit, but it has to be determined in a separate suit."

The husband's obstructionist lawyer either did not comprehend the legal aspects of the case, or understood and did not like the way things were going. He knew he preferred to be back before Judge Asner who had a reputation for favoring husbands in divorce cases. He decided to backpedal.

"Judge, I know everyone in the room appreciates the fact that you agreed to hear this matter in Judge Asner's absence. Neither of these parties wants to delay matters. They want to resolve things so they can get on with their lives, but I really think this matter should be reheard by Judge Asner. I mean, it's not like he is retired or anything."

Both lawyers and the judge knew this was correct. The agitated wife whispered something to her lawyer and the husband could not conceal a smirk when Judge AC agreed that the motion for rehearing should be heard by Judge Asner. He started to comment that Judge Asner was eminently correct in his ruling but thought better of it. He followed the parties as they filed out into the hallway and overheard the wife ask her lawyer to tell her what had happened. How could they lose when it was so clear? When the hallway had cleared, Judge AC popped in on some of his judge buddies to find out lunch plans but came up with no partners, so he returned to his clambers to see if he could get his desk cleared before noon. That would leave his afternoon free.

Restaurants in downtown Gainesville must not make money at lunch, thought AC, as he tried to decide where to dine. There were a few fast-food joints and, of course, the lunch counter at Wise's Drugs, but AC felt like a change. Harry's Seafood served a good Cajun gumbo, but it was always crowded. He should have taken an early lunch, he thought as he saw a large group of patrons milling about in front of Harry's waiting for a table. Wises it is, he decided, when he saw a familiar face in the crowd by Harry's. The balding head, the tortoise shell glasses, the tacky sport coat all told him it was none other the Judge "Jack-the-Ass" Asner. *Whoa*, wasn't there something about a soccer game? He started to go over and gently confront the judge about having to cover for him when he saw a second familiar face. He did not want to stare, and in fact averted his eyes and jaywalked across the street. Carlo of Vero was standing right next to Jack Asner. He quickly strode on toward Wise's without bothering to determine if the pair were lunching together or simply standing in the same line. AC remembered his lucky seat at the counter where he first struck up with Vicky. He headed for it but was stopped by lawyer friends at one of the small tables set up by the large window looking out on University Avenue.

"Hey, Judge, come join us."

The lawyers were John Cahill and Stacy Ann Maddox. AC really wanted to sit at the counter by himself and try to analyze his thoughts about Carlo, Sergeant Preston, and Asner. He wished he had gone back to Harry's and peeked into the window to see if Asner and Carlo were sitting together, but there was no way he could avoid these friendly lawyers, so he pulled back a chair and sat down. He ordered a cup of bean soup and a tuna salad on wheat toast from the waitress who had been with Wise's for forty years.

"OK," he said, "What's going on that I don't know about?"

"Judge, it has to be *quid pro quo*. You tell us who's going to retire from the bench, and we'll tell you scandal that will make you blush," said Stacy, the least reticent of the attorneys practicing before Judge AC.

"Blushing in public is truly enjoyable, but judges don't retire, they just fade away. I really have nothing to swap. You can tell me what's going on with the DCF contracts. Your firm used to represent almost all of the parents, and now I've got to deal with Hal Degan and Cindy Irving."

Stacy opened her mouth to reply but was quickly shushed by John Cahill, her senior partner.

"Judge, the new contract is not one we could financially justify. We took cases based on a flat fee per case. Some were resolved easily and some were not, but on the average we were able to provide quality representation and make enough to pay overhead. The new rule provides for an hourly payment which is not enough to survive on. As a result I think you'll see cases drag on and on as there is no incentive to bring the cases to a head."

At this point Trix, short for Beatrice, brought AC's soup and sandwich.

"I hope the bean is hot enough. It was the last bowl we had. I just never know how much to make. Let me know if you want it heated up some."

"I will, Trix, but could I have the pepper sauce.? That should add all the hot I'll need."

"Judge, as I was saying, I know the counter argument is that under our payment scheme, we would settle cases early so as not to have to work, but that's simply not true. You know, as we know, that in many cases the kids would be better removed from a sick parent. Our job was not to try to prevent that, but to assure that the parent was not being railroaded into giving up too soon, before she had a chance to prove herself. I'm probably talking too much, but in my opinion the new district legal counsel doesn't approve of our role at all. He would like to be the sole arbiter of which kids go and which kids stay."

AC liked John Cahill and admired his skill as a lawyer, but he was overly pedantic and really not much fun compared to Stacy who tried to jump into the conversation.

"Judge, I'll tell you what I think. I think this is..." but Judge AC shut her off.

"John, let me give you a bit of political philosophy. I'm not saying I agree with it in all cases, but Ulysses Grant once said the best way to eliminate a bad law was to strictly enforce it. This brings misery to a few but relieves many from the specter of an evil rule hanging over their heads. Once we start trying to find ways around bad laws or bad rules, they won't change. Enforce them and you get a change."

Stacy, at this point, had had enough. "I can arrange for joint soapboxes if you give me a few minutes."

"Stacy, you are too young to have a sense of history. You probably don't remember when parents had no right to appointed attorneys, even when the state sought to permanently remove their children. Now, we appoint lawyers even before the state has decided that termination of parental rights is called for. From your perspective I can sense the frustration you must have, but compare that to the devastation that would result if judges were removed from the process, and the DLC's made all the calls. That's the way it works in many parts of the world. I predict that in the long run these bumbling lawyers will mess up enough cases that they'll be removed. Stacy, are you intentionally rubbing my knee?"

It was Stacy's turn to blush as she searched her mind for a cute reply, but she was saved by the appearance of Doug Smith, a rather freewheeling member of the local bar.

"Jerge, yo honor," he said mimicking the black dialect, "What are you doing hanging around with these state tit lawyers? When are you going to rotate to civil so I can get a ruling on time?"

"That's not fair, Doug," said Stacy. "You've suckled everything from Republicans to roaches; you even moved to Country Club Estates, and you still pretend to be a liberal."

"Well, Ms Maddox, if you would come to work for me, you could have all the liberal work you want. All we do is sue the establishment, and we don't even ask for liberal, activist judges. Just judges who will go ahead and rule and not sit on cases forever."

"Well," said AC "I can take a hint. Doug thinks I should be back at work and he's right. Here Doug, take my seat and Stacy will try to make you blush. She failed with me as I am sheathed judicial armor."

AC left his tip and wandered over to the cash register clerk to settle up his bill. His mind was already rehashing all the events involving Carlo, the sinister con. That Carlo was up to no good was certain. Vicky had told him directly and Preston had told him the same in so many words. Asner had been in his office looking for the Jordan file and AC had been kicked off the Jordan case. Asner and Carlo were in line together at Harry's. What else? He was so distracted he almost walked into the traffic crossing Main Street.

He went back to his office and decided to draft a chart, an analytical time line, with all events and repercussions outlined on paper. He reached several conclusions. Do not call Preston about Asner being in line with Carlo. That would smack of totalitarian big brotherism. Tell Vicky about the cops being interested in Carlo without further delay, even though he would have to let on that she was linked with Carlo by the cops. Ask Vicky to check on the Jordan case for him. This last posed an ethical problem since once he had been removed from a case, even if wrongfully, he had absolutely no business interfering with the case. This was removal from the bench stuff. On the other hand, he knew the distinction between probable cause and a reasonable suspicion. His suspicion was reasonable in his mind and he would be remiss in his judicial responsibility if he did nothing. At least that is what he told himself as he told Shirley he had to go run some errands.

As he walked toward the elevator he ran into Dapper Dan Fox who was wearing new three hundred fifty dollar wing tips.

"Hey, AC, got a minute?"

"Sure."

"Come on down to my place. This isn't exactly a hallway conversation."

AC became as alert as his friend's namesake. He had not seen Judge Fox since their last conversation concerning Judge Asner, and he knew Judge Fox harbored many ill feelings toward Asner. Some of these ill feelings were, in AC's mind, a bit petty. He knew Dan was a case counter. The statistics from the office of the Clerk of the Court showed how many cases were pending in each division of court. Or at least they were supposed to. AC spent his time trying to correct his own obvious discrepancies, while Dan Fox used the numbers to try to show which judges were doing their jobs and which were not. AC had the feeling that this conversation was not going to be about counting cases, and he was correct.

"Remember the case you asked me about? The one involving Ricky Jordan?"

"Right. The one now assigned to Asner. That's not my case now, so I shouldn't really get involved."

"Bullshit. Asner was in your office trying to steal your file. It was your case then, not his. Anyway, this may not be significant, but I did some thinking and remembered more about Ricky Jordan. He is, as you say, a true Florida cracker, but his sister's married to Dan Hawthorne. Does that tell you something?"

"*The* Dan Hawthorne? Who owns Union County outright. *That* Dan Hawthorne?"

"I think there's a pine tree near Lake Butler that he doesn't own, but he is a person of considerable influence to say the least."

"Dan, I appreciate your checking on this for me. I'm out of the case now, but I was bothered by Asner's antics. If I hear anything I'll let you know."

Damn! thought AC as he left the chambers of Judge Fox. This information about Dan Hawthorne completely ruined AC's theory about Judge Asner being bribed by Carlo. If Asner was, indeed, corrupt, he would lean toward returning the baby to the Jordans who had, so it seemed, the requisite political influence. Dan Hawthorne owned a large trucking company, several limerock pits, a nursery, and several thousand acres of pine trees, and possibly even the sheriff.

***

AC picked up the ingredients for supper from Publix (where shopping was a pleasure), and, as he drove to Micanopy, he debated with himself about how to tell Vicky about his discoveries and suspicions. He did not want to hide anything from her, but he did not want to involve her in anything that might compromise her position with DCF. He now realized that there was no plausible connection between the Jordan case and Carlo, despite his sighting at Harry's restaurant line. That had all been total conjecture on his part. Stupid, he thought. That was the kind of logic that got federal prosecutors in trouble in conspiracy cases. He still had his suspicions about Jack the Asner and the District Legal Counsel. Vicky could prove helpful there. This was not a situation in which a bag of money would ever change hands. There might be a nod or a wink, but that would be about it. A year or two later Asner would get all the votes in Union County, except for the lonesome pine near Lake Butler, courtesy of Dan Hawthorne. Hard to hang a hat on that tree he thought.

AC was so preoccupied with these thoughts he overshot Vicky's driveway and had to do a U-turn to get back. Her car was not in the drive, so he knew he could have supper waiting when she got home. This pleased him. He had no pretensions of being a gourmet chef but thought he did a good job with country victuals. He started the yellow rice and chicken, set the table, put a bottle of Chardonnay in the freezer to chill, and found two candles in Vicky's drawer. As an afterthought he uncorked the wine and poured himself a glass and put it back in the freezer. *Move it down before it gets too cold*, he reminded himself as he sat on the couch and turned on the TV. The local news had already started and the screen showed a blond coed, a student journalist, from the University of Florida station standing in front of the Alachua County Courthouse talking about something that seemed familiar.

"The lawyer stated that it was a clear conflict of interest for Judge Weaver. When asked if he would report the matter to the Judicial Qualifications Commission he said that was not his goal. He stated that Judge Weaver's actions created an appearance of impropriety and that was what mattered. He stated he was certain Judge Weaver would grant the motion and disqualify himself from further proceedings. This is Jessica Roberts reporting from the Alachua County Courthouse."

Now what? thought AC. That has to be about the Wessex Industries case. The snakes versus the skunks. The only way Channel Five would have heard of the motion was if one of the lawyers called them. Stupid, stupid, stupid. So now they think I will welcome them with open arms? What jerks. I wonder which side could have been so dumb?

The barking of dogs announced Vicky's arrival. AC went outside and Vicky greeted him with her usual jump into his arms with her legs around his waist. AC could handle this but hoped Vicky remained trim. The quick kiss was fine, but the averted eyes let AC know all was not right.

"Long day in the pits?"

"AC, did you bring wine? I would like a glass and some comfort and counsel."

"Yes, love. I can provide all three for a modest *quid pro quo*."

"Well, you get the squid and whatever, while I change."

Vicky emerged barefooted from the bedroom wearing her favorite pink tank top and shorts. She curled up on the couch, cat fashion, and turned off the TV with the remote control. This was done with a snapping motion, as if to send a personal message to the television.

"AC, I just got a subpoena from the State Attorney's office. I called and they won't say what it's about. Our DCF attorneys are technically assistant state attorneys, but this subpoena is from Susan Spikes who has nothing to do with our office."

"When is the date? What is it? A deposition?"

"Yeah, deposition, I guess. It's two weeks away. AC, It has to be about that goddamned Carlo. I'm scared shitless."

If Vicky was scared shitless, AC was in worse shape. He should have been worried about Vicky, but his first reaction was to try to figure out how he could tell her what he had pledged himself to do. *You know, the cops were asking me all about you and Carlo and I just forgot to mention it.* He thought about tangled webs and deception and decided to come clean regardless of the consequences.

"Sweetheart, I know this is an awkward time to tell you, but a close friend of mine who happens to be a cop asked me if I knew Carlo. This was a few weeks ago. This was before you told me the Vero Beach story. I said we had met on the plaza and that was it. He told me to let him know if Carlo tried to contact me. The bad part is, well, somehow he knew you were a friend of Carlo. I should have mentioned it earlier, but I wanted for all that past stuff to go away."

He paused, not knowing where to go from there. Vicky said nothing but stared out the window at the darkening sky. AC suggested supper and Vicky asked if he was serious. "AC, I have to find out what is going on before I go in for this deposition. You know how these assholes work. Even if you've done nothing, they throw out a threat of obstruction of justice or whatever. I have to call Carlo."

"Not a good idea. His phone may be bugged or, if not, his answering machine will probably list your number for the cops to find."

"AC, I'm not going to ask you why you didn't tell me about the police and Carlo. I am deeply hurt, but there is no use dwelling on it. I know I didn't commit a criminal act. Thank goodness for that. Even so, if what I did do gets out, I'm through. Ruined. And I can only blame myself." A long pause, then "Shit."

Tears welled up in her eyes and she just let them run down her cheeks as she continued to stare out of the window. AC's emotions were a mixture of guilt and sadness. His first instinct was to try to comfort

Vicky, but he sensed she did not want a big hug from him under the circumstances.

"Vicky, love, what you are saying is totally speculative. There's no reason to conclude that the subpoena has anything to do with Carlo at all. Even if it has, there's no way anything could be held against you."

He had started to say 'pinned on you', and decided it was too much like cop talk.

Vicky gave him a condescending glance.

"AC, for a worldly-wise judge, you're sometimes so naive it hurts. OK. I won't jump to conclusions. You may be right. There's no way they can prove anything against me. I can simply lie my way through it. Carlo's word against mine. Fine. That gets me off the hook legally, and all I have to contend with is a headline that reads, 'Controversial DCF worker involved in baby adoption bribery scheme.' You ought to worry about your own butt. 'Judge's girlfriend linked to notorious fixer and millionaire pal wanting to buy baby. Speculation that children are being removed from families for purposes of adoption by wealthy clients.' That may be jumping to conclusions, but it scares me to death. I'm sorry, AC. You've not done anything to hurt the situation."

And with this she moved to his side of the couch and buried her face against his chest and did not try to control her sobbing. He held her for a long time, then gently suggested that a good meal would help them think things out. He was correct to some extent. Vicky was a good eater. Loved all sorts of greens and even ordered anchovies on pizza. She began to relax. To divert her attention he told her about the Jordan case, and about his initial suspicions connecting Asner and Carlo. He mentioned the Levy County domestic violence part in passing. Vicky perked up at this. Why hadn't he told her earlier? Didn't he trust her? Of course he did. But as she could see, he had been totally wrong. If Ricky Jordan had any outside source of influence, it was his brother-in-law, Dan Hawthorne, not Carlo Proenza.

Vicky now became agitated. "AC, if what you say is true, the result could be worse then the adoption business. If that baby is in jeopardy and is returned to the mother it could die. I know. Now *that's* something I *would* be willing to risk my career to stop."

"Vicky, please, all I have to go on is the phony recusal issue, and the fact that the brother-in-law of the grandfather is a person of influence in another county. Good grief."

"I know, I know," Vicky said in a much stronger, assertive tone. "But this is what *I* do for a living. I'm going to monitor that Jordan case, and stick my neck out if anything looks fishy. I've had one baby killed on my watch, and I know what it feels like. I'm not afraid of this jerk in Union County or Carlo, either, for that matter."

The food had done the trick after all, thought AC as they adjourned to the couch.

Vicky had made good logical points about all the possibilities and decided on positive action to resolve the situation. At least as far as the abused child was concerned. But Vicky's dilemma remained. They had to find out if Carlo was involved in Vicky's subpoena, and what he would testify to if things came to a head. There was no reason to trust Carlo, based on his occupation, but he did seem fond of Vicky. Maybe he would feel somewhat guilty for involving her in this whole scheme to begin with.

"Vicky, how far do you think you can trust Carlo? I mean, when you backed out on him, did he try to pressure you in any way to go through with the deal?"

"Actually, no. In fact he was real sweet now that I think of it. He said he was sorry. I may have even hugged him good-bye. It *was* good-bye. I do know that."

"Do you think he would agree to see you? To see us? In Vero maybe? I'm probably being paranoid about the phone tap. You know, I could have an attorney friend call him. That would mean telling all this to someone, but I think we have to be careful. My cop friend said that he was only helping out another agency, but it's a guess as to which one that would be. I can get Doug Smith to call. You know him? He's a former law partner of mine. He has the reputation of a gossip, but is really tight lipped as a clam."

"AC, my sweet, you have no business getting involved in all this mess. I should just say no. Period. I do know one thing. I know I'm glad that you sat down next to me at Wise's that time. I've never had anyone to lean on before you. Anyone that would stick up for me. I might cry at times, but I'm a tough cookie.

I've always had to go it alone. If you want to involve yourself and your friend there's no way I can refuse. This could turn out to be a big mistake on your part. Now slide down just a bit. That's right."

Vicky pulled off her tank top before rolling over on top of the thoroughly charmed AC.

IX

"Bastards! Shitheads! You won't believe it," said Judge Clem Weaver, spitting out the words as if they were coated with toxic residue.

"Do I detect a note of vexation in your tone?" asked AC, as he entered his chambers where Judge Clem had been pacing up and down waiting for his friend to arrive. "You don't normally froth at the mouth."

"Vexed. That's perfect. Good word. Much better than being so pissed off I can't see straight. Did you see the news? You know the damn case file in Wessex already has twenty-three volumes, and now they pull crap like this. OK. I admit it. I despise all the lawyers in the case, but I hate them all equally. The plaintiff is represented by a pompous, self-aggrandizing son-of-a-bitch with a few other faults besides, and the damn prissy-assed defense lawyer is an unctuous, sneaky, backstabbing whore with ethics hardly better than a Tallahassee lobbyist. I wouldn't give a French fart for the whole lot, but I feel equally sorry for both clients. No matter, it's your baby now."

"This is a bit awkward," said AC "I don't rotate to civil for another two months, and from what you say this case takes a full week out of the month for hearings. Is it even set for trial?"

"Trial? Trial? These people can't even set a deposition without having a court hearing. It's the damnedest mess I've ever seen. You know why I can't be fair? The basis for their motion to remove me?"

"Well, I can think of several reasons," responded AC. "But then I know you better than they do."

Judge Weaver hardly paused in his tirade. "You know the Spector firm, local counsel for the defense. They cover for the Philly bigshots on routine matters. Well, Alan Spector, the third, who has nothing to do with the Wessex case, is in my chambers doing an uncontested mortgage foreclosure while all the Wessex people are in my courtroom setting up for a hearing. You have to hold hearings in the courtroom; they won't all fit in a hearing room; so we finish the foreclosure and walk out together and the plaintiff's lawyer claims I'm holding ex-parte conferences with counsel for Wessex. Absurd. Totally absurd. The Spector firm has over a dozen lawyers. What are they supposed to do? Quit practicing before me until Wessex is over ten years from now? I'm telling you, they'll never get a trial set with all the garbage they are throwing out. Speaking of garbage, one side even accused the other of going through my garbage can, looking for evidence of God knows what. My Gallo wine bottles ought to be proof I'm not taking bribes. I won't say which side was the snoop, as I would never want to prejudice you."

Judge Weaver paused to catch his breath and recover his composure; he had really become agitated. Judge AC reflected on the situation and asked, "Am I going to have to read all twenty-three volumes to find out what is going on?"

Judge Weaver got up from the table he had been sitting on and began pacing around the chamber. He stopped and stared out of the window at the city hall building across University Avenue. "AC, I really am sorry about all this. I played things close to the chest and never let my frustration show. Never made snap rulings. This motion to disqualify is so bad I might go to the bar grievance committee with it."

He paused and AC let him think a bit. "I can fill you in on the case, but anything I say now could be interpreted as trying to influence you. We can't have that. What I would do is to schedule a case management conference to introduce yourself and give the lawyers a chance to summarize their positions on the status of everything. Timetables for depositions and the works."

The friends stared at each other a while. Clem Weaver, AC's fishing buddy and confidant offered no advice other than a parting, "Good luck. Oh, by the way, I'm sure my calendar has been freed up a bit by all this. Call me if you need any coverage."

Judge Clem Weaver left a very dejected Judge AC staring at his calendar for the day. He wanted to concentrate on something, anything. The mess with Vicky kept him from concentrating on his work and it in turn, kept him from concentrating on Vicky and Carlo. Even if Carlo was willing to talk what would he say? Maybe Carlo knew nothing of the investigation and a call would tip him off. Sgt. Preston said to call him if he heard from Carlo and now he was considering calling Carlo. What would Preston think of that?

"Judge, they are all here for your motion hearing. Do you want some more time? You have an easy calendar." Shirley could evidently sense something was wrong.

"Shirley, give me five minutes. I guess you could figure out why Judge Weaver was here?"

"In a word, Wessex would be my guess," was Shirley's reply as she closed the door.

Judge AC looked through the file for the pending hearing and decided that he and Vicky could resolve the Carlo predicament over the upcoming weekend. He got up and invited the lawyers into his lair.

The ability to focus on one problem at a time in the face of multiple distractions is certainly an asset for a judge. It is of benefit to most professions, except that of a stand-up comic, who has to jump from one subject to another constantly. It can sometimes be overdone, as in the case of the stereotypical absent-minded professor whose mind is not absent, only over-focused. Judge AC fell somewhere in between the two by nature, but training helped him complete his assigned tasks for the afternoon without dwelling on Vicky and Carlo. Once he was free of the office he reached several conclusions which he looked forward to sharing with Vicky.

The sun was low on the horizon as AC and Vicky sat on her patio with AC's usual bottle of wine, this time a Pinot Grigio, on the low table between them. They contemplated nature avoiding the subject on their minds, which had to come up sooner or later. Finally, AC jumped into the pond feet first.

"Vicky, what we know at this point is that Carlo is a con artist, Asner is an ass, and we are a pair of paranoids. All the rest of our imaginary problems are just that, imaginary."

"My problems, my sweet, not yours. I know what you say is the truth, but I'm still frightened. Paranoids only *think* people are talking about them. I know people are talking about me." Vicky took a sip of her wine and AC poured himself another glass. "People are paid to talk about you, so that's different. I just don't want to walk into that deposition without any clue as to what's up. Did you give any more thought about your lawyer friend talking to Carlo? Frankly, I think that would scare him. I think you would scare him. I think it has to be me. I really don't think he would intentionally hurt me. Why don't we drive down to Vero tomorrow? You can stay out of the picture, and I'll just ask him if there's any way the deal with the Cunninghams could have leaked out." Vicky looked at AC and batted her eyes. "I can drop into my West Virginia pretty-please mode and he'll talk. I'm sure of it."

AC did not like the thought of Vicky dropping into her pretty-please mode around Carlo, but agreed that her plan made sense. Plus, it would be a fun trip driving over to the coast with Vicky. In his wildest imagining a year ago he could not have dreamed of going to Vero Beach for the weekend with Vicky Carter. They could stay at the Driftwood, and it should still be warm enough to swim in the ocean. Body surfing in the fall was perfect. He could feel the water racing under his body and the foam swirling about his head, and he could picture Vicky waiting on the beach with a cool beer for him.

"Well, say something," said the perplexed Vicky.

His reverie snapped by reality, the now agreeable AC said he thought the idea was perfect. The trip would be fun and could possibly dispel all their anxieties.

"Sweetheart, I have to admit, though, that I am a bit jealous of this Carlo. He does have his charm and, although I'm no judge, he is good looking."

"Humph. AC, you're almost impossible. Come over here and let me show you how irresistible you are."

AC did not know if this was Vicky's pretty-please mode or some other West Virginia tactic, but it did not matter. He did as he was instructed and knew he would not trade places with a prince.

***

The trip from Micanopy to Vero Beach was an easy three-hour drive. The Florida Turnpike south of Orlando traversed one of the most remote regions of the state. It was from this area that the old-time cow hunters rounded up the wild Spanish cattle and drove them across the Florida scrub to Punta Rassa for shipment to Cuba. These crackers had been depicted by Fredrick Remington in the mid-nineties and looked as rough as any of the cowboys in his western scenes. The cow towns of Kissimmee and Arcadia, and most all of DeSoto County, were as tough as Texas and Dodge City combined, and remained so into the nineteen twenties. Rustling, regulators, rum running and range wars were the rule, not the exception. Cows in Florida were not even required to be fenced off the highways until after the Second World War. As they drove along, AC told Vicky some of his favorite tales about Bone Mizell, perhaps the most colorful of all the old cow hunters.

"Bone was in a card game which got busted up by the Sheriff. 'Hey we ain't done nothing wrong. These is just chips, not money,' 'Same as money' said the sheriff. In court Bone tried to pay his fine with chips, which the sheriff had testified was the same as money."

"AC, where do you get all this stuff?"

"Books mostly, but I do have some first-hand stories from Levy County. Lots of these old tales are folklore going back ages, then attributed to colorful characters like Bone."

The couple soon reached Yeehaw Junction where Highway Sixty crossed the turnpike. The 'Junction' part of the name was really the junction of 60 and 441 which was the old north-south highway from Orlando to Okeechobee. The aptly named "Desert Inn" had been serving burgers there since before almost anyone could remember.

"Believe it or not, this joint is on the national register of historic places," AC said, as they pulled up by the side entrance.

"Is it safe? Will Bone and his buddies have a shoot-out?"

"The dangers will be more internal than external. I would avoid the restrooms. They do serve a BLT that matches Wise's, but not yours," he remembered to add.

This had been an early lunch for the travelers, and they made it to Vero Beach just after noon. They passed the Dodgers' spring training facility, and crossed the Indian River to Orchid Island. Vicky had been to Vero Beach only one time and that had been hectic.

"Let's look for Carlo's condo. I know I'll remember it. Then we can look for a place for you to enjoy the scenery while I try to scare him up. Remember though, the scenery is for viewing only."

"We could go ahead and check into the Driftwood, unless you'd rather stay farther up the beach."

"Let's wait. We may have to try more than once. If I do find him, I would really like to stay somewhere else. Wait, this looks familiar, only I think we are going in the wrong direction."

"The Driftwood is the only place I remember," said AC, who had spent the night there once during the happier days of his marriage. "That's it, right there."

"OK, then keep going. You can see the Driftwood from Carlo's place. He pointed it out to me and said the first big storm would wipe it out. That one. Right there. Keep going. I wonder what those cop cars are doing in the parking lot. Never mind. Look, there's a public beach. You park and I'll walk back. It's only a few blocks. I should be back in an hour and I can call you on your cell phone if I'm held up."

Vicky gave him an excited but determined kiss and headed off, while AC located a newspaper vending machine and bought a local paper to read while he waited under the shade of a large-leaved tropical tree for Vicky's return. There was not much news of interest. He almost skipped over the article with the headline, "Body found in condo" , but some sixth sense drew him to it. He quickly skimmed the story. "Police are still investigating the discovery of a woman's body found yesterday in the oceanfront condo of a local businessman. Alex Brown, of the Vero Police department, has declined to release details of the event but it was learned from neighbors that the condo is owned by Carlo Proenza, a well-known citizen of Vero

Beach who has reportedly been out of state for several weeks. The police refused to disclose the cause of death or whether there was evidence of forced entry. Neighbors stated that a woman had been seen regularly going in and out of the apartment, and became suspicious when the lights to the condo remained on all night for several nights in a row."

AC reread the article twice and decided to walk down and try to find Vicky. This was not a time to be seen snooping around or leaving fingerprints on doors. He had gone only a block when he spied Vicky hurrying along on the other side of the street. Her face was in a scowl. She had not been gone long enough to have talked to Carlo, and he guessed correctly that she had been frightened away by the police.

"Hey, Vicky," he yelled, jaywalking across the street, not even looking for traffic.

Vicky's scowl immediately turned to an expression of relief, mixed with deep concern.

"AC, something's really going on. The cops were checking on everybody going in the whole condo. Carlo's unit is on the tenth floor so I walked around front and could see something going on inside."

AC interrupted her by holding up the paper. "Read this."

Vicky read as they walked back to AC's bench, where they sat under the tree in the park. She was very quiet and dropped the paper onto her lap.

"I hate stories like this," she finally said. "You can't tell if it's a drug overdose, a stroke, a victim of Jack-the-Ripper or what. It could be Carlo's mother for all we know. I know the cops need to preserve evidence, but suppose you were the next door neighbor? Maybe they tell *them* something. I don't know. Whatever it is, it's none of my business and I suggest we leave town by the shortest way possible."

"The AC express departs in three minutes for Melbourne via AIA. I remember a cute B&B right on the beach that admits lovers only. No married couples or kids. It's run by a real character. Hippie Harry's or something. I hope it hasn't been washed away."

"I'll beat you to the car. Last one there is a rotten egg," said Vicky in a halfhearted attempt to lighten the mood.

The road along the barrier island had lost some of its charm due to development, but was still spectacular. The glimpses of the Atlantic were post-card perfect and Vicky and AC began to relax and enjoy their new-found attachment toward each other. This was a good season to be in the area, as the summer crowd had left and the snowbirds had not yet migrated south. They stopped at Sebastian Inlet for a Coke and watched the fishermen along the jetties.

"Should have brought my tackle. I really ought to leave some in the truck. Oh, well."

"AC, look. That guy's got one. What kind is it?"

"Sheepshead. You have to jerk the hook just before you feel the bite to catch one. They're always around barnacles so the jetties are a perfect place to fish. OK. it's time to head on up to Melbourne so we'll have time for a swim."

ALL RISE

Actually, Indialantic, across Indian River from Melbourne, was where they found Woodstock Woody's B&B and checked in. Woody, or Harry the Hippie, as AC remembered him, had not changed and claimed he remembered AC. They were only about twenty five miles south of Cape Canaveral and the Kennedy Space Center, and had just missed a night launch by a week. Woody showed them spectacular pictures and promised to reserve a room for the next launch. The room was something less than spectacular. AC remembered the old country ballad about a cheap motel. "Cigarette burns on the table by the bed/ A King James Bible that ain't been read." They changed into swim suits and walked to the beach where AC had an exhilarating swim, but was not joined by his inlander girlfriend, due to the size of the surf.

"This place is a Mecca for East Coast surfers," said AC, toweling off. Swimming never failed to rejuvenate him and he grabbed a quick wet kiss from Vicky. "Let's go pig out."

Woody's could not even qualify as quaint, but did have indoor plumbing and, when AC was joined by Vicky in the hot shower, decor did not matter. Woody suggested a seafood joint for supper which only served locally caught fish. "Locals catch it, we serve it you eat it. No shirt, no shoes, no problem. That kind of place," he had told them. This trip was suddenly fun.

It was still fun next morning at the breakfast served personally by Woody. He chose what to serve- - take it or leave it. Lots of fruit. Mangos, papayas, plantains, and what he claimed was home baked bread. The honey was "Ulee's Gold" he smiled. Woody got a big fat hug from Vicky and gave AC a knowing wink as they left. The drive back to Gainesville was long and left no option but to discuss where things stood with Carlo.

"Vicky, I could call Ron Whittaker about the deposition. We go back a long way. I could call on a personal basis."

Ron Whittaker was the state attorney for the Eighth Judicial Circuit. His office prosecuted all the crime in the circuit and also hired the lawyers who handled juvenile dependency cases. These lawyers had once all been employed by the Department of Children and Families, but by giving them the title of assistant state attorney, their stature was increased, or so it was said. The District Legal Counsel remained a DCF employee creating some confusion in the chain of command.

"AC, dear, I got myself into this mess and can handle it OK. As I said before, if the word got out that you were involving yourself, it would make things worse. Look, I may have had some guilty thoughts, but that's not against the law. If they already know about my involvement, then my reputation is already shot."

"Well, let's think about the deal with Asner. The stated reason I got bumped from the case was that Jordan claimed he had influence with me. That's so much nonsense, and they knew it at the time. I think someone specifically wanted Asner on the case for some ulterior motive. I know for sure he got advance word of the transfer, so he must be part of some deal. I'm thinking he wanted to look in the file to see if he felt he could go along with whatever plan was being concocted. Well, there's nothing we can do now, so let's enjoy the trip. I wish we had added a day to check out the Canaveral National Seashore."

The route home was on the interstate along the coast past Cocoa and Titusville. The travelers' plans were to turn west and go through the Ocala National Forest before they got to Daytona. AC told Vicky how his father and mother had lived in Cocoa in the Thirties when people had to put screens on car windows to keep out mosquitoes. They stopped for lunch in Deland, which was on the edge of the vast forest which stretched almost to Vicky's home near Micanopy. Despite this proximity, and her interest in the outdoors, Vicky had never ventured into this land of clear lakes, pines and palmetto. She kept AC busy answering questions about the flora, fauna and hydrology which she called 'critters and stuff.' AC had read much of the area's natural history from the time of William Bartram up to the time of Archie Carr, who was Vicky's former neighbor, so was somewhat well informed. Finally he said, "Don't take it from me. Look on the back seat. I even marked the page for you."

Vicky reached for the worn paperback describing Bartram's Florida travels in the late seventeen hundreds. She read out loud:

"The Alachua Savanna is computed to be fifteen miles long by six or seven wide and near fifty miles round. The land about it very good and extremely proper for Indigo, would grow good corn, etc. The whole Savanna in the Summer and Fall a meadow of good kinds of grass, and here are abundance of very large fat Cattle and Horses, one-fifty or two hundred in droves all belonging to the Seminoles... would those Indians part with this land, it would admit a very valuable Settlement and would be a very considerable acquisition."

"What about Payne's Prairie?" Vicky asked.

"Batram was before Chief Payne's time. He called the prairie by its original name. It's fun to imagine what Florida must have been like back then. I'll share Archie Carr's books later. He lived not far from you. His wife gave the main impetus for stopping the infamous 'Cross Florida Barge Canal,' but they've still got the Ocklawaha River dammed damn them."

They stopped for a beer and cola at the store at Salt Springs, then walked over to the crystal clear pool which each day bubbled out thousands of gallons of slightly saline water. After a short run, the water found its way into Lake George, which was really just a wide spot in the St. Johns River. The spot was wide enough to qualify as Florida's second largest lake. Then, back in AC's pickup, they sang a bit. Vicky taught him the words to "Country Roads," which described West Virginia as "almost heaven." Vicky wondered aloud if the writer had spent much time in her native state.

"You know," said AC, "Stephen Foster never saw the Suwannee and didn't even know how to spell it. We need to write a song about Micanopy." Soon they had made it to Vicky's farm, and AC helped her unload her things. He departed reluctantly, but he had to get back to Gainesville to be ready for his trip to Levy County in the morning.

X

When AC got home from Micanopy there was a message on his answering machine from Shirley Blotch.

"Judge, I hope you get this. Don't go to Levy tomorrow. Judge Weaver will cover for you. He wants you to meet with the Wessex crew, as they are all scheduled to be in town for some motions he can't hear due to the reassignment. He thought this would be a good time for you to meet them and has instructed them to bring you up to date in the case. Call me if you don't get this."

Right, thought AC. Call me if you don't.... oh well, I *did* get it and I have to do this sooner or later. He would have preferred to set the initial meeting on his own terms and when he was more prepared. The defense lawyers were from Philadelphia making them "Philadephia lawyers", a term AC was familiar with, without knowing exactly what it meant. It did sound a bit intimidating to a small-town jurist. The plaintiffs were represented by a team from Miami, affectionately referred to as the "hurricanes" by the local bar, and Judge AC was well aware of their reputation. Their favorite tactic was to try a case in the media before presenting it to a jury. This, of course, made it harder to select a jury that had not formed an opinion of the case, and it gave the lawyers the advantage of influencing jurors by evidence not admissible in court. AC could anticipate the media statement: "Giant bloodsucking corporation is challenged by local firm that refuses to be bullied." Wessex was undoubtedly a bully, but the so-called "local firm" was now owned by a conglomerate from the Netherlands. Still, the firm was run by local folks active in Rotary and Youth Soccer, and they would have many friends among the prospective jurors.

AC called Vicky as he had promised, to wish her "night, night." She sounded like she had already gone to sleep as she murmured sweet things into his ear. He hung up, and as he lay in bed he contemplated his next day as well as the next decade or so of his future. He did not sleep well at all.

Judge AC rose early and donned his black pinstriped suit and power-red tie. He wanted to look a bit big city and not like some tweedy history professor. He cheated a bit with his formal attire by wearing rubber-soled black Rockport wingtips known as 'dress ports', and hoped no one would notice. He thought about wearing his robe. This might be more imposing, but the Wessex meeting was supposed to be an informal one with the attorneys. He had time to have a sit-down breakfast of raisin bran, while he read the Gainesville Sun. This was Monday, so half of the paper was full of wire service articles explaining that more exercise and less caloric intake was good for one's health. He finished the crossword in ten minutes flat. As he drove to work he thought about judge-lawyer relationships.

Almost all lawyers were polite to almost all judges almost all of the time. The elder statesmen of the bar treated judges, even junior judges, and even their opponents, with the utmost cordiality. After all, they had been admitted to the bar before advertising and Rambo tactics had come into vogue. They would, like duelists of an earlier era, fight to the death but never brawl in public. The younger lawyers, having been raised on television dramas, often argued with each other during a hearing. AC would have to remind them to "direct your arguments to the court; convince me; if you could convince your opponent you would not be here." Some difficulty was experienced from contemporaries. If the judge and lawyer had been classmates, it was difficult to change from a first name basis to "your honor," especially if the judge had been known as "Frog" in law school. Fortunately, AC was a Marine Corps veteran when he entered law school and this gave him a bit of an image lift above his fraternity-boy classmates.

Only five of the twenty-five volumes of the Wessex case had been delivered to Judge AC's office in advance of the hearing. These were not of much use in preparing for the scheduled briefing. They contained numerous documents entitled: "Notice to Produce" and "Objections to Notice to Produce." "Notice of Deposition of Party" and "Motion to Strike Notice of Deposition of Party." And on and on and on. Every request for information from one side was met with an objection from the other. The defendant wanted to look over the plaintiff's facilities. (Motion to View Premises). The plaintiff agreed to the motions but demanded to be present while the defendant was there. The defendant claimed that the plaintiff's lawyers should not be present, that they just wanted to learn what materials the defendant felt were important, in which case there would be an invasion of the lawyer-client privilege. The plaintiff claimed if the defendant was allowed on the premises without supervision, things would be stolen or pictures distorted. These were but a few of the issues needing to be resolved prior to trial. After mulling over all these dynamics, Judge AC concluded that to join into the hostilities as an antagonistic third party would only drag things on interminably. He determined the best strategy was to attempt to disarm the lawyers with charm.

When Judge AC pulled up to the electronic gate shielding the judges' courthouse parking area, he found that his magnetic card failed to open the cross-bar. He was about to call for help on his cellular phone, when Judge Moss pulled in behind him and started honking his horn. Obviously he knew it was his pal, AC, blocking the way, but the commotion caused a stir and bailiffs came from all directions. When they got inside AC turned to Ira and said, "I've always admired take-charge judges. I could have been there all day and missed the Wessex hearing your buddy set up for me."

"Wessex? Wait one. You're a family judge, a baby splitter. Division from Hell and all. Clem's supposed to split that baby."

"Clem was, until you assigned it to me. You *are* the chief judge, according to the last election."

Ira Moss was, in fact, the chief judge for the Eighth Judicial Circuit, a position of great power. He assigned judges to various divisions and was in charge of the budget and everything else of an administrative nature in the circuit. He signed orders by the stack. Most were routine and not read and did not need to be read. He had apparently not noticed the Wessex reassignment.

"What happened? You know, it seems to me someone should have told me what was going on. This is command decision stuff, not rubber stamp. Don't get me wrong. You are the man for the job, but that case is a bear."

AC knew Ira had been left in the dark. But it made no sense to assign the case to the current civil division judge who was scheduled to be replaced by AC in a few weeks.

"Hey, we can work it out. Clem is covering my division for all the hearings he had set in Wessex. The only thing we have to worry about is the three-to-four month trial, which I'm going to set for a 'date certain' come hell or high water. I just want you to back me up when that time comes. These jackasses are not going to disrupt the rest of our court no matter how important they think their case is."

"AC, you know you can count on me to support you. What's the current timetable?"

"I really have no idea. When Clem told me I had the case, he was too mad for me to go into details. A lot of it hinges on the amount of discovery allowed. The Plaintiff wants to engage in extensive discovery, but seems to be totally unrealistic when it comes to allocating enough time to get it all done before trial. The defense claims to want an early trial, but wants to limit discovery in a way that would help them hide past shenanigans. It's really a mess. I mean, we're talking about over three hundred depositions all over the country. All over the world, for that matter."

The two colleagues parted when the elevator reached the third floor, and AC noticed the crowd already assembled outside his courtroom. Several attorney-types were talking on cellular phones while aides carried charts and tripods into the courtroom. Overhead projectors had been replaced by power-point computers and there were several TV monitors being wheeled into the courtroom for the state-of-the-art high-tech performance.

AC gave a polite hello to Shirley as he entered his chambers and gave a cursory look at the crossword, but he knew there would be no time for this diversion. He decided to enter the courtroom from the public hallway rather than from the judge's entrance from the rear of the bench. This would give him the opportunity to shake hands with the lawyers and perhaps ease the tension. He had not called for a bailiff to go through the "all rise" routine and carried all five files into the courtroom himself. He knew this procedure was a calculated risk and that he would need to balance his cordiality with a firm control of the courtroom, or the big-city lawyers would try to intimidate him. Abe. Abe Lincoln, he thought. No doubt many tried to bully Abe, but with his resolve and sense of humor he prevailed. A perfect role model. He walked through the courtroom shaking hands and took the bench, assuming what he hoped would be the role of the alpha wolf.

"Ladies and gentlemen," (actually there was just one lady among the attorneys), "I am, as you know by now, Judge Alva Cason. I appreciate your agreeing to use this time to acquaint me with this case rather than arguing the motions which had been scheduled. I view my responsibility in this matter to administer justice impartially, but not to make a career of this case, if you get my meaning. Every litigant in this court views his case as the most important thing in his life, regardless of the amount in controversy, and I have hundreds of cases pending before me. My review of the case files leads me to believe the attorneys on both sides tend to rely too much on the court to resolve petty matters that could be handled by better cooperation between counsel. I want to make it clear from the start that I will be very intolerant of such behavior. There are many subtle sanctions that I can impose and will not hesitate to do so upon ample provocation. On the other hand, I recognize that this in an involved case, with out-of-town counsel and witnesses, and I will do everything in my power to expedite matters. I will work early and I will work late and even on weekends if we are making progress. Enough said. Will the plaintiff please give me an outline of the issues involved in the case and what needs to be done to bring the case to trial? I would appreciate it if the parties would refrain from arguing the case at this point."

"May it please the court. My name is Marc Goldman of Barish and Floyd. Our firm represents Aquatec, a small local firm specializing in water purification systems."

Marc Goldman, of Barish and Floyd, was an imposing figure with his slicked back dark hair and impeccable dress. Everyone had heard of Barish and Floyd, and he knew it and waited for the impression to sink in before continuing. Judge AC almost jumped in on the "small local firm" comment as he knew of the acquisition of Aquatec by ANG of the Netherlands, but he bit his tongue. He also knew the process involved desalinization not purification.

"Aquatec was founded twenty years ago by three professors from the University of Florida who had developed an economical and innovative process for the desalinization of seawater. The defendant in the case, Wessex Industries of Pennsylvania is also in the desalinization business as well as about every other business you can think of. Wessex is, of course, a Forbes 500 company."

That's two attempts to argue, thought Judge AC, making note that it was a "Fortune 500" company Goldman was attempting to disparage.

"Aquatec had marketed its process throughout the United States and Canada when, in 1984, Wessex, using base financial intimidation, coerced a contract with Aquatec whereby Wessex would own all the contracts Aquatec had acquired, and Aquatec would become a sort of servicing agent for Wessex. Aquatec thus became responsible for inspecting and servicing all of the operating plants, but the process and the contracts would now belong to Wessex. The plaintiff contends that Wessex illegally went from plant to plant throughout the country and poisoned the minds of the plant operators, who in turn canceled the servicing agreements with Aquatec. Wessex then used these cancellations as a basis for attempting to void its contract with Aquatic to service the plants, while at the same time keeping the rights to the desalinization process. We have alleged breach of contract, intentional interference with a business relationship, slander, and a violation of the RICO laws. We have encountered difficulties scheduling depositions in all the locations using Aquatec systems, and have found it almost impossible to schedule depositions of Wessex executives. We feel the court should impose the most severe sanctions against Wessex in order to enforce the plaintiff's discovery rights. If this is done we can be prepared for trial in six to eight months."

"And what is the other side of the coin?" asked Judge AC, looking at the defense table.

"Your Honor, most coins have two sides, but not this one." The lawyer now standing was dressed more casually then the plaintiff's lawyer. Usually it was the other way around. His hair was sandy and he wore what seemed to be a genuine smile. "I am Nathan Rouse of the Philadelphia branch of Burlington and Coving. As you know, this is the second team of lawyers the plaintiff has hired in an attempt to blackmail Wessex into some sort of settlement. We simply want to get this case before a jury and not try the matter in the press. The 'small local firm' is so much nonsense. ANG of the Netherlands is one of the largest conglomerates in the world and owns Aquatec lock stock and barrel."

Judge AC's mind wandered off at this point, wondering if Mr. Rouse of Burlington et.al. had any idea that he was making reference to the basic components of a flintlock rifle.

"We intend to present evidence that will conclusively demonstrate that Aquatec totally breached its contract to service the desalinization plants, and, in fact, Wessex was being sued by the owners of several plants whose systems had failed, due to improper servicing by Aquatec. We have repeatedly demanded the right to inspect the servicing records of Aquatec for all the plants in question and have been totally stonewalled. We, too, would like to bring this case to trial as soon as possible, but we are not optimistic at all, given the reluctance of the plaintiff to lay his cards on the table. How they plan to schedule over three hundred depositions in six months is beyond me."

With that said, the totally self-possessed and confident Philadelphia lawyer sat down behind the stacks of files on counsel table. He was too smooth to smirk; he simply looked at Judge AC with a bright expectant look which let all know he was in charge of the emotions of the courtroom, as well as the legalities of the case. His team of lawyers and assistants smiled too, as if on cue.

Judge AC had a few questions he wished to posit to both sides, but before he could get past the "Gent" in Gentlemen, Mr. Goldman was on his feet with a fake expression of outrage. Judge AC knew the emotion was fake, as lawyers as experienced as Goldman never lost their composure in court. Younger lawyers often did, to their detriment.

"Judge Cason. What you have just heard is a perfect example of the frustrations of this case. An examination of the file will demonstrate that it has been the defendant who has thwarted discovery, not the plaintiff. We are not here to reargue every motion that was heard by Judge Clem, I mean Judge Weaver, but he consistently ruled in our favor on discovery issues. An examination of the files will easily bear this out."

Judge Alva Cason told himself to remain as cool as a cucumber (or mango or something). It was, after all, the plaintiff who had kicked Judge Weaver off the case. This same plaintiff now urged him to review the files to see how Judge Weaver and Aquatec had been right all along.

"Gentlemen," said Judge AC, forgetting the woman lawyer, "I gather that the pleadings are now closed. I believe there were about five separate counts in the plaintiff's complaint and four counts in the defendant's counterclaim. Are any of these counts ready for a summary judgment hearing? That is, have any of the motions for summary judgment been scheduled for hearing?"

Judge AC immediately regretted this comment, as it was not directed at either party. Naturally, both lawyers jumped up at once and began talking at the same time and had to be quieted by Judge AC, who proceeded to ask a few more questions but was met with more accusations and recriminations and few answers. The only positive aspect of the hearing was that Judge AC gained the confidence that he needed to take charge of the situation and bring the case to a head. These big shots were good, but the huffing and puffing was the same stuff he was accustomed to. He thanked all present and retired to his office to draw up an order outlining a timetable for completing discovery and for a trial date in September of the following year.

XI

At the end of the Vero Beach trip when Vicky Carter had been dropped off in Micanopy by her new lover, she walked next door to thank Jim Bob (James Robert) O'Steen for feeding her livestock while she was gone, then headed straight for her big round tub, which she filled to the brim with an extra-warm spicy bubble bath. Although she had tried to persuade AC to stay over, she was really glad to have some time on her own to contemplate life. A lot of stuff had happened over a short period she thought, as she soaked in the luxury of her bath. She had not had a real boyfriend since she broke up with the vegetarian veterinarian she had lived with for five years. "Dr. VV and V," she had termed them. They had shared many interests, done some traveling, and Vicky proved to be a big help with the animals at the clinic when the technician was away. She had taken classes and had become duly qualified as a vet tech and shyly suggested that maybe she could make a career change and take the place of the current tech and live happily ever after with Dr. VV. As things turned out it was Vicky that was replaced, and Dr. VV and the tech moved to California to brush up on canine acupuncture.

The gals at work had fixed her up with dates a few times, but the guys were all sick puppies in Vicky's estimation. Carlo had not been a sick puppy by any stretch of the imagination. He had charm and wit and claimed he really liked her. She meant a lot to him, he had said. She had fallen for that line before in West Virginia and even though the accent changed, the lure was the name brand. AC was different. Although polished in the courtroom, he had to be led along in matters of romance. One of her more raunchy friends at work told her that men were easy to lead as a horse, if you knew what to hold them by. Well, he had been easy enough to catch, but she was not sure what to do with him now. Her cuckoo clock struck nine and she was out of the tub and in bed asleep well before the resident family of owls began their nightly hooting contest.

***

Case files in dependency matters contain the most private of information. What could be worse,

Vicky thought as she drove to work the next morning, than to have it known to the public that your own parent sexually abused you as a child? Those damn priests got away with it for years because everyone was too embarrassed to talk. Well, that was the thing about Freud wasn't it? Those nice Viennese gentlemen couldn't have been having sex with their own daughters, as the disturbed daughters claimed; the girls must have made it all up and had to be made to understand it was all in their minds. Or something like that. But what if the allegations were not true? The accusation was a conviction in the mind of the public. There was all this new stuff about memory being revived by hypnosis. It's a good thing the files are sealed. I wonder what my file would show if I were accused of plotting to accept a bribe to change the outcome in a dependency matter? I wonder if that would be sealed like a dependency file? I doubt it. That son-of-a-bitch Carlo, she thought as she began to tear up. Well, her motives might have been pure and that might sell to Saint Peter, but it would not sell to the public or DCF. When was that deposition anyway? She pulled into the parking lot at the Department of Children and Families well ahead of the rest of the workers.

All of her newly transferred files had to be reviewed, but the first one she opened was Jordan, Justine. The case worker was Sue Cudjo, perhaps the most inept of anyone on the staff, and African-American to boot. Sue's race was no problem for Vicky; her best friend at DCF, Rosa Banks, was black, but it was a potential problem in dealing with folks like the Jordans. *Maybe, maybe not,* thought Vicky as she read the file. It started off as a typical run-of-the-mill case. Rough bar. Drinking. Flirting. Lady says "no." "Ain't nobody gonna say no to me." Sir Galahad to the rescue. Spill over into the street. Sir Galahad not up to the task. Lady gets collarbone broken in struggle to intervene and faints or passes out and is taken to the hospital. Big problem. Jordan, Justine, age eighteen months, was in the back seat of mom's car, happily asleep, and not discovered for an hour or so.

Vicky skimmed over the parts of the file about the case being transferred from Putnam County to Alachua. She was particularly interested in two facets: the mother's history with DCF, and what AC had told her about the events in Levy County and the circumstances of his removal from the case. The lack of contact with the putative father of the child was also unusual. Normally, child support is sought even if the missing parent can not provide an alternative home. Was Ricky Jordan possibly the father as suggested in the domestic violence petition? There was nothing at all in the file about Mary Beth's parents having domestic violence problems. The child had been initially placed in foster care and a home study of the Jordan residence initiated, but no report was ever rendered. Some thirty-year-old criminal charge against Ricky Jordan had prevented the child from being placed with the Jordans to begin with, but under normal circumstances the child could have been placed with stable grandparents, even with the mother living in the home. Separation of a baby from its mother should be avoided if at all possible, especially when the case is one of neglect rather than abuse. Sometimes a single mother simply does not have the means of support to properly care for a child.

Then Vicky was transfixed by a letter bearing the letterhead of the district legal counsel. "Attention. Copies of all proceedings in this matter are to be made and forwarded to the Office of the District Legal Counsel immediately upon filing." There was some other bureauspeak in the letter but nothing worthy of attention. Vicky made a note of the date of the letter and when it had been clocked into the file. The mother's history was more disturbing than Vicky had anticipated. There had been three prior referrals to the Department, but only one had resulted in an initiation of a dependency proceeding. All three cases had involved some degree of disagreement among the workers handling the matter. Although the incidents leading to the referrals were minor, the attitude of unconcern by the mother was of great concern to the volunteer guardian ad litem. This volunteer had issued an inital report, but had resigned from the program due to her husband's new job in Texas, and had yet to be replaced.

Vicky thought about her pal, Rosa Banks. Vicky respected Rosa's judgement and found it hard to believe Rosa could have even considered covering up for Sue Cudjo, but she knew Sue was on probation for mishandling another case and another strike could mean Sue would lose her job. As a single mother with three children, she could turn from worker to client in a week. Sue was certainly not going to buck the higher-ups in the department. Vicky circled her calendar for the next court appearance in the case to make certain she personally appeared. Vicky's calendar had already been circled for a date later in the week. It read "depo with SA at ten," and she noticed it was for Wednesday.

Time flies when you are having fun, thought Judge AC. It also flies when you are taking a test and do not know the answers. He had not seen Vicky on Monday as his morning with the Wessex boys had been trying, and he still had to drive to Levy County for the afternoon. His assignment there was overloaded and he looked forward to his transfer to the civil division. As he drove home, he mulled over the weekend's events in Vero Beach which had certainly added to the tantalizing tidbits of information he had learned over the past few weeks. He had a lot of questions, but he also had a fulltime job and certainly had no aides to turn to and direct to investigate his suspicions. He made it a point to check out the Alachua County Public Library, which was next door to the courthouse and kept newspapers from all over the state. Over his lunch break on Tuesday he walked over and looked at the few past issues of the *Vero Beach Press Journal*. The paper from the past Saturday was not yet in the pile, but he did find the web address for the paper so he could check out the paper over the internet. He logged on back at his office, but found no new information about the body found in Carlo's condo. Well, he thought, some stories don't make the web pages. Maybe it was Carlo's mother after all. Old folks must die in condos by the dozens all over Florida. He called Vicky, got her voice mail, and left a message saying he would be responsible for dinner.

AC had recently been awarded a key to Vicky's farm house. He let himself in and started up a pot of pole beans and decided to pan fry the pork chops in olive oil with capers and his special Greek seasoning. There was some leftover rice which he threw out and started a fresh pot. Vicky did not maintain much of a liquor cabinet but he found some sherry, stretched out on the couch and turned on the local news. There, in full color, with his own courthouse serving as a backdrop, was the same University of Florida coed (student journalist) he had seen earlier, explaining that Mr. Marc Goldman had just called a press conference concerning the Aquatec case, "which would be coming to trial as soon as the local judiciary realized how important Aquatech was to the local economy." The scene cut to Marc Goldman himself, in shirtsleeves with a loosened tie, speaking of "giant bloodsucking corporations operating right here in Gainesville." *Right here in River City*, thought AC. This self-serving behavior was unheard of when AC began his legal career, or so he remembered in his purist's mind. Actually it was nothing new, but it was magnified by television. AC had forgotten reading of inflammatory accounts of trials such as the

Atlanta stories of the murder of little Mary Phagan and the conviction of Leo Frank, who was lynched in the press, and later, by a real mob. AC watched in disbelief as Goldman, pounding on his rented podium, told the crowd of three television crewmen:

"All we want is a jury. We feel sure our judge has no favors to return to Wessex, the giant corporation that unjustly and without warning terminated Aquatec's contract. Justice will prevail."

Well, thought a totally incensed Judge AC, Mr. Goldman will learn a lot about justice tomorrow morning. Does he not realize how he would feel if Wessex came on the air and ranted about greedy trial lawyers with frivolous lawsuits driving doctors and small businesses into bankruptcy? And "activist" judges bending over backward to support class action lawsuits against the very backbone of American industry. He had poured another large glass of sherry when Vicky bubbled in and distracted him by jumping up and throwing her legs about his waist.

"OK, enough, have you no respect for the elderly? Come and sit and tell me what you learned. Supper's all done except for the eating, and wine and cheese are on the way."

Vicky sat and sipped a bit of wine and thought about her findings in the Jordan case. She knew AC was primarily interested in the involvement of Judge Asner and the district legal counsel, while her primary interest was the welfare of the child. She thought it a bit strange that her sweet lover judge was not as concerned with the child as he was with two jerks in the system. At times he seemed so soft-hearted, but she knew his job required a hard side if he was going to sentence people to prison and even death.

"AC, my love, I found out that you may be right. This Jordan case may be a lot more involved than a simple redneck fight. I know you want to find out about Judge Jackass and this head decaf lawyer, but I need to find out a lot more to protect this baby. Unfortunately, I have a very weak caseworker, and even worse, the lawyer assigned to the mother is the biggest flake in the circuit. She's the most sincere person you could imagine, but she's like a mercy killer. Her heart may be in the right place, but her head is in space. Do you know her? Cindy Irving?"

Vicky then explained her suspicions and reservations concerning the true paternal sire of the child, and where it could end up being placed. Long-term relative placement could, in some cases, be a good alternative to termination of parental rights and adoption by strangers. The raising of a child by relatives was commonplace in the olden days. Parents became unable to care for their children for many reasons. Sickness, ill fortune, and the vagaries of life itself drove families apart. The children were given over to relatives and when, and if, the estranged parent recovered, the family could be reunited. There was no need to place a child out for adoption if a relative could cope with the situation on a long-term basis. For many years this was against DCF policy because it was felt the children needed permanency. As a result, parents contested giving their children up to strangers with no hope of reunification. The resulting trials were costly, lengthy, and emotional, and put a strain on the whole system. Long-term relative placement was finally seen as a workable solution, but it required not only that the relative have the means to care for the child, but also that the child would be protected from a potentially dangerous parent.

"Yeah," said AC, "I know Cindy Irving all too well. Vicky, I'm serious. I don't want to go into all the details, most of it is hearsay anyway, but this girl's been on the edge of a cliff for years. So far, her sincerity has been all that has saved her, but she's a true fanatic. You know, it's one thing to be a fruitcake on your own, but it's another for the State to provide you a fruitcake for a lawyer when the State wants to take your baby away on a permanent basis. Cindy is capable of anything. Buying the mom a ticket to Mexico; tricking her into signing termination papers. You name it. This is really a God-awful mess with Cindy and Asner and whatever is going on behind the scenes. It's really improper for me to even be involved in any way, but you need to watch this one."

This conversation had diverted Judge AC's attention away from the evening news about the Wessex case, or the Aquatec case as he now thought of it. Dinner was a culinary, if not dietary success. Vicky cleaned up while AC surfed the TV for something of interest. AC refused to watch anything with a laugh track, which eliminated most of the big networks. There was a "Christmas Special" reality show involving contestants competing to eat a bowl of reindeer testicles in the shortest time possible without vomiting. AC made a note to boycott the sponsors until he saw one was the US Postal Service. He soon gave up, clicked off the TV, and shared with Vicky his problems with the Wessex case.

"You see, the problem will be in selecting an impartial jury. With all the publicity going on, we could spend weeks just finding a panel that has not formed an opinion about the case. The lawyers consider this to be the only case in court and that I should make a career out of trying it. Well, if they want to try to prejudice the jury panel, we can just postpone the trial until things cool down. Maybe for a year. The only thing is; I don't want to postpone the trial. Oh well, they don't know that."

Vicky was listening with only one ear. Kids were more important than money. Justine Jordan might not have been worth the fifty million dollars sought by Aquatec, but she was to Vicky Carter. They went to bed and, as AC struggled through the newest Tom Wolfe novel, she contemplated the past few weeks and thought what an impact AC had made on her life. She finally had someone she could lean on. Not just anyone, but a person she could trust for the first time. Maybe he was a bit naive in some ways; he was solid where it counted. She snuggled her head against his chest and closed her eyes. This guy was not going to slip away.

XII

"Ms Carter. I'm Susan Spikes. We've not officially met, but I know you from court, and can say I wish all DCF workers were like you."

Vicky had gone to the office of the state attorney, which was located almost directly across University Avenue from Wise's Drugs, as directed in her subpoena. She had arrived on time, and had not been kept waiting a minute. She was ushered into a bleak room with a small window overlooking the state attorney's parking lot. There were no distracting pictures on the wall, only a small table with two straight backed chairs. The unsmiling court reporter had her own secretarial chair and steno machine. Susan Spikes appeared to be about Vicky's age, but was very short, perhaps less than five feet, and when she looked up to size up her deponent she did not look intimidating. This helped Vicky relax, but she remembered where she was.

AC had given Vicky some basic ground rules about depositions. Do not volunteer information. Do not try to explain things. Never argue. Always tell the truth and so forth. Susan Spikes' initial statement gave Vicky a pause, but she simply said "Thank you," and held her breath.

"Ms Carter, why don't you sit over here by the window? I'm sure you know why I need to take your statement."

Vicky was not sure at all, but followed AC's advice and said nothing. After all, no question had been asked.

"Well, as you probably know, we're prosecuting both the mother and boyfriend in the McKnight case. The shaken baby case. I'm sure you remember. We have to cover all bases. I've read the DCF files and can say that, had your initial recommendations been followed, we wouldn't be here today. Anyway, that's my opinion."

Vicky did not breathe a sigh of relief. She remained sphinx-like as directed. There could still be a trick.

"I need to ask you some questions, and if you don't understand the question you can ask me to clarify it. The reporter needs to swear you in to tell the truth."

This was done and Vicky began to relax.

"Your recommendation in the case was that DCF proceed to a termination proceeding after the first incident. Why was that?"

"I believe my report speaks for itself."

"Ms Carter, I promise you I'm not trying to trip you up. We're the good guys. We're prosecuting the people who killed this child. Can you tell me anything that would have led you to want to permanently remove this child from its mother? Juries like motives. Insurance, other lovers, revenge."

The court reporter interrupted at this point to add paper to her tray.

"What I need to know is this: What was it that made you think the child would still be in danger after the mother completed all her assignments?" Vicky remained silent, but her brain scrambled for answers.

"What kind of person could deliberately shake a year-old kid to death? That's what the jury will want to know."

Now Vicky audibly sighed.

"Ms Spikes, I've seen a lot in my job, and I understand what you are saying about juries. One time I had a paternal rape case where the most conservative member of the jury refused to convict. His rationale was that no father could do that to his own daughter. It wasn't that he thought the daughter was lying, just delusional. After two mistrials the sorry s.o.b was convicted."

Vicky looked the prosecutor directly in the eye. "What you're asking for is something that won't stand up in court. At least not from me. Maybe from a shrink or somebody, but not from a lowly social worker. I met the mom in the McKnight case and simply didn't believe her. Something about her attitude. I don't know. Sure, she jumped through all the DCF hoops and promised not to see the creep she'd been living with, but it was all a bunch of rehearsed crap. And let me tell you, this guy was as bad as they come. Self-centered, domineering, brutal, alcoholic. You name it." Susan Spikes started to interrupt, but thought better of it and Vicky continued. "So how would my testimony play before a jury? I can hear the cross-examination now. 'You had this *feeling* Ms Carter? Isn't it true that Ms McKnight successfully completed parenting classes? Did she not pass all the home inspections? Was she not holding down a responsible job? Do you have any knowledge of the facts of the night in question?' No, I doubt that I would be much help."

As an experienced assistant state attorney, Ms Spikes now saw she was dealing with an equal. She asked a few more questions to make sure Vicky could hold up to defense tactics and called it quits. She doubted she would call Vicky as a witness and suspected the defense attorney would not either, once he met her.

As Vicky walked away from the Prosecutor's office she wanted to call AC and tell him the good news, that the deposition had not been about Carlo and baby buying at all, but she realized that Jordan was still an ongoing case, and that it could lead anywhere. One arrow had been deflected, but what of the others? Well, anyway, Susan Spikes had boosted her ego. *What I recommended about termination of parental rights in McKnight had been with the purest of motives and I was right.* Then, as she waited for the light to change at University and Main, she remembered the pure motives of poor Cindy Irving, Mary Beth Jordan's lawyer.

***

Judge AC rose early Monday morning and, as he ate his breakfast cereal, dictated his Rule to Show Cause Order in the Wessex case. He dropped the dictation tape off at the courthouse and left Shirley a note to set a hearing three days later and to not check and see if the lawyers were "available." The general tone of the order had been thought out about three, AM, during the sleepless portion of AC's night, but he was pleased with the final result. He then drove over to Bronson to start his week's routine.

On Thursday, the morning of the hearing, Judge AC assumed his most stern demeanor. The parties had been given notice to appear at nine, AM, and the courtroom had been full well ahead of that time. The younger lawyers involved in the case were in the stairwell talking in shrill voices over cellular phones. Senior lawyers were whispering instructions to legal assistants. Charts with time schedules, outlined in three colors, were being placed on tripods. AC had requested Big Ben Stoker to open court in a formal manner. He meant business. Based on what these lawyers were paid, he figured this hearing would cost several thousand dollars. A drop in the bucket for a case in which each side had already spent millions in costs and fees.

"Good morning, ladies and gentlemen. No doubt you have read the court's rule to show cause order, and I hope you can understand my concern over the recent events that led to this order. First, I want to point out a few obvious facts about this case from the perspective of the court. I view the court's job as serving the public. You will not hear me refer to this as 'my courtroom,' for it is not. It belongs to the people. Thousands of issues are litigated each year in this building and all are very important to the people of this circuit. I realize that your case involves large sums of money, as well as lawyers and witnesses from all over the country, and I will do all within my power to bring it to a just conclusion. I will not, however, tolerate activity that will disrupt the other functions of this court. This trial is scheduled to last three months. During that time this courtroom will be exclusively devoted to your case. We will need to be able to select a jury which can devote three months to hear the case. Selecting that panel will be an involved task. We plan to impanel a special venire and will try to screen out potential jurors with preexisting conflicts. All of this is being done to facilitate your trial."

"Now, to the point of this hearing. I happened to see the so-called press conference conducted by the plaintiff's counsel on the steps of the courthouse. I also have been provided with a videotape of this presentation. Now, I believe in free speech. I have no problem with politicians and defense lawyers railing against greedy trial lawyers, and plaintiff's lawyers pointing out the evils of insurance companies and giant corporations, but when these statements come on the steps of this courthouse, on the eve of a trial, we do have a problem. Many statements I heard on TV would not be admissible in evidence in this case but have now been implanted in the minds of potential jurors. I'm sure you are all aware of the rules of professional conduct promulgated by the Florida Bar concerning extra-judicial statements. My concern here is not ethics, that issue can be dealt with elsewhere, but the practicalities of selecting a jury. Now that I've set a firm date for this trial, I plan to stick to it. I really don't need argument of counsel from either side on the issue of what to do or whether sanctions should or should not be imposed. I am aware of all the recriminations that have already occurred in this case, and I don't need a rehash of them all. I want the plaintiff to be forewarned that further activity of the nature of Friday's press conference will result in a lengthy delay of this trial. Thank you all for attending. Mr. Bailiff, court may be adjourned."

With a stern glance around the courtroom Judge AC walked off stage with a swirl of his black robe. *Curtain*, he thought.

***

As Christmas approached, Judge AC found he had more time on his hands. Any specially set hearing, such as a divorce, could require two lawyers, the husband and wife, and a number of witnesses including accountants, counselors, and other professionals. Many of these busy people had travel plans to Aspen and other exotic vacation spots, and all it took was one missing participant to cause a postponement. AC's son, Park, was going to spend the holidays in Aspen. As a student at the University of Colorado, in Boulder, he had the good fortune to meet a girl whose father "practically owned" Aspen. At least that was what AC heard during an excited telephone call from his son.

"Marty is super neat, dad. I *really* want you to meet her. Maybe we could come down over spring break. Some of the guys want to go to the Keys and we could easily swing by Gainesville for a day or so. The deal in Aspen is great. Marty's dad owns the waste disposal company for the whole county. They have a guest house at their place which sleeps eight with its own kitchen. Marty's uncle has some connection where we can get free lift tickets for a week. I mean, it won't cost a thing. Well, other than beer."

"Hey, it sounds great. Don't you need a chaperone? A Bible-carrying judge maybe?" Park did not need a judge in Aspen and downhill skiing had lost some of its allure for AC in any event. He had yet to tell Park of his romance with Vicky, but he expected it was known. Kids had a better network than the CIA.

ALL RISE

Even though the holiday season was not particularly busy for the courts, there was one category of hearings that multiplied near Christmas. Child visitation. The days when families drove over the river and through the trees to grandmother's house were long gone. Family permutations and dispersals made schedules almost impossible, and family law judges were supposed to work out all the details. Teenaged children made it all the more interesting if they had friends of the opposite sex, in which case they did not want to see relatives at all. Shunned parents blamed the ex-spouse for their child's rejection rather than the teenagers' affinity for a fellow teen. Even the lawyers became disgusted at much of the wrangling, and it takes a lot to disgust a lawyer. Not all the lawyers, however, and it was Judge AC's misfortune to catch the worst of the worst.

"Judge," called Shirley Bloch from her reception area, "Cindy Irving's on the line needing an emergency hearing. I told her we were booked, but she's insistent. I mean really insistent. Like she'll go to the governor unless she gets a hearing."

"Sounds like Christmas BS to me. Did she give the other side notice?"

"Wait, I'll check. No, she claims they won't return her calls."

Small wonder, AC thought.

"Find out who the other lawyer is and give her a fifteen-minute hearing time. Squeeze it in tomorrow. Over lunch if necessary. Or after five. Call the other lawyer and give him the time. Don't worry, everyone will show up."

Screw me, thought Judge AC. This is why I get paid the big bucks? Emergency? Snookums needs to wake up at Mommy's home on Christmas morning. Daddy demands the baby as he doesn't approve of mommy's new boyfriend, who is a hairy-headed hippie and is sure to spend the night with the mom. Irreparable damage will occur if either of the two options are chosen.

Prognostication in judicial matters did not pay as well as with the gaming industry, but it did bring some sense of self satisfaction to Judge AC, as he presided over the emergency hearing scheduled by Cindy Irving. His only error was that the roles were reversed. It was the mommy who did not approve of the daddy's new tattooed, nose-pierced girlfriend. He was able to exercise all his equanimity and achieve a draw that would last until the next holiday, or at least until he was transferred out of the family division.

As the parties were leaving his chambers Cindy Irving whispered something to her client and said, "Judge, can I see you a minute in private? It's nothing to do with this case at all."

This was awkward timing as well as being an awkward request. Judges are not supposed to discuss any matters in private, and certainly do not want to be seen doing so right after a contested hearing. Clem Weaver in the Wessex came to mind. Fortunately the opposing counsel knew Cindy Irving and Judge Cason very well. He knew he had nothing to worry about, plus he had prevailed in the emergency hearing. He gave an almost imperceptible nod to the judge and ushered his confused client out of the chambers.

"Judge, I have an ethical dilemma. I have this case over in dependency in which my client wants to give up the child to her parents, but that's not what's right. I think DCF might approve, but they are also talking termination. The mom doesn't want the kid, but doesn't want adoption either. My problem is that I can't let the child go to the grandparents. I think the granddad is actually the father of the child. Judge, I really don't know what to do. To make matters worse the granddad abuses his wife, or so she claims."

Judge AC stared out of the window for some time. He really hated to deal with Cindy but had to do something. Now he bit his lower lip. "Cindy."

She looked up expectantly at this familiarity. Judge AC was usually reserved and used only last names. Cindy was a plain woman who never wore any makeup. She was the devoted mother of two children and was once married to a lawyer who had clerked for Judge AC. She felt she could trust him completely. On the other hand Judge AC knew he might have to report her to the Florida Bar for misconduct unless she changed her ways.

"I have been disqualified in the case you describe. I think you know that. I can't possibly give you any advice in that case. The Florida Bar has a hotline for ethical questions. You might want to call the Bar, or you might want to call a local senior bar member like Clara Barber. You know her don't you?"

"But Judge, all I want is to do right. I don't want to get you in trouble or anything, but I don't know where to turn. People just don't seem to want to talk to me."

"Then try the hotline. They get paid to talk. And Cindy, remember, some people create their own problems. You shouldn't feel you can personally solve them all."

"But Judge, it's the baby I'm worried about. The baby didn't create any problems."

This statement made AC reflect a bit.

"I know, Cindy, but you represent the mother. The baby has a guardian and a caseworker. The department has good lawyers to protect the interests of the child."

Judge AC got up and walked from his hearing room into Shirley's area leaving Cindy Irving with no one to talk to. She left and Shirley Blotch said, "What a number. How would you like to have her for your lawyer?"

Judge AC made no reply.

XIII

The cuckoo clock in Vicky's living room cheerfully announced the hour as seven, but it was not yet morning on this shortest day of the year. AC was certain God was in his Heaven as he nestled his face against Vicky's nape.

BAM, BAM, BAM. "Hey, git up in there."

"That's Jim Bob. Got to be or the dogs would have raised a ruckus. Stay put. I'll handle it." Vicky said, pulling a terrycloth robe over her previously nude body.

Sure enough, it was Jim Bob wanting to organize a Christmas Eve party. He just *had* to try out his new deep fat fryer he had bought after Thanksgiving. He had been to a party where turkey was served which had been fried whole in deep fat, and thought one of Vicky's geese would be perfect for Christmas. All she had to do was designate the unlucky goose and he would do the rest. His current girlfriend made the best sweet potato casserole south of Tifton and other guests could bring the rest.

"We'll get your boyfriend to buy the booze. That way we'll know it's legal."

"That's fine Jim Bob. You can catch that gander son-of-a-bitch with the bad eye, but watch your back. He has friends."

Vicky tumbled back into bed and rolled on top of AC pinioning his arms down.

"You owe me one," she said as she pecked at his cheeks like a fowl. "Ugh, dragon breath and porcupine cheeks. Mother told me it would be like this, but I never believed her."

AC tried to roll her off, but she was surprisingly strong. She finally succeeded in forcing her chest onto his face and then relaxed.

"What do you want for Christmas? What that you don't already have?" she asked.

Christmas Eve came and the fried goose party was a culinary and social success, except for one of Jim Bob's friends who had been arrested a week earlier for driving under the influence, and who kept saying his goose was already cooked. It may have been his first and only *bon mot,* so everyone laughed with him the first ten or so times he repeated it. AC joined in with the crowd; after all, they were all voters, but he knew he was somewhat of a misfit. He felt he could politic and glad-hand with the best, but he still sensed the crowd looked at him the way they would a priest at a poker game. He did some defensive drinking, though not as heavily as Jim Bob's friend who had to be driven home. Finally, when everyone had gone and the leftover food was all put away, Vicky came up to AC and put her arms around him and said he was the perfect host.

"You put everyone at ease. You made them laugh. I thought you might have had too much Christmas cheer, but you were wonderful. I'm so lucky."

Vicky felt lucky the next morning when they exchanged gifts and she unwrapped the new riding mower seat AC had found for her. Not very sexy, but with it and the new umbrella which had not been wrapped, her hours mowing grass under a hot Florida sun would be vastly improved. AC opened Vicky's gift box and found a mackerel reel. He followed the reel's line to the garage and found the rod.

"I couldn't figure out how to wrap the rod without giving away the surprise. If it's not the right kind they'll take it back or swap it at the Tackle Box."

"It's perfect," said AC, who was touched to tears.

The week between Christmas and New Year's was even slower than the prior week, so AC had chosen this time to schedule two motions in the Wessex case, as he knew the lawyers would settle the matter among themselves rather than travel to Gainesville, and his prognostication proved correct, although they had not bothered to call and cancel the hearing until an hour before it was scheduled to be heard. Later that day he told Vicky about the lesbian divorce case he had resolved, which was the only interesting thing that happened all week.

"I thought they couldn't get married. How can they get a divorce?" she asked.

"Oh, they get married all right. Married with all the trimmings except a form from the courthouse. Double ring ceremony with a preacher, vows and honeymoon. The works. Then they set up house-keeping, buy a lot of furniture, fix up the house, all the usual stuff. Then, like any other married couple, something fails and they come to court wanting a judge to sort out the mess. Who gets the new TV? 'Well it's on my credit card,' says one. 'Yeah, well what about my credit card? We used it for food and the honeymoon. So does she have to pay her half of that?' And of course there are no receipts. So you can see we can call things by differing names: divorce or dissolution, marriage or civil partners, but we still end up having to deal with the mechanics of the situation. Of course, with unofficial civil unions, the parties can simply split and not come to court at all. Once you're legally married you do need to come to court and get a formal divorce, even if there's nothing to divide, otherwise you remain married, which can have all sorts of implications."

A mental image came to Vicky at this point. A suburban street in Charleston, West Virginia, with a cold rain falling and a man on the curb shaking his fist and yelling at her as she drove away. She had not taken the TV or anything else from the house. Just her clothes. Why was he so pissed? Was it the legal implications, whatever they were? She had meant to see a lawyer many times over the years, but could never force herself to bring up the memories of that miserably unhappy period. AC had never asked her about her past. It was as if he knew she would tell him when the time was right. Now did not seem to be that time.

"Well, they were lucky to have you as their judge. I'll bet many sanctimonious bastards would have thrown them out of court."

"Thank you, sweetheart. I would hate to be a sanctimonious bastard during the holidays."

***

Christmas in Vero Beach was not the same as in Micanopy. Or Chicago for that matter. The weather made a big difference. There was a parade of lighted boats, yachts really, cruising in formation down the Indian River and ending up at the "Club" for a seafood dinner. The *Osprey* led the parade as a result of a call from Carlo to the organizer of the festival. This pleased Captain Rita no end. Carlo and his new lady friend and another couple made up the crew. The second boat in line had been equipped by Disney to blare carols and other holiday music. Since no government money was involved, the Christmas carols were not perceived as establishing a religion.

Captain Rita and Reed sat up on the flying bridge, while their guests chatted below.

"I think my gift this Christmas will be my favorite of all my life," gushed Captain Rita. "I just don't know if I can wait until September for the big event."

"Sweetheart, everyone has to wait nine months. You should know that."

"Well, I don't want it to go sour, the way the Gainesville deal did."

"Nothing's certain, but that damned Carlo really knows his way around," Reed confided. "I hope his red tape scissors don't get dull."

"From what I hear about peddling influence in Russia, he must have felt entirely at home," Rita said with a bit of a smirk.

"He has guaranteed everything but the gender. The cost is all paid. I can stay here due to health reasons. You may have to spend some time over there, but so what?"

"I agree, my love. He just has a way with people. Look at the conversation down on the stern. He has the Wessexsons totally charmed. He does seem to ogle Sasha a bit too much. I wonder who dressed her for the evening. How long has she been with Harold?"

"Rita, dear, you know I don't keep up with that stuff. For all I know she could be his niece."

Reed instantly regretted this comment and hurriedly tried to cover it up.

"What I mean is, he never discusses anything with me but business."

ALL RISE

"Well that's business, if you ask me," sulked Rita. "Expensive and hard to write off."

"Rita, I'm the luckiest guy in the world. Let me go check on our crew."

Reed descended the ladder to the main deck and interrupted the conversation between his guests.

"All hands prepare for docking. Seaman Carlo, man the forward hawser. Lubbers stand clear of the aft cleats."

The *Osprey* glided into the slip without a bump or a grind. Captain Rita knew her stuff. The three couples made things fast and headed up the dock to the clubhouse. A casual observer would have had a hard time figuring out the relationship between the parties. Sasha, no last name had ever been given, led the way. Her hair was long and blond and she constantly fussed with it. The cocktail dress was red and white and was, as Rita observed, not yachting wear. She was followed by a woman about her same age. This was Rita Arroyo, Carlo's date for the evening. Her white slacks and navy sweater were appropriate, but there was a visible panty line under her skin-tight slacks. She wore her dark hair very short. Two distinguished looking gentlemen followed the young women but ignored them as Reed and Harold were engrossed in a private conversation. Carlo had stayed behind to help Rita, Captain Rita, double check *Osprey's* dock lines.

Rum and Coca Colas preceded dinner, which proved to be all any hungry sailor could expect after a hard day on the water. Seafood gumbo, crab cakes and coconut fried shrimp. A Jimmy Buffet imitator rendered calypso carols and the crowd was invited to participate in a limbo contest where lowering the bar signified success. Santa rolled in on a skateboard throwing candy kisses to the tune of Hoyt Axton's "Joy to the World." Everyone joined in on the chorus, "Joy to the world. All the boys and girls ___now. Joy to the fishes in the deep blue sea, ___Joy to you and me." A joyous time was had by all.

Back on the *Osprey* the men smoked real Cubans provided by Carlo and talked a little business on the stern deck while the "girls" watched a Christmas special on TV.

"Carlo, *mi amigo*," said Reed, almost exhausting his Spanish vocabulary, "my friend Harold has been spending a lot of time in Gainesville recently. It seems to me you have some connections there, know your way around there to some extent."

Carlo had never been given instructions in handling deposition questions, but his natural instinct told him how to react.

"I graduated from the University and bleed orange and blue once a year at the FSU game. Twice if we play Miami."

"Harold's interests are neither academic nor athletic, but more commercial in nature. Commercial and legal, as it were. His company, or the company he heads to be more precise, has been dragged into a frivolous lawsuit. The plaintiffs are represented by the infamous Marc Goldman, of whom you have probably heard. Miami guy. Harold isn't worried about the merits of the case, but needs some time to build up a more positive image in the community. The plaintiffs are all locals. Their kids are in school there and they're all Rotarians or what have you. This damn Goldman wants to try the case in the court of public opinion and not before an impartial jury. By the way, don't get me started on that or we'll be here all night. Just call my pal, Charles Keating. Anyway, we need to delay the trial for about a year and some jerk of a judge who has just been assigned to the case wants to rush to justice. The more our lawyers push, the more obstinate he becomes. He's crafty, no doubt. He hauled Goldman into court with all sorts of threats about improper conduct but didn't do a damn thing. We've checked out this judge and couldn't find anything to help us. I don't know why it took so long for you to come to mind. This is your specialty. *Comprare?*"

"*Si. Entiendo.*"

"Now wait a sec. I can do Hebrew and even some Russian, but let's keep this English," said Harold of Wessex Industries. "I admit all this small town shit is beyond me, and I don't want this to blow up in my face. If we're going to work a deal, it has to be clean. I mean, we're Fortune Five Hundred, not some sleazy New Jersey waste disposal outfit. Now Carlos, Reed says you got connections. Where I'm from that means one thing. Can I assume that's not the case in Gainesville?"

"Actually, it's Carlo, but that's ok. Yes, you're right. I don't have the kind of connections you speak of, I only persuade, never intimidate. I do know the judge in your case. At least I've met him, and my first impression is that he would not be an easy mark. I know another judge there that would be a gimmie, as they say on the links. It's a shame we don't have him to deal with."

Reed interjected himself as he did not like the tone of the conversation. "Well, gentlemen, what say we go topside and entertain the ladies? We can talk business later. After all, it is Christmas."

This proved to be a fortunate decision as Sasha and Carlo's Rita had not seen eye to eye on any subject of conversation, and Captain Rita had run out of conciliatory alternatives.

Carlo restored the ambiance of the group and all were laughing as the *Osprey* eased into the dock behind *Kissimmee Kiss*. As they disembarked, everyone was saying "good night," "happy holidays," "*feliz navidad*," and promising to call soon. No one said "y'all come back." Carlo felt Reed's hand on his elbow as they walked along the dock toward *Kissimmee Kiss*.

"Give me a call. We don't want to lose this one."

XIV

"All rise! The Eighth Judicial Circuit Court in, and for, Alachua County is now in session. The Honorable Jack Asner presiding." The bailiff paused until his honor was comfortably seated then announced: "You may be seated. There will be no talking in the court-room." He then assumed a military parade rest posture next to the podium. He had been well trained.

"Good morning, ladies and gentlemen. We have a number of dependency matters to deal with this morning. The first case is Ames, Mary. Will everyone interested in that case please approach the bench?"

Court dockets were always arranged alphabetically and everyone was given notice to appear at nine o'clock. It was much worse than a doctor's office, where there is some semblance of fair progression. Pity the poor Zambruckers, who had to sit through the whole morning, and sometimes the whole day, waiting for their case to be called, only to find out the case worker had continued it. Judge Asner moved through the docket at a reasonable pace. This was an improvement over Judge Wigglesworth, who could drag an uncontested divorce out to twenty minutes. He actually scheduled them thirty minutes apart. About ten-thirty the J's were reached.

"Jordan, Justine. Will everyone interested in this case please approach the bench?"

He addressed the approaching crowd in general. "Does this case involve any matters that will require the courtroom to be cleared?"

Everyone looked at each other and finally a rather plain looking woman carrying a heavy satchel spoke up. "Your honor, I anticipate some matters to arise that should be heard in private and would request the courtroom to be cleared."

"Yes, and who might you be?"

"My name is Cindy Irving, attorney for the mother."

"Well, Ms Irving, I hope you're not wasting the court's time. Mr. Bailiff, please clear the courtroom."

This act was performed and fully two minutes of the court's time was potentially wasted. The crowd gathered around the bench. Judge Asner now knew Cindy Irving, but other than the regulars, that was it. About then it dawned on him that this was the Jordan case. The one the district legal counsel had spoken to him about. The one he had discussed with Dan Hawthorne. Well, well, well.

"Well, let me get everyone straight. I know Ms Irving, but for the record could you all please identify yourselves starting from the right."

Two people began to speak at once as Judge Asner failed to say whether he meant his right or their right.

"Wait. One at a time. The reporter has to get all this down. OK, from this side, who do we have?"

"Judge, I'm Ricky Jordan and I have a few things to say. First of all I..."

"Mr. Jordan please. We are now calling roll. Your turn to talk will come later."

"Judge, I'm Amy Jordan. Rick's wife and Mary Beth's mom."

"Your honor, I'm Mary Blakewood, DCF attorney, standing in for Margie McGuire, who's on maternity leave."

"Sue Cudjo. DCF."

"Your honor, I'm Vicky Carter, the supervising caseworker for DCF in the case."

"Judge Asner, I'm Jane Jennings. Guardian's office. Our attorney is in another courtroom on a delinquency matter. The guardian we had assigned moved out of state, and we've not been able to get a replacement with the holidays and all. I'm sure we can get someone soon given the status of this case."

Cindy Irving spoke up. "Your, honor, my client, Mary Beth Jordan, was given notice of this hearing, but I don't think she'll appear. I'll reserve my comments until after I hear what DCF has to say."

"The court has read the file" (which was true in this case) "and would like to hear an up-date from the Department. Well, from everyone for that matter."

Mary Blakewood stated that the caseworker could report for the Department. Vicky Carter bit her lip as Sue Cudjo spoke up.

"Your honor, the department held a staffing in this case and is prepared to file a petition for termination of parental rights due to the lack of progress made by the mother in completing her assigned tasks."

Vicky noted that still no mention had been made of the father. The birth certificate did not list a dad. Vicky had checked on this. Sue Cudjo was also silent on the reasons for the mother's failure to complete her rehabilitation. *Shit*, thought Vicky. *Mary Beth had never been habilitated in the first place.* She held her tongue. The mom's lawyer was there to defend her client.

"Judge Asner, the guardian's office has a lot of questions about this case and certainly would like to have an opportunity to offer input once we have a guardian assigned."

"Well, Mrs. Jennings, this case has been in the system quite a while now, and, after all, it is the Department's role, as well as the guardian's, to look after the welfare of the child. And naturally, the family as a whole as well. I certainly want to hear from Ms Irving, but Ms Cudjo, why is the Department so insistent in terminating parental rights in this case?

ALL RISE

I know how things are these days, but I know there were many times when my momma left me in the car for a few minutes. Ms Jordan had no reason to suspect she would be attacked as she was in this case. And besides, living where she does out in, well, wherever, it is not easy to make it in to Gainesville to attend all these parenting classes that will teach her not to leave a baby in the car unattended. I think she now knows that already, wouldn't you think?"

Vicky looked over at Sue Cudjo who was staring at a point on the bench about two feet below Judge Asner. Vicky started to speak up, but she really knew very little about the case except what she had learned from the file. What she had learned from AC was strictly hearsay. Finally Sue Cudjo spoke up.

"Judge, your honor, I'm just reporting the result of the DCF staffing."

"Well, that's pretty obvious. What I can't see is why the kid can't live with the grandparents a year or so and give the mom a chance to grow up a bit. You know, get a job and a decent place to stay. What's she got, a high school education and no husband? This kind of stuff happens all the time. Why not let her and the baby live with her folks until she gets her feet on the ground?"

Ricky Jordan actually turned around with a grin and raised eyebrows and looked for an audience in the courtroom as if to ask for applause for the judge, but it had been cleared.

"Your honor," said Cindy Irving, giving her usual wild-eyed and distraught look, "We also have to look to the best interests of the child. I have some information to present to the court that might call that issue into question."

"Oh, you do? Well," said Judge Jack the Ass, "Since when did you start representing the child? You know, we now have lawyers for everybody but the judge. The DCF, the mom, the dad, the guardian ad litem, and now I suppose the kids need a lawyer paid for by the state. It's like we've got a lawyers' relief society passing the laws. Ms Irving, I don't mean to sound harsh, but your job is to represent the mom. We have, or will have, a guardian for the child who can speak up if the child's interests differ from the mom's, and of course DCF is supposed to consider the whole situation. Now, I don't know where the mom is, but if she doesn't care enough to show up in court, I don't know why the state should pay for a lawyer to represent her. Now, if she was in the hospital or something it would be different. I'm gonna continue this hearing for three weeks. At that time, Ms Irving, you can tell your client to be here, or I'll have the sheriff drag her in. I also expect the State to have a better and more complete explanation for termination than 'there was a staffing.' Before I calendar a termination trial, I need to have a clear idea of the contested issues and facts. Next case!"

There was nothing said as the group left the courtroom, but body postures could have told an observant spectator a great deal. Cindy was almost in tears. Jane Jenning's usually placid considerate face looked as agitated as a typical basketball coach.

Ricky Jordan strutted while Amy skulked like an Iraqi POW. Vicky looked miffed but was composed enough to notice for the first time that the district legal counsel had been lurking in a corner of the courtroom during the entire proceeding.

Back in the DCF office Vicky summoned Sue Cudjo and asked in a voice as gentle as she could muster; "Sue, what in the world is going on in the Jordan case? According to the file we haven't even given notice to the father who may be in the service somewhere. Cindy Irving is making vague noises about some serious matters and her client doesn't even show up for court. Well, you heard the Judge. Why can't the kid stay with the grandparents? I mean, I know the department's official policy about permanency, but this doesn't look like a termination case from what's in the file. Does Marge Mcguire think she can win a termination trial even against that idiot, Cindy Irving?"

"Well, Vicky, I admit it's a complicated mess, but I don't really know what to do. I don't even know where to start to explain things."

"Why don't you start with the father? Where is he? One note said he is in the Marines in North Carolina."

Sue Cudjo moved her head in a way that was not really a nod or a shake. "Well, Mary Beth says that ain't the case. That that was just something her dad made up because she don't really know who the dad is. She says she slept with a couple of guys after partying but doesn't know their names or where to find them. She claims she hardly knows this Marine guy."

"It sounds as if she knew the others even less. Well, we can always publish a notice in the paper. What about the mom? Why won't she jump through the hoops and take a few parenting classes and so forth?"

"You need to meet Mary Beth, Vicky. It's like she don't care at all. She refuses to go to any program we set up. She says just let her folks have the kid."

"What's wrong with that?" asked Vicky, already suspecting the answer.

"Ricky's got a record. Some kind of crime."

"Sue, you know we need more than that. What kind of crime? How long ago?"

"Then there was some recent incident. Ricky's wife called the cops, but was gone when they got there. She called back and said it was all a misunderstanding. They made her come in for an exam to see she wasn't hurt or nothing and that was about it."

Vicky thought for a minute in silence, hoping Sue would blurt out something. She remembered that AC had told her about some sort of domestic violence hearing over in Levy County, but she did not remember the details and did not want to push Sue too hard. At least not yet. Violence between the grandparents would certainly be a big factor in placing a child with them.

"Vicky, you know Mr. Grimmage, the new legal counsel at DFC?"

"I've never really met him. I know who he is. He was in court today."

"Well, for some reason he is onto this case. He said to me some stuff about not wanting to waste time on weak cases. Like we got enough bad cases that we can't get to trial, so we shouldn't fool with weak ones."

"Look, Sue, you report to me and I report to Mary Barnes and she reports to Tallahassee. Not Grimmage."

"I know that, Vicky. It's just that I'm low man on the totem pole and I got kids to look after. I really don't know what to do. And another thing: Cindy Irving, and I know you don't approve of her, well, she says she's going to drop a bombshell if the kid goes to the grands. Go to the governor and so on. She says she's got proof that Ricky Jordan is the real father of the baby."

***

Vicky wanted desperately to talk over the events of the day with AC. She knew that he had been removed from the case on phony grounds, but, as he said, he was not on the case and shouldn't discuss it. She knew he would like to get something on Judge Asner, but nothing really improper had happened in court. Maybe Asner had acted like a jerk, so what's new? She did think she could get by asking one thing if she used a hypothetical example.

"AC, I need some free legal advice. Let me give you a hypothetical."

AC thought, *here it comes.* This was a common way for legal questions to be put to a judge. It was usually easy to figure out that the question was not hypothetical at all, but a true-life situation needing a lawyer's advice. What the hell, thought AC as he poked up the fire he had built in Vicky's pot-bellied stove, I'll play along. After all, it's Vicky and I can always back out. "Shoot."

"OK. There's this lawyer who has a client who wants her lawyer to do something and the lawyer thinks it's not right. Does the lawyer have to do it anyway?"

So simple thought AC. So simple that huge treatises had been written on the subject. Ask a lawyer a simple question and he gives you a book for an answer and you are still no better off. How often had he heard that one? Even when he asked direct questions of lawyers in court it was the same. "Well, let me ask, is it a legal thing this client wants to do? I mean, is it not against the law?"

"Legal? Yeah, I guess so. It's not a crime exactly, but it would be immoral. That's the thing, AC. You lawyers always bring in extra stuff like that."

"Well, for example, if a client wants to take the stand and lie, that would be a crime and the lawyer could not ethically participate. The lawyer would have to withdraw, but in criminal cases that poses a problem because accused persons are entitled to a lawyer."

"OK," said Vicky. "That makes sense. But what about if the lawyer then tells on the client? Tells other people what the client's up to."

"That's a separate can of worms, but related in a way. Clients are entitled to tell lawyers things in confidence. Those communications are privileged from disclosure. There could be exceptions. Like, if the client says I'm going out and shoot my wife."

"AC, you've been a great help. Maybe you could give me a dozen more exceptions to the rule."

"There's always the "smart-ass" exception. They get no protection at all," said AC heading for the bathroom in an attempt to end the conversation.

"Wait. One more second. Suppose the lawyer learns something from somewhere else. Not from the client I mean. Can he then tell about it?"

AC had to think about that one. "The questions always get harder toward the end. I would say the lawyer can't continue to represent the client and disclose harmful material. If the lawyer withdraws, I can see that in some cases it might be OK to disclose some things, but never something the lawyer learned from the client. Let's go to bed and I'll give you enough examples to put you to sleep. Guaranteed."

XV

Judge Ira Moss did not enjoy being chief judge of the Eighth Judicial Circuit. His undergraduate degree had been in history, and at times he felt like a history professor who had been thrust into college administration, university provost or something. There was a court administrator to handle most of the details, but he had to make the final decisions on such matters as judicial assignments and case loads. There were ten county judges in the six counties of the circuit and nine circuit judges. Dealing with them was much like conducting an opera with nineteen divas. His position was not even permanent. Elections among the judges were held every other year and tradition had it that two terms were about right. The former chief could then be bossed about like any other judge. Citizens would often complain to the chief judge about anything to do with the system. Many of these complaints, such as lack of juror parking, could be shuffled off to various administrative assistants, but there were complaints directed at judges that he had to deal with. Adverse judicial rulings brought complaints, but most people understood that legal appeals went to higher courts, not to the chief judge. Aggrieved parties could be referred to the Judicial Qualifications Commission if the matter involved misconduct as opposed to a judicial decision. This body had the power to conduct inquiries and recommend a judge's removal from office. The Supreme Court of Florida had the final decision. Judge Moss did not like to receive complaints about his fellow judges, but there were times when the complaint was more administrative in nature rather than one involving a judge's decision or misconduct.

"He insists on speaking to you, judge. Says it's about the guardian program. The administrator's office referred him up here so apparently they couldn't handle him. His name is Dan Hawthorne."

"OK, put him on," said an already irate Ira. He started to be polite, but thought better of it. Nobody was going to push his guardians around.

"Judge Moss."

"Judge Moss, this is Dan Hawthorne. You've got some problems over there that you ought to know about."

This was met by silence on the part of Judge Moss.

"Pardon me, did you hear me, judge?"

"Yes, I can hear you fine. You haven't said anything yet," said Ira coolly but calmly.

"Well, it's about those guardians over there. They can't seem to get their act together on a case I have an interest in. I've spoken several times with Judge Asner, who's a good friend of mine, and he says he can't do anything until they get a guardian. He says it's just a formality, that he already knows what he is going to do and everything; he just can't seem to get anything out of the guardian's office. I mean, we got H and RS and everything; why do we need a guardian to boot?"

Judge Moss was about to give the usual apologetic reply about guardians being volunteers, and how they helped children who might have a conflict with DCF findings, and how helpful they were to the courts, and so forth until it dawned on him what this jerk had said about talking to Asner.

"Mr. Hawthorne, I appreciate your call. I'll check out the matter thoroughly. I assume it's a dependency matter. What is the name of the case?"

"It's Jordan, Ricky Jordan. Well, I guess it's in the name of the kid, Justine. Justine's mom is Mary Beth."

"And, Mr. Hawthorne, how are you involved in the case and how can you be reached?"

"I'm not involved in the case at all. My sister's married to Ricky. I live just outside Lake Butler on One-Twenty-One. Everybody knows where I live."

Judge Moss explained he needed a telephone number, thanked Mr. Hawthorne for his time and hung up. He sat at his desk a long time thinking about what he should do. This was not the sort of thing he could delegate to his administrator. Well, maybe the part about the lack of a guardian, but not the part about the ex-parte communications by Judge Asner. This was serious business. Removal from office business.

"Charlotte, call Judge Fox and see if he's available to come up for a few minutes. I could go down there, but Brunhilda might have the drawbridge up."

Judge Fox had served two terms on the JQC and would know a lot more than Ira about its internal workings. Ira knew that it was composed of several judges, some lawyers and a few lay people. It had prosecutors just like the Inquisition and just as vicious from the perspective of the judges who were charged. Ira felt the information he had just heard was not enough to report Judge Asner to the JQC, but he also knew it was very likely true. As it turned out Judge Fox was available and on his way up to see his chief before Brunhilda finished complaining to Charlotte about surly clerks.

"What's up, sport? It had better be important. I was just about to place a buy order with my broker for some Enron stock."

"Hey, Dan. Sit down. It could be serious and I need to pick your brain about JQC proceedings."

"Let me guess. Judge Asner, right?"

"Yes, Dan. Your perception amazes me."

Judge Moss then related his conversation with Dan Hawthorne which just took a minute. "The reason I called you, Dan, is that you know all about the workings of the JQC. I just don't see how I can report such sketchy information. There should be some kind of investigation it seems to me. I'm not a detective and once someone starts snooping around everyone will clam up."

"Well Ira, we already have a snoop. AC asked me about this situation a couple of weeks ago, but we really need to keep him out of it since he has recused from the case. And, of course, he is seeing that little vixen of a case worker at DFC. I don't know if she has anything to do with the case or not. I do agree that we should have more before going to the JQC."

"Dan, you've completely lost me. Do you think AC is somehow in cahoots with DCF?"

"Absolutely not. But it could look that way if he got directly involved."

Dapper Dan Fox then told Ira of his visit from AC and all about Asner's weekend visit to AC's office and the motion to disqualify AC.

"Ira, do you know any of these people? Ricky Jordan has been in the system a long time. He was the guy Ellen had the bailiffs tail every time he came to the courthouse, and Ellen Kravitz is not a wimpy judge. Jordan's not really a hoodlum, but overly insistent and persistent. His sister married Dan Hawthorne over in Lake Butler. You must know Hawthorne. Has the limerock trucks and timber. Good Tallahassee connections so I'm told."

"OK, OK. I didn't pay much attention to his name, but now I know who he is. Could he have something to do with this new district legal counsel for DCF? I just don't know. I probably should have tried to find out more. Dan, why don't you do this? Watch the case and see what happens. I know you remember the traffic ticket situation with Asner. If we go to the JQC any future collegiality is out the window. This one has to stick."

"Aye aye, chief. After all I am the administrative judge of the family law division. It does bother me that this is a dependency case and a child could be put at risk. It might be better to reassign the case and forget about Asner."

Chief Judge Ira Moss thought for awhile.

"Yeah, that's true, but if we have a snake in our midst we need to nail him, or who knows what could happen in the future? Keep me posted."

***

"Civil" according to Judge AC's dictionary refers to the interrelations of citizens with one another or with the state. It can also mean polite or not rude. Courteous. The civil division of circuit court was more concerned with the first definition than the latter. The Wessex case was totally excluded from the second definition. Fortunately for Judge AC, one of his responsibilities in the civil division in the Eighth Judicial Circuit was to oversee probate matters where politeness prevailed. Almost all of the work in probate court consisted of filling out forms. When a person died the estate had to be probated, which meant that creditors had to be properly notified and paid, and that heirs had to be properly notified and given their proper distributions from the estate. In Hollywood where estates such as those of Howard Hughes and Marlon Brando required probate, it could become a circus, but in Gainesville it was usually quite simple and almost all of the work was done by the clerk's office and a staff attorney and her assistant who presented the properly filled out forms to the judge for signature. To ensure that matters were progressing on a timely basis Judge AC required attorneys to attend case management conferences on a regular basis and explain why the case had not been closed. This effective procedure was resented by a few attorneys. The clients of these procrastinating attorneys were the unknowing beneficiaries of case management. Once, when one of the slower attorneys complained about the pushy probate staff, Judge AC was prompted to remark that never in the history of court proceedings did so many owe so much to so few. This drew an uncomprehending simper from the attorney who apparently was not a big fan of Sir Winston. During one of these case management sessions Shirley Bloch interrupted the proceedings and told Judge AC he was needed in the Chief Judge's office as soon as it was convenient.

"He said don't stop work or anything. Just come on up when you can."

"Did he say what it was about?" asked an anxious AC.

"No. He just said Judge Fox and he wanted to see you."

These CMCs, as they were called, were entertaining in a way. Judge AC got to see many of his old friends and could joke, gossip and relax. This annoyed his ultra-efficient staff attorney who presented the cases to the judge, since she had other work to do.

"I'll tell you what," said AC to his staff of two, "I'll go see what's up with the chief. If there are judicial decisions to be made, make the attorneys wait until I get back. Most of them will just need the cases continued another month which is OK. You can do that."

Darcy Lewis gave a wan smile. She knew the attorneys derided her as "Judge Lewis," and she would have preferred to have Judge AC present to provide a little authority to her requests for diligence.

"Yo, whazup?" AC said as he pulled back a chair in the chambers of the chief judge.

Judge Fox spoke first. He was serious, but he was always serious compared to AC and Judge Weaver.

"AC. I know you remember our conversation about Asner and the file in your office. Well, some

things have come up you should know about. I don't
want to get personal, but some of it may involve Vicky
Carter."

"Do I need a lawyer?"

"No, no, nothing like that," said Ira. "It's just an
awkward situation. I don't know whether you and
Vicky talk about work or not, but it's about that
Jordan case and Judge Asner."

AC held back his questions with great effort.

"Why don't you lay it out, Dan?" said Ira Moss.

"Well, Ira got a call from Dan Hawthorne about
the case, complaining about the guardian's office.
Said they were stalling and wouldn't do anything and
so on. He mentioned that he had talked to his good
friend Jack Asner several times about the case, and
poor Jack's hands were tied by the lack of a guardian. Good old Jack, of course, was ready to rule but
couldn't do so until he had a guardian."

"Rule about what?" asked AC.

"Well, he didn't specifically say, but from what we
now know, he wants to place the baby in long-term
relative care with the grandparents, Ricky and his
wife, who is Hawthorne's sister. At least that was what
Asner stated in open court. We have a transcript of
the proceedings. The mother apparently doesn't care
about raising the child and wants it to go to her folks.
Anyway, some nutty attorney for the mom..."

"Cindy Irving, no doubt."

"Yeah, that one. Well, on her own she prepares a
motion requesting DCF to investigate whether Ricky
is in fact the natural father of the kid. Claims she has

proof, but doesn't say what it is or how she got it. Now remember, she's supposed to represent the mother. She doesn't actually file the motion but attaches it to a letter she sends to everybody from the governor on down, detailing the whole situation, including a suggestion that Asner obviously had his mind already made up about the disposition."

"Let me know when you want me to chime in," said a rather chagrined AC.

"Well, of course, the mom's attorney has been hired by DCF to represent the mom who wants nothing to do with the situation. DCF then fires what's-her-name, Cindy, for a conflict of interest throwing the case into limbo."

"Let me interject," said AC. "Vicky and I don't talk shop, but I do know she's the supervising case worker on the case. You both know about how I was disqualified by a bogus motion and that Asner was in my office looking for the file before the motion was even filed. I did tell her to watch the case closely. Now that I think about it, I remember some vague allegation about the true father of the baby in a domestic violence case filed over in Levy County. I doubt that I told Vicky the details of that, since at that time I was still on the case. She did ask me a curious 'hypothetical' question recently. She wanted to know if an attorney had to do what a client wanted even if the attorney knew it was wrong, or something like that."

"Well, we have two problems," put in Ira. "I don't see how I can leave Asner on the case after the call from Hawthorne, especially in light of what's happened. I plan to reassign it. I just don't know whether I have enough to report him to the JQC. All I really have is someone spouting off about being friends with a judge. Lord knows how many times that happens. Thousands."

"I'm ready to vote," AC said.

"I'm with AC," Dapper Dan Fox said, "but my bias is well known."

"OK, gang, I appreciate your opinions. I need to sit on this. When does my term end anyway?" Chief Judge Moss said, rising to signal an end to the conference.

XVI

Carlo Proenza had the top down on his Volvo as he drove toward his condo in Vero Beach after a good workout at his fitness center, which had once been nothing more than a gym. His cellular phone rang like an old-fashioned telephone. The ring was one of the fifteen options offered and he rather liked the nostalgic sound of a bell. After all it was BellSouth, not BleepSouth. On picking up the phone he heard Reed Cunningham's pleasant, soothing voice. Reed always sounded like he was imparting some great secret. One that he could share with no one but you.

"Listen, Carlo, meet me at the Ocean Grill at noon. We have some big business to discuss. Can do?"

"Sure, do I need to change? I'm on my way home from the gym?"

"No, no," Reed said. "It's just the two of us, but it's not a cell phone topic."

Carlo had developed a true affection toward Reed. He was sorry Reed had gotten into all that trouble in the savings and loan business. He was, after all, guilty of doing nothing but what everyone else was doing. Reed had charm and wit and Rita to boot. He also had connections to very rich and powerful people. Harold Wessexson came to mind.

"Sit down, *amigo*. You have earned a toddy with all that physical exertion. You and Rita. I wish I had the determination."

"Amstel sounds fine. Reed, you must worry off weight. I work all the time and you still have me beat. Let's order then you can tell me what's up."

Both listened to the waitress recite the list of unprinted daily specials, naming not only the dish but all the seasonings and method of cooking.

"Bring us both the salmon thing with capers," said Reed who, as a take charge guy, was anxious to get on with the business at hand.

"Let me guess," said Carlo. "Harold Wessexson."

"Bingo. And it's right up your alley. He's a lucky man to have found us. What he needs is not much. Nothing illegal. It's just what we talked about on the *Osprey*. A simple continuance. I know a little of what's going on, but all you need to know is it involves big bucks. I mean very big bucks. Mergers and so on, but the deal is this; he needs the case continued for a year and is willing to offer handsome compensation to anyone who can achieve his ends. His hotshot lawyers claim to have hit a brick wall. Do you think you can help?"

"All I know of the case I get from the papers. I've been in Gainesville a lot recently, dealing with a bunch of stuff to do with widening roads. I happen to know the judge a little. Remember Vicky? The DCF worker I told you about? Well, she ended up dating this judge. Heavy dating if you know what I mean. His reputation is that he's sometimes flippant and irreverent, but impervious to outside influence all the same. Nor is he burdened by "invincible ignorance," to use Walker Percy's phrase. I can think of no way to approach him on a matter like this."

"He's not one of those God damn activist judges is he?"

"No, he is a bit lethargic from what I hear."

"OK, Carlo, that was good, but this is your specialty, not mine. Let me throw out a few ideas. Let's start with this girlfriend. I know you think highly of her, but she did almost accept a bribe. Well, she did accept it; she just backed out at the last minute. Suppose all that would come out in the press? They would really hang her."

"Then we would surely all hang together. See, that's what I have been saying about intimidation. I want happy clients, not threatened ones," said Carlo, who did not like the direction of the conversation.

"I have had some experience with intimidation at the hands of federal prosecutors. It can be a very effective tool. Let's explore this a bit. Let us suppose this Vicky person could be intimidated in a way that she thought she had all the risk and we had little. Do you think she could persuade her boyfriend judge to see things our way?"

"Reed, I just don't see how…"

"Stop for a minute. Skip the details of how we could get to Vicky. Could she influence the judge?"

"Possibly. I would have to do some checking. He really shouldn't be dating her anyway. Or at least he shouldn't have when he was handling DCF cases. I feel she has quite a hold on him. He wouldn't want to see her destroyed for sure."

"OK," said Reed in his most soothing voice. "Let's not threaten her; let's play on her sympathy with a bit of a threat in the background. You did say you thought she sort of liked you some?"

The waitperson served the salmon special with a vegetable medley.

"Let's eat this fish for now. You check things out and think on it. Call me in a week with your plan. Say, are you still dating that chick you had over at Christmas? Maybe the two of you can come over for dinner? If this works out you can buy her a Volvo to match yours, and get cash back as well."

***

With all the breaking news in the Jordan case, AC and Vicky had almost forgotten about the Vero Beach intrigue. Jordan was a Judge Jack-the-ass problem, and had nothing to do with Carlo and babies for sale. Based on further comments by Dan Hawthorne, Judge Moss had decided to refer Judge Asner to the Judicial Qualifications Commission for knowingly accepting out-of-court communications. He had also requested the Florida Bar to check out the involvement of the district legal counsel, Grimmage. These referrals were confidential, but Vicky heard of them at the beauty parlor where she went to get her nails filed and ears filled. Charlotte, Judge Moss's judicial assistant had typed the referral letters, and told Brunhilda who told Vicky's beauticians who, in turn, told Vicky, who told AC.

Vicky had other news for AC which she shared over a dinner of Chinese take-out.

"The letter Cindy Irving sent out to the world prompted poor Mary Beth to open up. She now admits her father has been sexually abusing her since she was a child. Well, she's still a child, really, but you know what I mean. At least he is out of the house."

"What about the true father of the child?" AC asked quietly. He was beyond being shocked, having heard many similar tales in his career, "Is it Ricky?"

"She claims no, but that can, and will, be checked out. What's so awful is that she was willing to abandon her own child to such a home. AC, I'm really torn between wanting to help people in situations like this, and wanting to wash my hands of it all."

"I know you want to protect this baby, that's the most important thing, but did you learn anything new about Jack-the-Ass?"

"No. Not really. Now that he's off the case, all we have is what he said on the record in court. He was obviously inclined to place the child with the grandparents, but he didn't know about the abuse. At least it hadn't come out in court. We finally have a guardian assigned to the case. Jane Jennings has taken on the case herself. Poor Cindy Irving got fired, but she was replaced by Stacy Ann Maddox, who is a fighter, and who has uncommon sense, if you know what I mean."

The couple talked long into the night. All the ramifications of the case were discussed. If Mary Beth had been abused as a child, it would explain much of her behavior. Ricky Jordan had dominated her and her mother, and now that he was out of the house there was a chance that Mary Beth and her mother could make a go of it. Mary Beth's mother was still somewhat in denial, but now that things were in the open she might come forward and tell the whole truth. Mary Beth's older siblings might even have something interesting to add to the sordid story.

As they snuggled into bed, AC felt closer to Vicky than he ever had, but knew this was not the time to discuss their future. As the couple drifted off into dreamland, AC felt Vicky experience a series of shivers as if some foreboding image had crossed her mind. What was the old expression? A rabbit jumped over my grave?

***

ALL RISE

The grave-jumping rabbit had been right. Vicky was at home alone the next night heating up a frozen dinner when the phone rang. AC was at his fly fishing club meeting, *so, who could it be?* Vicky thought as she picked up the receiver. She was not one to screen calls, but was on the government's do not call list.

"Vicky, it's Carlo."

There was a long period of silence. Vicky gave no acknowledgment that she recognized the caller.

"Vicky, how have you been?"

Still no response, but not a hang up click either.

"Look, I don't want to intrude, but I do have something important to discuss with you."

Still there was no click, but no response either. Carlo knew he was often not the person people wished to hear from, so was not discouraged by the silence.

"Vicky, this is very awkward for me, as well as you. I'm in somewhat of a bind and it involves you and also that nice judge you introduced me to."

Carlo knew that with this comment he had her hooked. He went on.

"A lot has happened since I last saw you. You remember our friend we were going to see when you were here in Vero? Well, he's turned out to be a scoundrel. I can't go into details now, but I do need to talk to you. I can be in Gainesville anytime you say. We can meet anywhere you suggest, but I suggest that it be private, and Vicky, this does involve your friend, the judge, who needs to be kept out of things for now."

Vicky's stomach was churning, like a traveler in the Atlanta airport who suddenly discovers he is in the wrong concourse with a flight leaving in ten minutes. She finally spoke. "Carlo, I suggest you go out and buy body armor as I am on my way over to Vero to erase you from the face of the earth. You creep! First me, and now you want to involve AC. Shit. I was suckered once, but I'll be God damned if I will fall for your crap again."

Carlo remained calm. Negotiations like this were, after all, what he did for a living.

"Vicky, think for a minute. When I first met you we were complete strangers. I didn't appreciate your principles. I never pressured you to do anything once you set me straight. Now I do need to talk to you or I would never have called. I won't say 'trust me.' I know better than that, but I can say that there's a great potential that we, and I mean you, me, and maybe the judge, can get into deep trouble unless certain steps are taken."

"Wear your body armor and meet me at noon at the Waldo Road Sonny's this Wednesday."

***

"Ira," said Judge AC over his lunch of black beans and rice, "the gossip mongers all know about your sending Judge Asner to the JQC. I want you to know that I never breathed a word, but you had to do it. Look, I was almost in the same box. Ricky Jordan said I was putty in his hands, but you know that's

239

crap. The calls from Dan Hawthorne were for real. He even called you. Do you have enough to make it stick?"

"AC *mi amigo*, I would rather not go into it. I will say I felt the referral was justified. But look, I need for you to bring me up to date on Wessex and Aquatec. Are we really set for trial in August or September? Do you have any suggestions about coverage? We have to get someone to either cover the trial or cover your docket. You can't do both at the same time, and we can't just close down half the civil division for three or four months. The esteemed Senior Judge, Harold Brown, may be available for the trial, but I would anticipate some objections from the lawyers."

"Ira, this case is a nightmare. Clem did all he could and you know how competent he is. He called it the snakes versus the skunks and he was right. My take on it is, now that I have set a date for trial, we need to stick by it. We can't be the ones to blink. Will it settle? God only knows, but I know it won't unless there's a firm trial date. We have to assign a judge and let them know we mean business. I can check around, but it will ultimately be your call. One possibility is that retired appellate judge living out by you. He's sharp as a tack and is what some call a no-nonsense judge."

"Why would Stan possibly want to take the case?"

"Virility. Who wants to be over-the-hill? Stan would be perfect. It would appeal to his ego. You handle his wife and I'll do my best to charm Stan into doing it. My job will be easier. I know damn well Stan's wife doesn't want him tied up for three or four months. We can even give him a choice: my docket or the trial. My bet is he will pick the trial."

***

"Vicky, I'm embarrassed to have called you," said Carlo as he slid into the seat opposite Vicky at the original Sonny's Bar-B-Q on Waldo Road, "but I really am in a jam. Let me bring you up to date. After our deal with the Cunninghams fell through..."

"Your deal," interjected Vicky.

"My deal," agreed Carlo. "Well, we became friends, or so I thought."

At that time a seasoned waitress handed them a menu and asked if they were ready to order. Most of her customers had the menu memorized. After all, this was the original Sonny's Fat Boy's before it became a franchised chain. Vicky assumed command much as Reed had done in Vero Beach.

"Give us both pork lunch specials with beans and coleslaw," she said. "And half and half tea if that's ok."

Carlo nodded. He had been around long enough to know what half sweet and half regular iced tea meant.

Carlo was, however, a bit uneasy by his surroundings. The place was not really what he had in mind. The tables were crowded with workers from the adjacent industrial park, as well as a number of uniformed officers of the law. Oh well, he thought, the purloined letter had been out in the open and it had not been discovered. Having lunch with Vicky in public made more sense than sneaking away somewhere.

"Well, I guess I called the meeting."

"You sure did, and it'd better be important," said Vicky.

Carlo remembered the plan of action he had worked out with Reed Cunningham.

"Vicky, I was bringing you up to date. After our... my deal, fell through with Reed Cunningham, I had a very unfortunate and traumatic experience. I was out of town in Chicago and my mother was staying in my condo. She had a stroke and died. I told you how close we were, so I won't go into details about how I felt. The problem was, that I was not there and the cops entered my place and took the opportunity to snoop around. They found some things that had nothing to do with my mother's death. They asked me questions which I referred to my lawyer."

"Carlo, I'm really sorry about your mom. We never met, but I know how important she was to you."

"Thank you, Vicky. Well, as you know, my reputation is somewhat mixed. The incident got a little press and I got a call from Reed about it. He was very polite, and we became friends. Oh, by the way, I was able to arrange a Russian adoption for Reed and his wife. Anyway, as things turned out, I found he has other friends. Much better friends than me, it seems. Friends with more money and influence. Friends who need a favor. This involves a lawsuit in

Gainesville. You can guess who the judge is. Vicky, I'm really sorry to put you in this position."

"You can shut your fucking con artist mouth right now. If you think I'm going to do anything to influence AC, you'd better get a new brain."

"Vicky, Vicky, I know. But if you don't help, these creeps will find some other way to get to your judge. Reed obviously knows about the adoption matter and is threatening to report it to the cops. If he does, it could mean that we'll be subpoenaed to testify; which would mean that you'll be ruined regardless of the outcome; that your judge will be dragged into the mess and possibly ruined as well. Don't you see?"

Vicky was beginning to crumble. They finished their meal in silence, and neither diner would have won a clean plate award. The waitress came with the check without being summoned, and said it could be paid at the check-out counter. By this time Vicky was openly weeping. This drew the attention of several of the sheet metal workers at the adjacent table. Carlo decided it was time to withdraw to less threatening surroundings, and put his arm on Vicky's shoulder and escorted her out of Sonny's, leaving an overly generous tip.

"Vicky," said Carlo as they sat in his Volvo, "it's just a continuance. That's all they want. No throwing the case or anything like that at all. These cases usually drag on for years, and this one's not that old at all anyway. If there was any way I could pull it off without involving you I would do it. It may all be a bluff but it's not one I want to call."

Vicky sat still for a long time. She did not look at Carlo. Finally she looked at him with an expression of utter contempt.

"I can hear myself now. 'Oh, AC, sweetie pie, I would just love it if you would continue that old case for a year. It's not all that old anyway, and it would mean *so* much to me.' Carlo, as a professional briber you have the brains of a goose."

Now it was Carlo's time to think. What Vicky said made sense.

"Well, maybe you'll just have to lay it out on the table. Tell him it's his decision.

"Don't *ask* him to do it; just tell him what will happen if he doesn't. Tell him not to continue the case. Tell him you're willing to take the hit, but you just thought he ought to know."

Vicky breathed very deeply, and let the air out very slowly. An observer, such as one of the sheet metal gang, would have marveled at her change in composure. She smiled, which Carlo noted with some apprehension. This was not a circumstance for smiles.

"Carlo, if I go through with this, is there anything in it for me?"

"Like what?"

"Well, whores usually get paid don't they? Street hookers may have a fixed price, but us high class babes expect some reward too. I don't know why this continuance is so damn important but even a West Virginia gal knows when money is changing hands. How about half your cut? And don't insult me with that 'bad old Reed' crap. I know you're in cahoots with him."

Carlo grinned. "That sounds almost like a proposed pre-nuptial agreement, but I agree. Fifty-fifty it is. Vicky, to tell the honest truth I have no idea what my reward might be. All I got was a hint of benefits and a bit of a threat. Pretty much what you got. In my line of work that's not uncommon. I think we could make a great team. I'll leave things in your lovely hands."

Vicky gave him a peck on the cheek and drove back to the DCF office down the street.

***

The lunch counter at Wise's was jam packed. Judge AC started to leave when he noticed Stacy Ann Maddox seated next to an elderly diner who was reaching into his pocket for change for a tip. Some of the old timers were light tippers as they could remember when coffee went from five to ten cents a cup. A dollar tip for a sandwich was something they could not fathom.

"Ms Maddox, what an unexpected pleasure. I'm glad you left that obnoxious Cahill at work. He won't let you get a word in edgewise."

"Judge Cason, how have you been? Are you glad to get out of Family Division? Would it be sucking up to say we miss you?"

"Yes, as a matter of fact it would. You know how judges despise being flattered. I remember one time…"

"Quit it, judge, or I won't let you in on the Jordan case."

"Straight for the jugular. Sign of a real lawyer. You win. I give up."

"Well, I think it's going to work out for the best. Grimmage has backed off, and run for cover. Rumor has it that he was receiving his marching orders from Tallahassee connections not associated with DCF. He's been reported to the Florida Bar, but I doubt that anything will come of it, the way ethics are treated these days. Judge Lee now has the case and considers it a priority item. The best news is that Mary Beth now has the support she needs to start fresh. Her brothers and sisters have come forward and her mom has left Ricky for good. There might be criminal repercussions, but that's not my concern. You know, Judge, this is one of those cases that should not have been rushed to a speedy conclusion despite DCF policy."

"Ms Maddox, you may very well win a gold star on this one. You'll certainly not get rich. Why don't you see if Doug Smith is really serious about giving you a job? Personal injury stuff is where it's at. Suing understaffed nursing homes is like taking candy from a baby, or so I've been told. You do a public good and get paid well to boot."

"Oh, Judge, I don't know. I've even thought about going back to school and leaving all this crap. Study anthropology or something. I really don't need the money. My dad owns about a jillion acres in the Panhandle. All my boyfriend is interested in is his band over in St. Augustine. What did they say in your day? Crazy mixed up kid? That may be me."

"Hey, Stacy, wait till you have your first midlife crisis. Then it's too late to go back to school and start over, so you need to look for the gold stars wherever you can find them. They won't be on your report cards, but they'll be there all the same. When I was a lawyer, I don't think anyone ever thanked me for a job well done. If I lost a case, the client was pissed. If I won, they thought they deserved to win anyway. I learned to pat myself on the back, and it surely has come in handy as a judge. Would you like a pat on the back?"

All Stacy Ann Maddox could do was to look at AC with an expression of total vulnerability, and with a weak smile, briefly put her head on AC's shoulder.

XVI

Paynes Prairie was shrouded in mist as AC drove down to Micanopy. The sandhill cranes, that had earlier migrated from points north, seemed content as they foraged among the high spots for crane tid-bits. The few bison that had been turned loose on the prairie were reclusive and not to be seen. AC felt as content as the cranes as he thought how well things had worked out with the Jordan case. There would always be other problematic cases. *Did I really think that word?* AC thought as he sped along. Maybe I should have my vocabulary thoroughly expunged. I'll be thinking words such as "seamless" and "marginal-ize" soon. He had promised Vicky supper and planned to smother some ham with pineapple and have sweet potato on the side. A chilled bottle of Chardonnay sat by his side.

"Yoo hoo. I hope you're in the mood for some hammy-wammy," yelled AC as he entered.

"Chef AC, what a treat. Come over here and let me give you an advance thank you."

AC uncorked the wine and spread some cheese on some somewhat stale crackers and brought them to the table in front of the TV.

"Let me get this stuff started," said AC as he turned toward the kitchen. "Tell me if we made the news."

"I never ever want to make the news again." said Vicky. But deep down she knew she would. There was no alternative this time.

"Hey, lover, what was the name of that cop you told me about? The one with the funny name," Vicky shouted to AC, as he put the sweet potatoes in the oven.

"What cop? What funny name?"

"Oh, you know. Like the one in the old-time radio show. The one you said asked about me and Carlo that time."

"Sergeant Preston of the Yukon. Why do you ask?"

"Well, you said his wife was an artist, and some-body was talking about her today. They said she was really good. She paints animals and stuff. I'm pretty sure she was the one. Preston."

"Yeah, Valerie. Shows her work at a gallery up in High Springs. Let's go up and look for it this weekend.

I have one of her early works showing some hounds running through the woods. You know the one. It's over the sofa in the den."

"Sounds fun to me," said Vicky as she walked back to the bedroom to change.

***

Sergeant Jim Preston was at his desk early the next morning filling out a report when his phone rang.

"Preston here."

Sergeant Preston, this is Vicky Carter. We've not met, but I think you know who I am. I work at the Department for Children and Families."

"Yes, Ms Carter. We have a mutual friend."

"Right. Well, you talked to our mutual friend awhile back, and I need to talk to you now. I would prefer not to talk over the phone if that's all right."

Jim Preston knew enough not to ask what it was all about.

"Fine, Ms Carter, let's meet... well I can meet any-where. Do you have anyplace in mind?"

"How about Morningside Park tomorrow at noon? I'll bring some KFC and drinks on me."

"That'll be perfect. See you then. Oh, by the way, I'm not in uniform these days. I'll have my dog with me, a black lab. He loves the park. His name really is King."

Vicky felt reassured by the warmth of Preston's voice. She knew what she had to do, but it had to be done right. AC seemed to trust this guy, Preston, implicitly, but she needed to check him out for herself. As she pulled into the parking lot at Morningside Park, she saw a man throwing a ball to a large black dog. She watched for some time to see how he reacted with the dog. That could be important. Satisfied, she left her car and walked directly up to the dog.

"Hi, King. Want to play fetch? Give me the ball."

King dropped the tennis ball at her feet, She picked it up and threw it into a clump of palmettos. As she turned she said, "Hi Jim, I'm Vicky. Want to play cops and robbers?"

Jim Preston tried to assess this self-assured woman. He liked and respected Judge Cason, and did not think he would hook up with just anybody. Still, he knew she once had connections with one Carlo Proenza, who had an unsavory reputation. He felt he had to play things very close to the chest. While King looked for the ball, Vicky spread out the picnic lunch on a concrete table.

"Ms Carter, any friend of Judge Cason's is a friend of mine, but I doubt that you have come here to talk about him."

"You're right, Sergeant. I've come to talk about Carlo Proenza and Reed Cunningham, if you are interested."

Straight and to the point, thought Sergeant Preston.

"Yeah, I've heard of Proenza, but you've got to understand, he's not really in my jurisdiction. I did ask AC, I mean Judge Cason, about Proenza, but that was as a favor for another law enforcement agency. I did tell him you knew Proenza, but that was because one of our guys saw you with him at the gym. For obvious reasons, I can't share why we are interested in Proenza. In fact I suggested that the judge not discuss this with you, but I'm sure he had his reasons to do so."

"AC knows nothing of this. Nothing at all." Vicky took a deep breath. "I'm here to spill the beans, or blab, or whatever it is they do."

And blab she did. Jim Preston was a good listener. He did not take notes or pull out his recorder. He just listened and thought. Vicky told him of meeting Carlo in the gym and how she felt under pressure about the shaken baby case. She told of the trip to Vero and the appointment with the Cunninghams and how she had backed out at the last minute.

"I felt so guilty. To think I almost committed a felony. Well, maybe I did. Like a conspiracy or something."

"Vicky, I really appreciate your coming to me like this, but it seems to me that nothing ever happened. Evil thoughts don't constitute a crime." Except in politics, he thought. "What do you expect me to do with this information? Right now it would be just your word against his. And that's simply not enough."

Vicky had not thought through her plan to this extent. She certainly was not going to tell Jim of Carlo's threat. That would involve AC. Her idea was to expose Carlo and Reed and take the heat herself. Then she remembered Watergate and "Deep Throat."

"Follow the money."

"What money?"

"The two hundred thousand dollar check I just told you about. To some charity or something. Carlo said he had it in trust. That should nail Carlo or at least make him squirm."

"How do we find out about the money, the check?"

"You're the cop, not me, but if I were a cop, I might check with the locals."

"And what about you, Vicky? How will this look if it hits the press. 'Controversial DCF worker involved in baby buying scam'."

"I know, Jim, I know. I do know what I'm doing though. Chalk it up to civic duty or whatever. I just want them exposed for what they are. Obviously, AC has no idea I'm here with you. Just follow up on the money. Here, King, fetch the ball."

***

Jim Preston did a lot of thinking on his way back to his office. He had taken an immediate liking to Vicky. She liked AC and she liked King and King liked her. He knew there was something she was not telling him. It must involve AC somehow, he thought as he pulled into the Alachua County Sheriff's Office parking lot on the Hawthorne Road just around the corner from Morningside Park, which was now "Morningside Nature Center" in keeping with the renaming of institutions. His involvement in the Proenza matter had been through the Florida Department of Law Enforcement. Bill Blessing, an old friend and fellow Gator he had met at FBI school years ago, was his contact in Tallahassee. He felt safe in imparting his new information to Bill, even though he could not figure out Vicky's motive in coming to see him.

He got through to his friend right away. "Hey, Bill, thought I would just call and see if you need help with the savage 'Noles'. Should I dispatch the Gator Cavalry?"

"No, I'm safe as long as the Gators keep losing up here. What's up in the swamp?"

"Remember last fall when you said to be on the lookout for this guy, Proenza, from Vero who was snooping around Gatortown?"

"Yeah, you said some guys spotted him in a gym or something."

"Well, his name popped up from a very curious source. I just got back from a clandestine meeting with a local DCF worker who had dated Proenza a couple of times. I can't remember whether I told you about her or not. Anyway, she told me how Proenza had lured her into some scam in Vero, and how she backed out at the last minute, much to her credit. I'm sure, from talking with her, that her motives were pure, but the bottom line was that it involved a bribe from some rich guy, Reed Cunningham, to help him adopt a DCF foster child. Are you interested in the rest; do you have time for the whole story?"

"Jim, I have all day to listen to anything about Carlo Proenza. He somehow stays a step ahead of us.

We get tips, but nothing ever sticks. We know damn well he's much more than a lobbyist or 'consultant' as they say, but can never prove it. We know this kind of crap goes on all over the state, or world for that matter. What do they say in South America, the oil for the machinery? I forget the Spanish. Somehow or another, on every controversial project in the state, this guy's name pops up. A bridge to nowhere in the Panhandle, offshore oil leases, you name it. We know he's not registered as a lobbyist and could maybe go after him on that, but that wouldn't be much of a charge. About like fishing without a license or something. What do you have? I would love to hear more."

Jim told more. All he knew. Neither Jim nor Bill knew of the discovery by the Vero Beach Police of the check in Carlo's condo, and, of course, neither had any reason to suspect that Carlo had threatened Vicky.

"Jim, when you talked to this confidential source, didn't she realize that if this story breaks everything will come out in public? That she can't remain a confidential informant?"

"Yes, she knows all that and is willing to take the heat. To be honest, I can't figure out her motive for coming to me. I know she wants to stick it to Carlo. I have no idea about this Cunningham guy. Is he an FDLE target?"

Bill Blessing paused a moment and said, "Perhaps a person of interest. Well, it's public record that he was convicted in one of the biggest S and L scandals in the country and spent some time at Eglin. He's now retired, but his lifestyle suggests more income than Social Security."

"Billy Boy, what I would do if I were FDLE, is check with the Indian River Sheriff and Vero police about this mysterious check. Two hundred grand, supposedly. My Deep Throat source emphasized we should follow the money and to talk to the locals. I don't know if she's holding anything back or not, but I'm sure she's a straight shooter. With a check you would have some tangible evidence, not just a bunch of conversation. Bye now."

Jim Preston felt he had done a good day's work, however he could not ignore the nagging voice in the back of his brain that repeated, AC, AC, AC. He felt some moral obligation to call his old friend, the only judge he really trusted, and tell him of Vicky's visit. Some inherent cop instinct told him not to.

XVIII

Judge Jack Asner was in chambers sipping his second cup of coffee of the afternoon while his courtroom full of juvenile delinquents, their attorneys, their prosecutors, court bailiffs and clerks awaited his return to court. Judge Asner felt it helped things for the participants to wait before his grand entrance. That way they could settle down a bit.

"Judge, do you want to take a call from some Judge Frisbee or something in Tampa?" asked his judicial assistant, who was known in the legal community as Sally the Snip. "He didn't say what it was about; said it was personal to you, and he can call back if you're already in court."

"Yeah, put him on," replied Jack.

Name sounds familiar he thought. Somebody who had something to do with the Conference of Circuit Judges.

"Hello, Jack, this is Frank Friesling. As you probably know, I am the conference rep on the JQC."

"Sure, Frank, old buddy. What's happening?"

"Well, Jack, I just called to give you a heads up. The JQC found probable cause in a case of yours about some alleged ex-parte communication with someone named Hawthorne. The Jordan case, I believe it was. You'll get a formal notice in the mail, but I didn't want it to come as a shock. As you know, probable cause just means they found enough evidence to proceed. They haven't even heard your side of the story, of course. Now, as a member, I'm not allowed to go into details, but you might want to consider retaining a lawyer. Once the JQC elects to proceed, the usual practice is to inquire into every other complaint ever lodged against a judge. I find that somewhat unfair, but if the judge has a clean record it can work to the judge's advantage. Anyway, I'm sorry to be the bearer of bad news, but I didn't want you to open the mail without some warning."

As there was no response after a decent interval, Judge Frank Friesling said, "Good luck, Jack," and hung up.

"Some son-of-a-bitch is going to pay for this," threatened Judge Asner to his empty chamber. He knew his old pal, Frank, would not say who the complaining party was, but he suspected that shithead Cason. "Sally," he called in a louder voice, "Call Judge

Moss and get coverage for this morning's docket. I have sort of a family emergency to attend to."

Judge Asner waited while Sally called, but it was not a patient wait. Goddamn it. He *had* talked to Dan Hawthorne. And that little prick at DCF to boot. Both had dropped the name of a person in Tallahassee to whom Asner felt he owed his judicial appointment. Maybe he should call *him.* Maybe not. Especially after what Frank Friesling had said. Now he was not as mad at Frank as he was when he hung up. Hell, Frank did him a favor. Call a lawyer, he said.

"Judge, they won't answer."

"Well, go up there. Go to the court administrator. Cancel court. I don't care. I have an emergency and have to leave."

"When will you be back?"

"Sally, what do I look like, a fortune teller? I don't know. Just tell anybody who calls that I'm out on an emergency and take a message. If it's important, take it upstairs to the administrator."

Judge Jack Asner had a few drawbacks from a judicial standpoint but he was crafty and not especially dumb. He did have dumb friends though, and he drove directly to the offices of the dumbest of them all.

"Good morning, sir, can we help you?" said a rather seedy-looking receptionist/secretary/file clerk.

"Tell Degan Judge Asner is here to see him."

"Yes sir. How is that spelled?"

"J-U-D-G-E."

"Do you have an appointment?"

"Just tell him my name is Asner, A-S-N-E-R, and that my wife was just run over by a drunk doctor and I need a lawyer in a hurry."

Thirty seconds later Hal Degan swept Judge Asner into his office telling Girl Friday to hold all calls, and bring in a fresh pot of coffee.

"Hal, I may need a lawyer. Let me lay out what I know and you can tell me what you think. I just got a call from a judge pal of mine on the JQC. Heads-up call, he called it. Well, some s.o.b apparently turned me in for talking out of court. I mean, shit, what am I supposed to do when a constituent calls me up? Hang up in his face?"

"OK, Jack, take it easy. Start from the top. What kind of case is this?"

"Dependency. Something to do with a kid snatched because the mother went into a bar and left the kid asleep in the car. Well, you do that DCF stuff, don't you? Didn't you just get the contract? Anyway, I get this call from the uncle who only wants to know how the case is going. I say, fine, but I need to get a guardian appointed. Pretty soon we'll need a guardian for the guardian to make sure they're doing a good job. The next thing I know, I get this call from the JQC. You figure. I think it's some kind of set-up."

"Jack, you know me. I say never give an inch. Come out swinging. I wouldn't be where I am today if I was a quitter. Have you gotten any papers or anything from the JQC?"

"No. Just this 'friendly' call."

"Good. That gives us time to do some planning. From what I hear, all the judges brought before the JQC bow and scrape and roll over and play dead. I think it's time somebody made a stand. Let me know when you get something I can work on."

"Do you need a retainer or something?" asked an anxious Asner.

"Judge, I am embarrassed that you should even ask. Of course not. Professional courtesy isn't yet dead in this country. My time is your time. And by the way, I'll instruct my paralegal to be sure to put you directly through when you call. You can't imagine what we have to go through to get decent help these days."

Judge Asner felt much relieved after his visit to Hal Deagan. He considered whether to return to court. No, that would not do. He would never want his personal problems to interfere with his decision making. He decided to go by Lillian's for a relaxing toddy.

Lillian's Music Store had been a music store selling pianos and so forth. Now it was a piano bar selling booze and so forth. It was a bit earlier than his usual stopover on his way home, but the "crowd was there as usual, and the usual crowd was there." On his left stood Mike O'Something, *never could remember that guy's name* he thought as he placed his order.

"Fret," he called, giving his best imitation of the black dialect, "Gimmie a happy hour special margarita."

Fred instantly produced the requested drink. Judge Asner was not a good tipper, but might come in handy sometime.

Jack Asner thought about the day's events. This was a bunch of junk. *This could be serious.* Frisbee what's-his-name had said something about looking into all a judge's past behavior on the bench. Well, he was no different from all the rest was he? Look at Cason. He was supposedly screwing some DCF worker. Happy hour resulted in two drinks having been placed before him. By the time he started on the second his attention turned to the girl two stools down who was talking on a cellular phone. The conversation sounded unpleasant and ended with a "Yeah, screw you too."

"Sweetie, let me buy you a drink. Fret, serve one up for this gal. She seems unhappy, and that's a bad image for Lillian's. My name's Jack. You look familiar."

"Mary Beth... You look familiar too. Thanks." And to Fred she said, "I'll have a Bud Lite."

Mary Beth had not been in court the day Judge Asner heard the Jordan case, so he had no reason to suspect that this young woman was the subject of his new concerns. Mary Beth had, in fact, seen Judge Asner on the bench, but did not recognize him without his robe. This was a common occurrence in the lives of judges, much like supporting actors who are remembered from somewhere, but remain nameless.

Even if Judge Asner had seen Mary Beth in court it is doubtful that he would have identified her with the wretched creature who had presented herself to Judge Cason several months ago. Stacy Ann Maddox had personally driven her to the beauty parlor for a tint and style, and to the Junior League thrift store for some lightly worn stylish garb. Mary Beth now had a respectable job and a schedule that gave her one early afternoon a week on the town. Lillian's was a bit of a throwback to her former partying days, but it seemed refined to Mary Beth. Young townies stopped by after work and talked about their hot prospects and how Gator football recruiting was going. She hoped Stacy Ann did not stop by. That would be awful.

She was curious about this old bald-headed fart everyone seemed to know. He kept up a typical bar-room conversation which was not really a conversation, but a monologue. She occasionally had to say "yes" or "no" to some question, but she did not listen or care what he said. Well, a free drink is better than no drink, she thought, and her funds were definitely limited. She could afford to be as pleasant to him as if he were an uncle. Not Uncle Dan though, her mom's brother. She had learned of his role in her current mess. How his buddies in Tallahassee would get H and RS off their backs. Her face saddened as these events were recalled.

"Hey, why so down in the mouth?" asked the bald-headed old fart. "Fret, give this lass another special. We got to cheer her up."

"Thanks, but no thanks. I got to go pick up my kid."

"OK, babe. You know what's best. But look, here's my card. If you ever need a favor, give me a call."

***

Three days later Mary Beth gave the card to Stacy Ann Maddox, and related her conversation at Lillian's.

"Now Stacy, I know what you're going to think, but really, I just stopped in for one quick drink and left, and was home by six. I made the seven o'clock homemaking class at Santa Fe."

Stacy decided not to lecture Mary Beth considering all the progress she had made, but she certainly made a mental note of the events in Lillian's.

The review hearing later that day went perfectly. Mary Beth was praised all around the table. The guardian, the case worker, and Judge Lee all gave her high marks. Ricky Jordan was said to be out of the state on business.

After the hearing and hugs all around, it was with some hesitation that Stacy Ann Maddox called Judge Alva Cason, her confidant on the bench. As a mere mortal she did not want to become involved in a fight among the gods, but she knew there was going to be a fight, as Cindy Irving had told her of Judge Asner's visit to Hal Degan, Cindy's boss. Hal had naturally bragged all over the office about how vigorously he would defend his good friend, Judge Asner, who was so wrongfully accused. Cindy was now looking for another job.

Judge AC was alone in chambers, and against his own better judgment, answered the telephone. An agitated voice on the other end said, "Judge, it's awful. I just don't see how it can get any worse than this. We've got a circuit judge hitting on a dependency mom at Lillian's. I know it's not his case now, but yuck. He has to be reported."

"Stacy, right?"

"Yes, judge."

"Tell me who, what, when, and where? Well, I can guess the who part. Tell me what's up."

Stacey did. She told the story as far as she knew it.

"I'm as repulsed as you, but we have to think things through. Although it's not official, and as much as I would like to crucify Asner, (he refrained from calling him Jack-the-Ass) Judge Asner has already been reported to the JQC. I understand he is now represented by Hal Degan. I question whether we want to subject Mary Beth to cross examination on this point? As dumb as Degan is, I doubt Mary Beth could hold up. I can hear it now. 'You were in this saloon, it was a saloon wasn't it? Coming on to Judge Asner, weren't you? Admit it, you saw a chance to make up to a circuit judge who could help with your case. He felt sorry for you and bought you a drink, but wouldn't take the next step, so now you want to punish him?' I just don't think so."

"Judge, as Mary Beth's lawyer, and a member of the Bar I felt I had an obligation to report this. I think I'm going somewhere and cry. When I finish will you buy me a drink at Lillian's?"

After Stacy Ann hung up, Judge AC thought about proceedings before the Judicial Qualifications Commission. *The Fear and Loathing Commission,* as Hunter Thompson would have styled it. He did not know the exact extent of the evidence that would be presented against Judge Jack Asner, but grinned with pleasure at the thought of Hal Degan addressing that august body. In his mind, one more nail would not be needed to close Asner's coffin so there was no need to report the incident at Lillian's Music Store.

XIX

"Carlo. What the hell is going on?"

"Reed, my friend. I was just going to call. I just got back from Gainesville and everything is on track just the way you predicted. You really know your stuff. Vicky even gave me a kiss and a promise I didn't expect. I think she can handle this judge with no problem."

"Carlo, Carlo, Carlo. Where is my goddamn check?"

"What check?" asked Carlo, as it dawned on him exactly what Reed was asking.

"The check the cops just asked me about. The one made out to the esteemed Sara Beville Foundation.

Mrs. Beville is very disappointed that it was not delivered. You know damn well what check."

Carlo Proenza had been in many compromising situations. He was not one to lose his composure, but he could not help but feel as if a doctor was approaching him with a very large medical instrument. He had intended to shred the check once the deal with Vicky fell through, but he could not remember doing so.

"Hold on, Reed. I'm sure I left it in a safe place or destroyed it."

He hastily scrounged through his desk and, sure enough, found the check in a file labeled–what?– *Adoption!* Jesus Christ! Mary, Mother of God!

"Reed, I have it. It was in my desk. What are you saying about cops?"

"I just got a call from a very polite man at the Florida Department of Law Enforcement. Says his name is Blessing. He asked me what I knew about the Sara Beville Foundation. My initial reaction was to tell him to piss off, then I remembered your phony charity, so I fell back on my usual routine about speaking only through my attorneys. I was very courteous and explained that, with my past, I had been instructed by them never to talk directly to law enforcement as much as I would like to help them and so forth. How did they know about the check, Carlo? This could screw up things big time."

"Let's think this through. You, me and Vicky knew, but Vicky never saw the actual check. Reed, there is some possibility that the check was discovered by the cops when they came in to investigate my mother's death. I know they looked through some of my things. It was probably an illegal search, but nothing was taken to my knowledge. The check was not in plain open view as they say in legalese. Even if they saw it, why would it raise any suspicion? Granted, it's a large check, but that's it."

Reed softened his voice some.

"I made an appointment with my lawyer in West Palm. I suggest you get this Carter woman off our case, although it may be too late for that. Our, or I should say my, intimidation plan no longer seems tenable. I can't believe you left that check lying around."

Carlo appreciated the fact that Reed had taken the blame for the plan to threaten Vicky. *Could she be behind this?* he wondered.

"I feel awful about the check. All I can say is that it seemed inconsequential at the time, with the deal off and everything. I find it hard to believe that Vicky could be behind this, given her own vulnerability. She even asked for some kind of cut for influencing the judge in the other matter. None of this adds up. My guess is that the cops saw the check and are on a fishing expedition. I know I've been a target for some time."

"You're probably right, Carlo. Nothing will come of the Sara Beville check. Nothing happened. No foundation. So what? Maybe we were going to found one. Adopt a baby? The only way they could know that would be from Vicky, and they've not mentioned adoption at all. What baby? When? Why not? What

I worry about is Wessex. If Vicky talks about that it means big trouble. I mean really big trouble."

"I agree," said a less-than-contrite Carlo, "But remember it was Wessexson who proposed the deal."

"Hey, I've been to jail once and don't plan to go again. No matter who my roommates are. That's why the *Osprey* always has full tanks. I'm only kidding, or half kidding. Tell me more about this Vicky. Maybe we've misjudged her."

"She's an enigma, and that's about all I can say for sure," said Carlo, almost thinking out loud. "At times she seems very protective of her judge friend, and a minute later she wants to cut in on the profits. Maybe she's the con, and we are the chumps. My best assessment is that she'll protect her judge at all costs. That was her motive in the adoption business; to protect some kid, not to make money. No, she's not going to sell her judge down the river. The Wessex case will never come up. I'm willing to bet the farm on it."

Reed Cunningham had taken many risks in his career. Only one had backfired. He made quick accurate decisions.

"Carlo, my man, I agree. Let's stonewall the bastards."

***

Sergeant Jim Preston was a long way from the Yukon, but still complained about being chilly as he walked with his wife, Valerie, and dog King, along a trail beside the Santa Fe River in a cool North Florida breeze. King was not fazed a bit by the cold, and fetched the sticks Jim tossed into the coffee-colored Santa Fe.

"A jacket would help," suggested his wife Valerie, as she tried to avoid the spray from King's happy shaking.

The couple had driven over to O'leno State Park to give King some exercise. This stretch of the Santa Fe was known as "The Natural Bridge," since the river could be crossed without a man-made bridge. There was no beautiful arch spanning the river; it obligingly sank beneath the surface and reappeared at "River Rise" several miles downstream.

"Oh, by the way, our friend, the judge came by the studio yesterday with his girlfriend. They didn't buy anything, but I did sort of put one on reserve for them. They seemed more interested in each other than the painting, but I have a feeling they'll be back."

As soon as Jim got to his office the next day he telephoned Bill Blessing to get an update on the information Vicky had provided him about Carlo Proenza.

"I'm glad you called," said Bill. "The deal is this. I called Vero as you suggested, and after a lot of hassling, found someone willing to talk. I knew they would be nervous, considering the way they got their information, but thanks to you and your source, I convinced them that all we wanted was a confirmation about some money changing hands. They had entered Proenza's apartment on a valid legal basis, and found his mother had died of a stroke while he was out of town. They decided to do some snooping and found a two hundred thousand dollar check made out to something called the Sara Beville Foundation, which doesn't seem to exist. I called our pal Reed Cunningham, who signed the check, and got a referral to his lawyer which was to be expected. Now this is the interesting part. Two days later I get this call from Cunningham's lawyer who wants to set up a meeting. I still doubt that it will lead to anything we could rely on in court. Lot of 'he said, she said' stuff. Proenza did have a check, but it's bound to be gone by now. The cop's testimony that he saw it would probably be ruled inadmissible due to the intrusive nature of the search of the condo. Do you think you could set up a meeting with your source? From what you say she's a decent person. I would really hate to drag her into this mess unless we had some chance of building a solid case against Proenza. I can get her immunity from prosecution, but not immunity from *persecution* by DCF and the inkslingers of the press."

Jim Preston jumped in, "She'll meet and she'll talk. I'm sure of it. What I can't figure out is her motive. You don't know it, but she's already gotten a black eye on a shaken baby case. Wasn't her fault at all, but it was on her watch. She's bound to understand the political consequences."

Bill Blessing gave an audible sigh. Jim Preston waited for him to speak.

"Let me ask you this, Jim. Do you consider me to be an honorable cop, one with morals and ethics and everything?"

"Of course I do," truthfully answered Jim, who considered himself to be equally moral and ethical.

"What if I told you I would be willing to use the law to ruin Proenza's reputation even if I knew I couldn't convict him. What then?"

Now it was Jim Preston's turn to take a long pause.

"Come on down, Bill. I'll set up a meeting with Vicky. We can talk more then."

Jim hung up and wished he had some sort of spiritual advisor to call. Ruin a jackal's reputation and Vicky's at the same time, he wondered?

***

When Carlo Proenza got the call from his lawyer saying that a warrant had been issued for his arrest and that arrangements for a bond had already been made, he chalked it up to business as usual. His lawyer assured him that the case would never withstand a motion to dismiss, once depositions were taken, certain evidence suppressed, and the state's case was exposed as a sham. A sham costing him a hundred thousand dollars in lawyer's fees, he thought as he pulled into the driveway of Kissimmee Kiss. The ornate gate did not open when he punched the private code numbers Reed had given him into the electronic switch. He had expected as much when Reed had not returned his calls. From his vantage point he could see the empty dock where *"Osprey"* was usually at rest. With both tanks full she could easily be in the islands by now. Fine, he thought. One less witness, but I doubt that will reduce my lawyer's fees.

After going through the formalities of an arrest, Carlo planned to drive to Fort Pierce to see his lawyer the next day. He had considered calling Vicky. His lawyer had, of course, advised him to talk to no one. He trusted this lawyer who had served six years on the bench in Fort Pierce, and who had swapped his seeming sinecure and sanctity of black robes for a handful of silver three years ago. Carlo felt he understood people as well as his lawyer, or any lawyer for that matter. He would call Vicky if he felt like it. Up until this current situation, Carlo had always maintained a clear conscience. To his way of thinking, no one had ever been hurt by his dealings. He was just a facilitator. Why, then, had he threatened Vicky? *Why!* This went against his basic principles. What was it that he had assured Reed? She would never let her judge be exposed to scandal? Why had he not realized this before threatening her? Well he had, that was why he felt safe in his proposition to her. As he crossed the Indian River on the way from the courthouse to his condo, it suddenly dawned on him. This was her gallant gesture. Her own private "Beau Geste." The next day he drove to Fort Pierce to see his lawyer with a continuing feeling of remorse unlike anything he had ever experienced in all his sordid dealings.

***

The tiny story about Carlo, Vicky, and Reed in the *Vero Beach Press Journal* was not so deep as a well or wide as a church door, but it was enough; enough to guarantee the demise of the career of the valiant Vicky Carter as sure as Tybalt's scratch doomed the valiant Mercutio. AC immediately called Vicky when he read the story in *The Gainesville Sun* as reported by the Associated Press. There was no answer at her house. He expected this as she had told him she would be out of town on an educational conference for several days. After a frantic trip across the prairie he arrived at her empty house. At least the animals were there. Jim Bob's truck was in his driveway and all his outside floodlights were on. Suppertime for the livestock, thought AC as he hurried next door.

"She said to give you this," said Jim Bob. He made no effort to hide his tears. He was a tough old cracker, and knew a lot about life. He knew real men cried when the time was right and this was one of those times.

AC read the first line, thanked Jim Bob, and walked back to his truck.

My Dearest Darling Angel,

By the time you read this I'll be in Phoenix or somewhere. Please forgive the blotches on the paper. They're simply love spots to remind you that I love you more than anyone I have ever loved in my whole life. This past year has shown me more of the joy of life than I have ever known. It's beyond my scope of being to know how to let go, but I know I have to. I won't say goodbye. Somehow I just can't. I want to put some closure to this chapter of my life, but I can't, so I'll just have to let things resolve themselves.

After all that's happened, I simply can't stay in Gainesville. Jim Bob is going to buy my farm and most of the livestock. I know he doesn't look it, but he got really rich when I-75 came through his property and put in an interchange.

AC, love, I've had it with social work. It's not worth the effort when the government cuts our funding and the clients don't even seem to care about anything. I know you'll stand firm and sort out the mess. I have to go to some place where my help will be appreciated, like dealing with animals. Maybe I'm too old to get into vet school, but I know I can get a job in a clinic, and who knows after that? I made a bunch of money on the sale of my farm. I have everything I need but you. Please remember me with love. You will be in my heart forever.

The letter was not signed or dated. AC read it over several times by the weak map light of his truck. He thought of other endings to chapters in people's lives. He thought of the fictional Fredrick Henry leaving the hospital and walking back to the hotel in the rain, and Gabriel Conroy watching the flakes, silver and dark, falling obliquely against the lamplight and finally faintly falling, like the descent of their last end, upon all the living and the dead.

What eventually happened to old Fred and Gabe, AC wondered, as he sat in the front seat of his pickup, holding his face in his large bony hands and listening to the soft mealtime nickering of horses in the adjacent field?

XX

Spring came to North Florida and with it crowds of spring breakers. The Sandhill cranes as well as the robins had already migrated north to make room. Pollen was in the air dusting the azalea and dogwood blossoms. As Judge AC drove down to Orlando to pick up his son, Park, he spotted the land Jim Bob had sold around the Micanopy interchange of Interstate 75. A billboard advised him that here was the best Bar-B-Que in the land. AC was making the two hour drive to Mickeyville, Park's term, due to its better airline and cheaper connections from Denver. The logistics of Park's spring break, as presented to AC, had been planned with the precision of the Normandy invasion. Denver to Orlando. Pick up by Dad. Spend onc night with Dad. One night with Mom. Vince picks me up in G'ville on his way down from Atlanta. Drive straight through in Vince's van to Miami and pick up Sean. Continue to Islamorada where Bernie's folks have a condo. The rest was classified.

It was great to be with Park, AC thought as they drove back through the freeze-damaged orange groves north of Orlando, and Park rattled on and on about how great college was.

"What ever happened to Miss Vail?" asked AC.

"Oh, you mean Marty. Miss Aspen really. Well, these thing happen you know. That's the nice thing about being young; there's always another one around the corner."

Park Cason had always been an extraordinarily perceptive youth. The minute his words were out of his mouth he regretted them. "Aunt" Mimi had kept him somewhat abreast of his dad's affairs, and he knew of Vicky and her departure. Mimi was really a next door neighbor who had known Park since he was a baby, and who provided refuge during the stormier times of AC's divorce. Park decided to jump right in and find out for himself what was going on.

"Dad, speaking of girlfriends, you've been keeping me a bit in the dark, haven't you?" AC knew this was true, and thought how to best reply. He knew he should have given the same flip reply Park had, but the words would not come. Only a small unnoticed tear he brushed away with a fake cough. "Well, we were just sort of getting to know each other you know. There's not really a lot to tell."

ALL RISE

And that was about it. Park felt he could not press the issue, and AC felt foolish trying to discuss his love affairs with a college freshman, even if it was his own son. The talk soon turned to fishing, football and the fabulous Florida Keys where AC had gone every year during his youth.

"Be careful of the coral and sea urchins if you dive. And remember that time I stuck the fillet knife through my finger with that stupid stingray."

"Yes, dad, you've always served as a good example for avoiding injury."

They both laughed as they remembered all the other mishaps that had inevitably occurred during adventurous undertakings. After an hour's wait, they had mediocre steaks at Outback's. AC told Park he had ordered medium, not mediocre, and Park was bubbly happy. As was his proud father.

***

Despite all his rationalizations–she wasn't a fling, a passing fancy, really not cut out to be a judge's wife and so on–AC remained depressed for weeks after Vicky's sudden exit. Where was she? Where had she gone? He knew that if the case against Carlo was to proceed she would have to testify. He considered calling Sergeant Preston but did not. Vicky was entitled to her life without having him pull on her. He was not in a position to quit his job and join her in some shack in the wilderness or on a desert isle. For some reason he could not fathom, she had left him, and that was that. He had kept her parting letter and occasionally read it over and over. It gave him no clue as to how everything in Vero Beach had been discovered. Everything in Gainesville had been hushed up. There were no follow-up stories to the original short piece he had read about an unnamed DCF worker being involved in a baby buying scheme, but the unnamed worker was, nevertheless, gone from his life.

The cases in court came and went. Mortgage foreclosures, the occasional will contest, contract disputes, and, of course, the multitude of whiplash injuries generated by lawyer advertising. "If you have been injured come to see us. It is always someone else's fault." Well, AC did not really believe that, but the ads made it seem that way. He thought about retirement. Six years at the least.

Summer had now returned to North Florida with a vengeance. Judge AC debated with himself about opening a can of soup and staying in his office for lunch or trying to find a partner. Glancing out his window he sized up the possibilities of rain. With the dark clouds to the west a walk to Wise's was out of the question. He decided to stroll the halls and see who was in the building. It was a bit early for lunch and many of the courtrooms were still in session. He noted that Judge Wigglesworth's was still almost full of domestic violence cases. Judge Lee's was dark, a mark of efficiency. He stood for a moment at the door to 3A where Judge Moss presided and tried to catch his eye through the glass window in the door.

ALL RISE

Using judicial sign language he could mimic someone eating soup and determine if Ira was available,
but something was happening in the courtroom that
demanded Ira's full attention. AC decided to go in
and took a seat on the back row. The bailiff gave him
a nod of recognition. Suddenly he recognized the
man seated at the defense table. He was wearing a
suit and tie and had a fresh haircut, but it was Ricky
Jordan without a doubt. AC knew the public defender's office maintained a wardrobe of decent suits for
their clients. Judges occasionally recognized some
of their own donated hand-me-downs on the defendants standing before a jury.

Judge Moss, now in an imperious tone, commanded, "The defendant will approach the bench."

The defendant and his attorney, a youngster looking no older than AC's son, Park, did as they were
told. AC had heard nothing more about the Jordan
family since Stacy Ann Maddox had told him of Mary
Beth's remarkable resurrection.

"Mr. Jordan, you have pled guilty to the crime of
contributing to the delinquency of a minor, a misde-
meanor of the first degree. Do you have anything to
say before the judgment and sentence of the court is
pronounced?"

Ricky opened his mouth as if to speak, but his attorney quickly gave him a nudge and said, "No your
honor. The defendant elects to remain silent." This
was met by a coarse whisper from Ricky, which received an equally coarse admonition from the young
attorney.

"Very well, the court adjudicates you guilty and sentences you to one year in the county jail, and im poses the statutory court costs. Please report to the bailiff to be fingerprinted."

Ricky gave a couple of twists to his shoulders and looked to the almost empty courtroom for sympathy. The only person he saw was some guy hiding behind a newspaper. Big Ben Stoker whispered something in his ear, and that was that. Judge Moss waited to sign the judgment and sentence forms being prepared by the clerk, then asked the bailiffs to adjourn court.

"All Rise," Big Ben said "This court is now adjourned."

AC put down the newspaper he had been using as a shield and met Ira as he was removing his robe in chambers. "That was a surprise," AC said. "Let's grab a bite and you can fill me in."

Emiliano's was now closed for lunch, so Ira suggested Wise's. "Nah," AC said. "It's about to rain. Let's pig out on Archer Road. Wise's is a bit public anyway. We have a bit of catching up to do."

AC drove to the Olive Garden restaurant on Archer Road where there were booths and a few tour- ists fresh from 1-75. The students were now gone, but a few had jobs in Gainesville for the summer. The waitress was one of these and asked if AC and Ira were interested in the luncheon wine specials. They were not.

"On second thought," said AC, "Let's share a bottle. I checked your schedule before we left and you're free all afternoon and we have a lot to talk about."

Ira might have been the chief judge, but AC was several years his senior and commanded some force of persuasion.

"Chianti sounds fine," Ira said. "Ask if they have Ruffino. I once had a shrink named Ruffino, and he always calmed my nerves. So you want the story on Jordan? Long or short version?"

"You know, Ira, I'm really not all that interested in Ricky now, but I sort of need to know the story." He hesitated, "It might come up some time in the future."

"Yes, in all probability it will come up in the future. As you could guess, the plea deal down from a felony was part of a bargain, the kind that always pisses me off. There's convincing evidence that Ricky was sexually molesting his daughter, but you know how hard those cases are. Hard to prove and hard on the emotions so they took a plea down to contributing. They thought for a while that he was the father of the baby, but that was not the case according to DNA."

"Who is?" asked AC as he filled the long-stemmed wine glasses.

"Can't say. Well, I could say if I knew, but I don't. Anyway, Ricky was in on conversations between his brother-in-law and Grimage when they discussed returning what's her name and the baby to the Jordan home, and he's agreed to testify if Grimage is ever charged with anything. Or brought up before the Bar's disciplinary board. Agreed to testify truthfully, but his story will probably change several times before things come to a head. Anyway, it's a start."

"I'm more interested in our brother," AC said, "but I expect you know that."

"That's out of my hands. I told the JQC all I knew."

AC felt his friend was beginning to clam up and decided not to push things. Then he thought, why not? "I haven't told the JQC all I know."

Ira raised his brows in mock horror. "Covering up judicial misbehavior is an ethical violation. It may be necessary to report you. I would myself, but I'm too busy being chief judge." He paused, pleased with his humor, then curiosity got the better of him. "Tell me yours and I'll tell you mine."

"You won't believe my story, so you should go first."

This time Ira refilled the wine glasses. "Mine is part speculation and part fact and you know enough to keep it top secret. You know the background. Ricky whose sister is married to Dan Hawthorne, asks for Dan's help in the dependency matter. Switch to Tallahassee where Representative Buel, from Lake City, is in line to become Speaker next year. His biggest campaign contributor is Dan Hawthorne. Buel calls somebody at DCF, who calls Grimage, who talks to Asner. Hawthorne admits he talked to Asner about the case," Ira Moss had rushed through all this in his usual rapid fire fashion. "Lot of gaps to fill in, but that's it in a nutshell. How much of this can actually be proven is another matter. It depends on who is the biggest rat."

"But Asner didn't actually do anything," AC said, "Or did he?"

"The JQC has the ball and they are running with it. Or plodding with it I should say. It will be at least a year before it's all sorted out. I have no idea of the status of any proceedings against Grimage or the rest. What's your story?"

"The Jordan girl, the mom, is Mary Beth. One afternoon she stops by Lillian's, and who tries to pick her up but Jack-the-Ass Asner."

"Bullshit."

"I said you wouldn't believe me, but it's accurate. Jack bought her a drink, offered another and gave her his card. Apparently she was never actually in his courtroom so they didn't recognize each other. She gave the card to her lawyer."

"AC, this Chianti is about gone, but you get no more. You're hallucinating."

"Well, I wanted to run it by you. If you don't believe it, neither will the JQC. It is true though. In my opinion Ms Jordan should not risk involvement. After all, she wasn't really offended. I'm the one offended."

Ira nodded in agreement, and poured the remaining wine for himself. He considered asking AC about Vicky but decided it was too personal, so he changed the subject and they finished their meal with typical banal judicial gossiping.

NATH DOUGHTIE

***

Park Cason had taken a summer job in Estes Park, Colorado, so AC had few domestic responsibilities. Park had lived with him after the divorce and he had enjoyed cooking for two and Park's praise over his culinary expertise. It was not much, but maybe it beat Park's macaroni and tuna casserole and the student union at CU. The "Alfred Packer Grill" had been named for an early citizen of Colorado who ate some of his fellow snow-bound travelers. Vicky had been a good eater too, he remembered. Always won a clean plate award even when AC cooked broccoli. Vicky. Oh well, AC thought as he popped a "Healthy One" into the microwave and poured another glass of cabernet.

As he waited for the TV dinner to cook, he opened the sliding glass door to his balcony. The first day of October had brought a slight, ever-so-slight hint of fall. AC figured the mackerel would be back on Seahorse reef by now. Maybe a first cousin of Big Spic, Vicky's fish. Vicky. Vicky where are you? He jumped at the sound of the phone as if he had been caught peeking in a window. He did not recognize the number that flashed on the phone's screen and started to let the answering machine take the call. No one calls at dinnertime except solicitors he thought as he picked up the receiver, *I'll give them a piece of my mind.*

"Hello," he barked. "Who's calling?" He was prepared to identify himself as the butler when he heard a soft woman's voice ask,

"AC, is that you? This is Valerie. You sound so gruff. Are you OK?"

"Valerie. Oh, I'm fine. I thought you must be one of those damn phone solicitors that always call at dinnertime."

"Well, that's true to some extent." Valerie laughed. "I really wanted to know if you and your friend, Vicky wasn't it?, still wanted the painting you picked out. I sort of put it on hold for you just in case. Vicky seemed to especially like it. Liked the movement of the horses. Does she still have birthdays?"

AC remembered the painting well. Three running horses tossing their manes and seeming to float on a cloud. Light seemed to come from all directions. Vicky had...

"Yes, I do want the picture. A lot has happened or I would have called sooner. How are Sergeant Preston and King getting along?"

"They're fine, Judge. Look I'm having a sort of gallery exhibition in High Springs Saturday afternoon. Why don't you and Vicky drive up and you can surprise her. Jim is helping with some refreshments and I know he would like to see you. King, too."

"Sounds great. Where is the place?"

"On the left as you come into town. We'll have out balloons or something."

"Look for me about three."

NATH DOUGHTIE

*****

The highway between Gainesville and High Springs threaded through some of the most charming scenery in the whole of the Eighth Circuit, rolling hills covered with luxuriant grass used for grazing or hay and an occasional house surrounded by ancient live oaks set far back from the road. Some cows, each with an escorting egret poised for grasshoppers, were spread out in a field. A few years and it would be gone. AC counted the new developments that had arisen in the past few years. Progress. That is what it is all about he thought as he passed "Progress Center" on the outskirts of the town of Alachua. Progress had converted corn fields into distribution warehouses for Dollar General and Wal-Mart with others to follow. The people that had fled progress in South Florida were now complaining about progress following them north.

High Springs, like many towns in the area, was once supported by the early phosphate industry. The mine pits were all that were left of that era, but High Springs had been rejuvenated by the antique trade. The "Shoppes" were on every corner, and there were a number that sold curios and local art. Valerie Preston had arranged for a private showing in a vacant building that was in-between tenants. AC located the exhibition and worked his way in through the white wine and quiche crowd from Gainesville who were being served white wine and quiche by a smiling Jim Preston.

ALL RISE

"Wow! This beats a tent at the Sante Fe Arts Festival," AC said, reaching for a glass of the wine.

"We just have it for the weekend, a contribution from one of Val's admirers, actually. Have you seen her yet? She told me you were coming. And Judge, I told her that Vicky might not be with you."

The friends exchanged what could be described as a "knowing look," although AC wondered what in hell Jim knew. Valerie came up and gave AC a hug and a kiss on the cheek. She had dressed in a gray smock with dabs of paint all over the front. This identified her as the artist. Underneath he could see something that looked like an exotic crimson Indian sari which could be exposed when the photographers arrived. AC thought she was plenty photogenic without a costume.

"AC, come with me." She took his hand and led him to a room in the rear of the gallery. When she turned on the switch, a flood of light lit up the floating horse painting, framed and standing on an easel. It was just as he had remembered it when he first saw it with Vicky.

"You saved it for me. Thank you. Thank you so much. This really means a lot."

"I saved it for you *and* Vicky. You have to pick it up together."

AC avoided Valerie's eyes and instead stared at the painting. There was a long silence.

"I don't know where Vicky is these days."

"Jim might. You need to talk to him."

As AC tried to think of what to say, he thought about his relationship with the Prestons. Casual friends, yes, and trusted, but not...not what? Not people he could let down his guard with? They might see him cry, and that would never do. Judges are impassive. They maintain a front. They are like actors who never break character.

"AC, Jim told me some things about Vicky that you don't know. Come over tonight at eight. To our house. You need to see King anyway. Promise you'll come."

"I'll come. How about if I bring a pizza? Anchovies on the side?"

***

AC had a couple of hours to kill before going to the Preston's modest house in Northeast Gainesville. He stopped by Hitchcock's grocery in Alachua and bought beer and a large soup bone for King. He continued on into Gainesville and turned left onto University Avenue. It was still a bit early for his visit, so he ordered a pizza from Leonardo's and asked them to have it ready a little before eight. He continued his drive toward downtown and the courthouse square where he turned south toward Biven's Arm Nature Center. The gate to the parking lot was down so he just pulled his pickup into a cleared area across the road.

No use letting Mr. Sam Adams get warm, he thought as he grasped one of the beers and tried to twist off the bottle cap. It was a bit dark to see if it was a twist cap so he used the opener on his Swiss army knife. He took a long pull from the bottle and tried to organize his thoughts. What could Jim know about Vicky that he did not? Why she left town? *She said that in her letter.* The letter that rested in the top drawer of his desk at home. He saw a police patrol car drive by and felt a bit guilty about his open bottle of beer. Maybe he should just go to Leonardo's and wait there. The parking lot was almost full, but AC found the last place and pulled in. Then he just sat there and finished his beer and listened as Garrison Keillor entertained the NPR crowd on the radio. His thoughts remained a confused jumble of emotions. A little before eight he went in and picked up his pizza. Pepperoni and mushrooms with anchovies on the side.

The Preston's house was not hard to spot once AC found the right street. He had relied on his memory, but had only been by once to pick up a painting he bought from Valerie at an art show. All the streets looked alike and he drove down several before seeing the multicolored house he was looking for. No simple gated community beige here. More of a Van Gogh splash.

"Judge, you made it," Jim said ushering him in past an excited King. "Hush up, King, or you go to your box."

AC produced the huge bone. "Can he take this out back or something?"

"Watch this. King, sit, hold." King did as he was told and Jim balanced the bone on King's long muzzle. "OK King, show Judge how you can count. One, two, three, four, five."

At the word "five" King deftly tossed the bone in the air, caught it and, without a thank you, exited through a dog door in the rear of the house.

Valerie entered wiping her hands on a dish towel. She had changed from her sari and wore jeans and baggy tee shirt. "Judge, we thought you might have been lost. Let's sit here at the table. You guys must be starved."

The guys did as they were told although AC was worried that the beer was too warm and the pizza too cool. Both were fine however, and everyone dug in. Although AC had only one topic on his mind he engaged in polite chit-chat. "So how many paintings did you sell today?"

Valerie had sold only one, a charcoal sketch of an English Setter, but did obtain a commission to paint the portrait of an Arab stallion in Ocala. "I really am hesitant to do these as most people want a photographic image of their horse, but I figure if they saw my work they must know what I will do. My art dealer friend says I don't charge enough. You and Vicky better hurry up and buy my cloud horses before the price goes up."

"Well, yes," AC said, wondering how to get to the subject of Vicky, hoping Jim would say something. Jim just sat there munching his pizza and swilling his Sam Adams.

"Well, I guess I called this meeting," Valerie said. "Maybe I'd better take charge. Jim, you need to tell AC what you know about Vicky. He is on a need-to-know basis."

"Judge," Jim said, "I really don't know what you know, and what you don't know, but there is one thing I learned from this Proenza guy that I think you don't know."

AC reached for another Sam Adams thinking he was glad he had brought a twelve-pack. Valerie had put several on ice in a small cooler by the table. "Like I told Valerie, I don't know where Vicky even is. She left about the same time that story about baby buying came out. I haven't tried to track her down. She seemed to want it that way. I guess she didn't exactly say so, but she hasn't called or anything."

Valerie said, "I just met Vicky once. The time you all came up and saw the painting. She is definitely in love with you. An artist knows these things."

"I only met Vicky once, well twice, but I'm just a cop. I don't have the emotional instincts of an artist," said Jim, "but I do know something about motives."

"Well, I don't." said AC, becoming somewhat annoyed.

"Now be patient Judge. That's your specialty. OK, let's start from the top from what I know. Some of our guys were sort of monitoring Proenza and saw him at the gym where they work out over lunch. Saw him with Vicky. I heard you started seeing Vicky. Courthouse gossip, you know, so I mentioned Proenza to you. Sometimes later, several months I guess, I get a call from Vicky out of the blue. Wants to meet in the park, over at Morningside, and give me information. We meet, and she tells me all about a deal with Proenza and a rich guy from Vero Beach wanting to adopt a baby."

"She told me all about that," said AC. "Well, I mean about what went on in Vero. Not about meeting you. She said she backed out of the deal with Proenza before anything took place. She did think, for awhile, that the State had somehow gotten wind of it, but it was a false alarm. Now, from what you say, Vicky was the one that told law enforcement. It makes no sense. None."

"Well, it will. Or might. After our meeting, I called my contact at FDLE and we set up an interview with Vicky. She basically told the same story."

"When was this?" interrupted AC.

"Sometime after Christmas. I would have to check. Anyway, this time she mentioned a check passing hands. Or *maybe* passing hands. Carlo Proenza told her something about having the funds. If that could be proved it might establish a conspiracy, so FDLE decided to pursue the matter. Local law enforcement confirmed the existence of a large check in Proenza's condo, but they had no grounds to seize it."

"You guys want any more pizza, or can I give it to King?" asked Valerie, walking toward the kitchen.

"He'll get fat, but go ahead. So, as I was saying, based on Vicky's story and some knowledge of the check she described, FDLE goes in for a warrant, and arrests Proenza, but can't locate the other guy, Cunningham."

"All this is intriguing, but why would Vicky expose herself to it? Maybe she wanted to get back at Carlo for something, but her name would still get dragged through the mud."

"Patience, your honor. I'm coming to that. The rich guy, Cunningham, has his lawyer call the prosecutor and offer to cooperate. In exchange for immunity naturally. Proenza hears of this and is pissed. I go down for a depo in Vero and finally meet Proenza, who, despite his reputation, is a slick cookie. After all is said and done, the state attorney decides not to prosecute, to 'no information' the case. Lack of compelling evidence. So I'm in the hall with Proenza waiting for the lawyers to finish up and, Valerie, come back in here. You'll want to hear this part."

"King says thanks. His paws are too muddy for indoors, or he would woof in person. Where are you in the story?"

"This is what Proenza told me just standing in the hall. I don't know what his motive was in telling me. Maybe to get back at Cunningham for finking on him. He did say a couple of things that made me think he sincerely felt sorry for Vicky. It could also be that none of it's true. Anyway, he says 'Jim (we're first name buddies now) if you see Vicky tell her I'm sorry for everything. She is one brave woman. That judge is really a lucky man.' I say that I will do so, then ask him, why did she do it? Was she that mad at you? He said, 'She did it for her judge. Cunningham threatened to expose her involvement unless she influenced her judge to take some specific action in a civil case in Gainesville. To grant a continuance or something. She wouldn't put the judge in the position of having to choose between his judicial honor and her honor, so she told on herself. And on us, of course.' That was his story."

The table was quiet for a long time. King whined at the garage door, but was ignored. Finally AC broke the silence with a sigh. Then he spoke. "What he said was true. I was under a lot of pressure to continue a major case. The Wessex case. You may have heard of it. I didn't continue it and the parties settled right before trial last month. I have absolutely no idea how Proenza and Cunningham are, or were, involved in the case. I can't figure out how they even heard of the case, but they must have or Proenza would not have said what he did. Vicky might know. Do you know where she is now?"

"No," said Jim, "but her address would be in the file. It would be easy to find."

"I know where she is," Valerie said to the stunned men. "She called about the horses. The painting. That was why I called AC. Well, one reason I called AC. I didn't want to say more until I found out what was going on."

"Was she mad at me or anything?"

"No, of course not, Judge." Valerie looked exasperated. "She simply felt she had to start her life over. After everything that had happened. She had no job, or any prospect of getting one in her field. She couldn't tell you what she had done. She was mixed up and distraught. She just left."

"But she did call about the painting?"

"Yes, she did call about the painting."

"Well, where is she?" asked AC in apparent anguish.

"I think she has to answer that." Valerie said. "I plan to give her a call and let her know what has happened. I plan to tell her you want the painting too. It's something you might have to work out together. If she wants to, she will call you."

They sat looking at the pizza crumbs and the round wet spots on the table. There were a couple of bottles left in the refrigerator, but all in the cooler were gone. "It's pretty late," said AC, pushing back his chair a bit.

"All rise," said Valerie, standing.

THE END

Printed in the United States
95587LV00006B/1-6/A